KU-350-981

SUSAN DEXTER

The Winter King's War

The Ring
of Allaire

FONTANA/Collins

First published in Great Britain by Fontana Paperbacks 1987

Copyright © 1981 by Susan Dexter

Printed and bound in Great Britain by
William Collins Sons & Co. Ltd, Glasgow

Conditions of Sale
This book is sold subject to the condition
that it shall not, by way of trade or otherwise,
be lent, re-sold, hired out or otherwise circulated
without the publisher's prior consent in any form of
binding or cover other than that in which it is
published and without a similar condition
including this condition being imposed
on the subsequent purchaser

## The Ring of Allaire

Susan Dexter was born in 1955 in Pennsylvania, USA, where she still lives. She works as a fashion illustrator and freelance artist. It was her interest in illustration that led her to adult fantasy via its many award-winning cover designs, but she has had a deep love for fairy tales since childhood.

*The Ring of Allaire* is her first novel, and the first of a trilogy, *The Winter King's War*. The sequels, to be published in Fontana during 1987, are *The Sword of Calandra* and *The Mountains of Channadran*.

*By the same author*

This book is for:

My mother, for loving me and putting up with me and eventually reading this.

Sherryl, for being herself, and my friend.

Pat, who offered to read this before I even asked him to.

Thomas Becket, the only cat I ever loved.

Waldo Pepper, my blue and white canary who truly believed he could sing winter out of existence.

And for Fritz Leiber, whose stories have been a never ending fascination and pleasure, and whose friendship has been a never ending wonder and joy.

# Contents

# PROLOG

His hooves took him far and fast, for he was of an ancient breeding, older almost than the moors he ran over. Bred to magic, he fled down the wind, away from the field where the last King of Calandra and Esdragon's Duke, late his master, lay dying, their decimated armies ranged wearily around them. He was frightened, he who had never known fear before. He had battled chimeras and trampled tigers, cried fierce challenges to armed hosts, carried his Dukes to battles and perilous midnight trysts, but a dark-frosted doom lay before his flying body now, opening black under him, and all his fabled fleetness of foot could not save him.

The world began to spin, to whirl, colors brightening and fading, whipping by like piles of long-dead leaves. All his many masters appeared, and the lovely maidens who had once waved to them from battlements now dust. Unstable as water, the ground rolled beneath him. Against his will, he turned, struggling all the while to straighten his course. His limbs grew heavy now, unsupple and wooden. His mane no longer blew free upon his neck. There was a bright, hot pain through his middle, as if he had leaped into a beast-trap and been impaled upon its spike. The circling became more rapid. The dark crystals filled all the air.

He screamed, wildly despairing, and that scream was spun away. A voice began to laugh, softly, and ice formed on a field of flowers somewhere, and deepened layer by layer.

And the laughter grew louder.

The flowers blackened and fell away, and the laughter was shriller, changed in tempo, became a calliope. And the world went around, and around, and around . . .

# The Brass Dog

IN OTHER LANDS, folk worshipped things as diverse as serpents and trees and the great sun itself. But in Calandra, and for her, there was only the Word that began it all, and the Twenty Original Grimoires of the mages' dissertations upon that Word. It was not quite a religion, the way the world reckoned such things. The wizards and mages were not quite priests, and what might otherwise have passed for temples were often nothing more than thatched huts, devoted as much to all forms of life and learning as to magic. No, not quite a religion. Only life itself, to the wizards . . .

It was going to rain again.

The air was blue with the look and feel of it, the colors of the trees and flowers wet and intense. The sun was a watery lemon yellow, and the air was cool and full of scents. There was a sound of moving water everywhere, running along the ground, dripping from the tips of leaves. The world sparkled with it.

Tristan savored the early evening light, as his feet hurried him home. He was hardly wet, the latest storm not having lasted long. Besides, he had the use of a fairly good spell for keeping rain off. It had only worn thin a little, toward the storm's end. Just where his nose had managed to poke through the spell's shield. Nothing to worry over.

He'd escaped the wind's worst gusts and most of the hailstorm that accompanied them because he'd been scavenging for magic-stones at the bottom of a brush-overgrown, dry streambed. And if he'd had a bad moment getting out of the streambed before the rainwater came in, what of that? At his age, near-misses could be quickly forgotten.

He patted the reassuring fullness of the pouch at his belt. Blais would be pleased—his apprentice had searched well

today. Small stones of power had seemed to gather themselves eagerly under his usually fumbling fingers. He'd
been often sidetracked, and wandered a long way, and was
late coming home with the storm and all, but they'd have
plenty of charms to peddle, come next market day. And
tucked safely deep within his worn wool sweater was a major find, an object so manifestly full of power that he'd
briefly feared to touch it barehanded. The huge black
feather still smelled of thunder and lightning flash.

He was eager to show that to his master—it was much
the best find he'd ever made. Better even than a sea-eagle's
pinion, maybe. Not that he had the skill to wield such a
thing—but he had recognized it, so surely there was some
hope for him.

Those magical things that came so easily to Blais were
beyond him still, as much as if he should try to lift their
cottage with a single finger. He shrugged, as if to hide his
yearning even from himself. Oh, to be able to call fire
from wet wood with one glance, or charm a sailor into
faithfulness! To hold converse with the shifting stars, learning their secrets, sharing their dreams. To know that your
magic was going to do what you expected it to, and not
whatever it pleased—oh, to be a wizard, in truth! That goal
was still a long way off, even after nineteen-odd years. A
good thing he'd been started at his career early—at birth,
in fact—if his progress was to be this slow.

Slow. The word seemed to catch in his mind. I've got to
get home now, Tristan thought, inexplicably panic-stricken.
He'd dallied too long seeking out wild strawberries as well
as stones, and there'd been something disquieting about
that storm. He'd expected more than hail when the air had
once grown so cold. And he'd been so far from home, yet
he was sure he'd only been brushed by the storm's fringe.

The sun shone here now, and everything sparkled and
looked peaceful, but there *were* signs of damage. A lot of
leaves lay soggily in his path, and that looked like a branch
hanging attached to its tree by only shreds of bark, there in
the orchard.

Blais would expect him to be home, helping to repair
whatever damage there was. And he'd earned a tongue-
lashing, wandering around woolgathering both before and

after the storm when he should have been getting himself home before Blais worried.

Well, fine. He deserved a scolding, and it would be quickly over and forgotten. Why then this queasy feeling, almost of dread? He could see the cottage there before him, and nothing looked amiss with it. What kind of silly fancy had he fallen prey to?

He crossed over the rain-swollen brook somewhat gingerly. The footlog wobbled, and crossing running water was always tricky for wizards, even apprentice ones. No sense risking a ducking.

Intent upon his feet, he scarcely noted the empty look of the cottage windows or that the door stood slackly ajar. Wind, he thought, when he finally did notice. It had blown the door open and probably the hearth fire out—that would explain the lack of smoke from the chimney. It had been quite a storm.

He fully expected to find Blais within, muttering incantations over the logs. Not that the job would take him long—why even Tristan could handle fire-lighting, more or less. It was the first spellcraft Blais had taught him.

The cottage's single room was empty.

"Blais?" Tristan paused in the doorway, his shadow falling across the beaten earth floor and Blais' grimoire. The book lay open to a formula for the calling of unicorns, and its brightly illuminated pages riffled gently in the breeze.

In point of fact, there were books everywhere. Actually, there always were books everywhere in the cottage, since they never had shelves enough. But Tristan was always careful to stack the volumes neatly, whether on floor or chair or chimney-piece. Certainly he never scattered them about like this, tumbled all anyhow, pages and covers bent. And what was this? Their oak table turned on its side? What sort of wind could have done this? He righted the table and picked up the grimoire, glancing around nervously as he did so. Ashes from the blown-out fire were thick over everything.

"Blais?" Maybe Blais was in the herb garden, speaking encouragement to the tender lavender, no doubt, or reviving branches mashed flat by the rain.

It took Tristan only seconds to determine that he wasn't.

He was not in the orchard either, or the lean-to that housed their cow and the seasoned firewood. Might he have been called away? Not without his spellbook, surely. And a quick glance showed Tristan the wizard's yew walking-staff still leaning in the corner by the door.

A little feeling of uneasiness stood up in Tristan's stomach and walked heavily into his throat. The cottage was dark inside now. The sun had dipped low, and the rectangle of light through the door was blood-red. Tristan shivered.

"Tristan."

He spun around with a cry of relief.

"*Blais!*"

There was no one there.

He looked very carefully, but the shadow of the cypress beside the door stayed just that—a shadow—no matter how long or closely he looked. Perhaps a cloak of invisibility? He knew full well that Blais did not possess one. Yet it had been Blais' voice.

"Tristan."

The voice was behind him, inside the cottage. He whipped around again, tangled his feet and fell to his knees, hard. The room before him was still empty.

Light! He needed a light and wanted it very badly. The cottage was too dark inside now to make out details.

He had to make the necessary passes twice, stumbling over the words, before the tinder caught. His firestone felt cold, useless. His hands were shaking around it. He'd bruised his left knee badly, and his head was spinning giddily.

Be your age, Tristan ordered himself sternly. A child would be beaten for behaving this way, and you're long past that. Aren't you just a bit old to be spooked by the dark? He pushed his hair back from his eyes and willed his fingers to stop their trembling.

The firelight was heartening. Tristan hung the kettle over the yellow flames and stayed close, warming himself, though the cold in him seemed set too deep for mere flames to reach.

He's been called away—normal enough—and I work myself into hearing voices. He'll be back by morning and laugh when I tell him about this. If I tell him. He might at least have left a note, a corner of Tristan's mind added with a touch of irritation.

Blais generally left his messages written in silver within the tall mirror. But it was blank of anything now except Tristan's uncertain reflection.

"Tristan."

The firelight sparked off the brass lion-dog that sat on the carven werewood table, next to the crystal sphere in its tripod. It held incense in its hollow body, and smoke drifted out of its mouth now.

"Tristan." Another puff of smoke.

Tristan stared at it.

"Listen to me. I may not have much time to say this." Smoke rings of varying sizes punctuated every word.

"Blais?" Tristan's voice sounded very small, perhaps because he had very little air left in his lungs to back it.

"Yes. Listen carefully, Tristan, there will be time to say this only once. I have held on a very long time, waiting for you to come home."

"I'm sorry, I was—Where are you?"

"No time for that, blast it! You saw the storm? Then you should have guessed its cause. Nímir has slain me, but in the end I cheated him! He couldn't claim all my magic or the knowledge he destroyed me for having."

"The Winter King here?" Frost nipped at the tip of Tristan's nose as he looked wildly about the shadowed room.

"Stop asking so many questions! I tell you, there's no time. Tristan, listen to me! Attend closely now. I may not come back but I can pass my knowledge on to you, before I fade utterly. I have left you a word, a clue, which none but you may find or use. Read it, and the spell is yours to command, with all attendant instructions."

Spell?

The lion-dog belched more honeysuckle-scented smoke, anticipating his question.

"It concerns Allaire of the Nine Rings, she who has been the special quest of wizards since Nímir stole her away, for only by magic may she be found. She lies in Darkenkeep, beyond the uttermost Gates, and there she shall lie in her enchanted sleep until the mage comes who can awaken her.

"Nine rings of silver are on her fingers, rings old in power but powerless without the proper ring to mate her tenth finger. With those rings she may defeat Nímir, and the threat of everlasting Winternight shall be banished from this world forever. She will wed the King of Calandra, as was long ago intended, and peace will reign with them.

"Three things are needed, say the prophecies of the time, to win the lady from the Winter King's hold: a wizard well-skilled in power; the rightful heir to Calandra's throne; and Valadan, the warhorse of Esdragon."

"But those last two are as well hidden as Allaire herself," Tristan said, bemused. Other wizards in Blais' volumes of magely history—which were just now supporting a board which served as a shelf for yet other books—had spoken of the quest, embarked gloriously upon it, and were never seen again. Blais had called them fools and worse, and had himself always remained at home. Why was he now repeating a useless legend Tristan had cut his reading-teeth on?

"Not so," Blais went on, in response to Tristan's last words. "You will have the information needed to seek out Valadan, and the rightful Heir is Polassar. Him you will find at Lassair Castle, which he holds—for the moment. Calandra's throne has many claimants, and they war with him. Do not be deceived, for they are creatures of Nímir, or inspired by him. Polassar is the true Heir."

The lion-dog breathed sparks, its sides glowing cherry-red. Blais was clearly nearing the end of his powers.

"When you have found Allaire, you must awaken her. This only you can do, for Polassar will not be able to help you. You must find the key yourself, in yourself, and I think you will only know what it is when the time comes to use it. Then seek for the last ring. Of this I have no knowledge. It is written that Allaire will know the ring when it is on her finger, but that she cannot lead you to it. Nor can I help you further. I should have told you before this, but it was dangerous knowledge for a child, and I left it too long. My duty was to pass on the quest, and I have now done so." A puff of smoke passed from the lion-dog's mouth like a sigh. "I realize you are ill-prepared for this—but you do have a certain talent. Trust to it. It may be enough."

"That doesn't sound hopeful," Tristan ventured.

"Tristan, if you do but find her, you will have accomplished more than any of the six thousand and forty-three mages who have sought before you . . ."

A last cloud of mist came out of the brass mouth, scarcely even smoke now. Tristan waited, but no more came after it. He put a hand out and finally, gently, touched the golden mane. The metal still held a last hint of warmth.

# The Search

TRISTAN SAT A LONG time in the dark, wondering.

And then he got up, collected Blais' books from the floor, and began to read them, page by carefully written page. Some he had never been permitted to touch before, and those he fingered nervously a long while before unclasping their covers. Still, if Blais had left him a clue about Valadan, then it was here, somewhere. That and all the rest the old mage had learned concerning Allaire and everything else in the long years of his life. Blais might at least have told him where to begin, Tristan mused sourly.

Allaire was the special quest of wizards, he read, because only by a wizard could she be wakened and released from her bondage.

Much of the story was familiar to him. After all, he was as well-drilled in history as any wizard's apprentice was expected to be. He'd never had any trouble with that. And this woman was the pivot on which much of Calandra's past turned. It was a famous and fabulous time in which she'd lived, and the events made a famous story, full of marvels and heroes and hopes and tragedy. It had rightly become a classic tale, but it had the added virtue of being true as well. Blais had made an exhaustive study of it.

It was every mage's duty to aid the search for Allaire, whether actively—which had thus far always failed—or by research, which was safe but had come to seem pointless.

Every mage so far who'd chosen the first course had impatiently despaired of finding Valadan, believed him destroyed, and set off without him. Every quest therefore ended in failure, though many had won quite close to their goal. Their epic stories were passed down from mages to wide-eyed apprentices over the centuries.

Without Valadan, every quest was doomed to fail. And now Blais had found a clue—and died for it. It was still here, somewhere.

I should have been here, Tristan thought, rubbing at a tear that blurred the words on the page before him. I should have known that he was in trouble. Maybe I could have helped him. The thought that he almost certainly would not have been of the slightest use was troubling, shameful. He bent his head over the page again.

Tristan read through the night, and the dawn. Never lifting his head, he moved from page to page, from book to grimoire, until it was time to light the candles again. He was distracted only once, by an intriguing formula for the casting of rainbows from a single raindrop which he'd somehow overlooked before. Otherwise he worked with commendable dedication, ignoring burning eyes and physical and mental exhaustion. When sleep seemed too alluring, he put the kettle on the fire again and brewed a noxious smelling tea which kept him wakeful.

The last candle was guttering when he found it—a single word in a small green volume no larger than his hand. *Carrousel.* The page about it seemed to glow.

He didn't know what it meant, and yet he somehow did. Words, other words that he'd just read, and some that he hadn't, began dropping into place as if they were part of some inevitable formula triggered by that one word. His brain felt as if it were stretching, to hold the new words. The sensation was momentarily unpleasant.

He knew where to search now, to come to the place where that one word would lead him to Valadan.

Strange languages came to him, words barely making sense, yet he must speak them. The path he was set to follow looked long and treacherous, a kind of journeying he'd never dreamed of. It looked worrisomely difficult too, and he was nervous about undertaking such a trip, but a sort of ensorcelled confidence overrode all but the smallest feeling of unease. Blais' spell would look after him, if he executed it properly.

There was no question now of how to accomplish his mission. And no doubt, either, that in the end he would come to Valadan.

Valadan was the black warhorse of the mighty Dukes of Esdragon. He had served them all with magic speed, high courage, and deeds of valor until the last Duke was slain fighting his king, the last King of Calandra. Valadan!

The temptation to fall instantly asleep was very strong after so many hours of reading, searching, and anxiety. But somehow he was dressing in the first clothes that came under his fingers and was taking up Blais' grimoire and opening it, tracing spells with one forefinger while his lips faintly moved.

He stopped. The pull of the infant spell was strong, but he resisted it. Other duties called to him more pressingly.

Tristan laid the grimoire carefully on the table, and walked quickly to the lean-to that snuggled against the back of the cottage. The cow raised soft eyes to him, then returned to nosing through the straw at her feet. If Tristan carried no bucket of feed, then she'd give him scant attention.

He couldn't just leave her here with no one to take care of her feeding and milking. He could put her in the orchard—plenty of grass there and a fence that would doubtless fall down the first time she scratched her rump on it. She could leave any time she took the urge to wander, but he'd need some sort of spell to keep her milked. Maybe there was something in the grimoire. For sure they hadn't any neighbors near or willing enough to stop in and take care of the chore, and he had no time to ask for any help anyway.

He fetched the grimoire, thinking the while.

Eventually he found a promising charm, if it would work for him. He rather hoped it would, since he intended trying to direct the milk into a certain pot in a certain house—that of a poor widow struggling alone with two small children. She'd certainly have a good use for the milk.

It was a pretty finely directed spell for his meager abilities, though. It could go wrong on any number of points, and small wonder that he spoke it with little confidence. The cow looked at him with perplexity, but nothing else happened. Tristan let out his breath slowly, with relief. The way his luck tended to run, he might equally have expected her to sprout wings, or grow green fur on her hooves. He didn't like to tempt fate by trying the spell a second time.

Perhaps a simple compulsion. It wasn't too far to the widow's—the cow would be there long before she was in any distress over milking. It was also a much easier spell, and maybe easier on the cow too, better than having her udder pulled at by invisible hands and her milk vanishing into the very air—though a wizard's animals were used to almost anything.

He read the second spell with much more command, and something must have smiled on his magic at last. As he made a last economical gesture with his forefinger, in the direction of the widow's home, the cow lifted her head and mooed softly. She looked puzzled. Then, with more speed than she'd shown in years—except at feeding times—she swayed off toward the road, turned and moved out of sight. Tristan smiled thinly.

He let the hen out of her coop, and dumped all of Blais' tadpoles into the pond. Would he be back before they'd all grown into bullfrogs? Tristan wished he knew.

He'd delayed as long as he safely might. Wrapping his travelling cloak about him, Tristan took up the grimoire and his own box of powerful stones. His mind cleared of workaday distractions and filled with instructions once more. He hugged Blais' knowledge convulsively tight to him, briefly, and then opened the grimoire.

Two pages, previously sealed together so that they appeared as one—with no gaps in the subject matter contained on them either—slipped apart. Tristan looked at them curiously, and felt his lips beginning to move.

It was time. Whether he liked it or not, felt equal to the task or not, Blais' spell was working in him.

As he solemnly chanted the final words upon the page, Tristan's eyes widened, for the air before him had begun to shimmer, like the heat-haze of a summer noon. He could still see the room about him—the outlines of the doorposts and the cypress beyond them, at least—but they had become outlines only and soon faded till they were fainter than the lines which connect the stars into constellations. Then they were gone, leaving not even an afterimage before his eyes. Tristan swallowed hard, surprised that he still had air to breathe. Only the grimoire in his hands was solid and real, and he gripped it far tighter than he needed to.

The book seemed to drop forward in his hands. Alarmed, he took a step forward to catch his balance. As he did so he felt the book give another tug. Thus led, he took several more steps, watching the grimoire and darting nervous glances out the sides of his eyes, not daring to turn his head. Whenever a word glowed on the page before him he spoke it carefully, making gestures with whichever hand came free for them, in whatever manner his fingers found good.

Once he paused briefly, having stumbled when the book ceased to move. A whole page flipped over then, and half the next sheet flamed green. He spoke the words limned there and, as the book pulled ahead again, felt gentle bumpings against his skin, soft and moist on his face as if many soap bubbles burst there. Tristan blinked.

He opened his eyes to a far different scene.

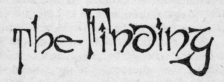

# The Finding

TRISTAN HAD WALKED many a dusty mile on the trail of this caravan, always just a little behind it, a few hours and miles late. He hadn't quite been reduced to stealing food; it was summer here, so he found berries in plenty, and wild duck eggs beside ponds, and begged a few meals as well. But his feet ached clean up to his hip-bones and Tristan was having a difficult time holding the object of his quest firmly in mind, especially at day's end or beginning. Sleeping under hedges did not clarify his thoughts in the least— and he could sleep only when absolutely necessary, never for more than an hour or two. His eyes felt as if someone had poured grit between their lids and stirred it around.

Tristan had no idea where he might be, except that he

was on a road, somewhere, mostly dirt and sometimes gravelled, and that just now it ran between rose hedges. The roses were as withered as he felt, dropping faded petals into the dust under his feet.

He had passed through two towns so far, their cobbles now only dimly remembered. He hadn't recognized either of them, hadn't expected to. Both places had held faint signs of his quarry—remnants of festivities, paper streamers and bits of food lying in the roadway, flattened patches of grass outside the town proper. And always, in answer to his question, yes, the carnival had gone on. That way. Some hours ago.

He hoped to catch up the next time they stopped in a town. It was his only hope, for the caravan travelled by wagon, and afoot he'd never catch them otherwise. The traces of magic that he followed were faint, but he wasn't sure if that might be due to time and distance or if they'd simply begun so.

Asking about shortcuts had been futile. He had the greatest difficulty making himself understood. There seemed to be something the matter with his voice.

It sounded just the same to his own ears, but whenever he spoke, Tristan was conscious of startled glances, not to mention the trouble people seemed to have understanding him. Someone sicced a fortunately mild-mannered dog on him once, and he had no way of knowing what he'd said or done to cause the misunderstanding. He'd noted that the folk he questioned all possessed the same weird accent to their speech; but, trained to languages as he had been in the course of his apprenticeship, Tristan was used to far worse. He hadn't yet reasoned that the speech difference might be alarming to someone without that experience.

By midmorning he was no longer alone on the road. He fell in with a herd of geese first, then passed a wagon laden with early vegetables and later on a jostling woolly confusion of sheep and lambs. The quality of the road improved, and a village came in sight at the edge of a broad lea. Between Tristan and the town lay a bright, noisy jumble, surrounded by people and produce.

Most of the past few days and all of his current surroundings dissolved into a sort of haze through which he passed without taking much notice. His goal was in sight. It was market day, and a crowd was gathered about the infrequent novelty of the travelling carnival.

Tristan slipped heedlessly through the crowd. Blais' spell sang in his head, the same pleased sort of sound as a cat's purr.

*Carrousel.* What, or who might that be? His conviction that Blais' spell had contained everything he'd need for his quest vanished.

Well, it would have to be something concerning horses, anyway. Tristan strolled casually past piles of foodstuffs, trying to quiet his empty belly. A sweetmeat seller was a further trial, but not a temptation. He hadn't a single coin of any sort on him and doubted that his money would have been acceptable here in any case. He hoped he was in the right place, at least. The slightest mistake in his reading of the incantation could have had all sorts of unexpected and unpleasant consequences, he knew. Still, it wasn't as if he'd been all on his own. At the time it had felt more as if the spell was reading him, and he'd been aware of Blais' firm control over his every word and motion.

A shriek ripped the air. Tristan whirled, eyes wide. *Toadstools*, what sort of idiot would pull up a mandrake root in the midst of such a crowd?

He steadied himself. Hearing the scream a mandrake gave as it was uprooted was instantly fatal. Harvesting had to be done at the dark of the moon, and the harvester had best stuff his ears well with wax. But he wasn't dead, and no one around him seemed to be either. So what—

The sound was repeated several times, in bursts of varying duration. Tristan steered toward it, through the press of marketers. After a few more preliminary shrieks, the noises steadied into something that he could recognize as music, though he didn't know the tune.

A puff of smoke rose into the air over the bobbing heads of the crowd. No, not smoke. Too white for that. It looked more like steam. Was there a travelling blacksmith among the farmers and tradesmen? Tristan drifted to the edge of the crowd.

And beheld the carrousel.

It could be nothing else, by the thrilling that ran through him at the sight of it. He seemed to see it through two sets of eyes. The grimoire, though tucked safe inside the pack

he wore strapped across his sho___
jump.

Its touch against his spine seemed to commu___ little eager
to Tristan. The thing making all the noise—for it plays
lustily now—was an instrument called a calliope, and those
puffs of steam which rose through its dozen pipes produced the sound. The larger thing behind it—that was the
carrousel.

Its workings consisted of many whirling gears and turning rods, in baffling profusion, and there was a hint of
steam about it too. Tristan was vaguely reminded of a
water-driven grain mill, but it wasn't the workings of the
thing which interested him. What the workings served to
move, that was his goal.

The wheel carried perhaps two dozen wooden horses, ar-
rayed in a double circle about a central hub. Poles ran
through their middles and attached them to the wheel under their feet and to something in the shadowy framework
above them, mostly hidden by the gaudy cloth which
formed a peaked canopy over them.

That was on the wagons I followed? Tristan wondered,
nearly aloud. Someone elbowed him roughly aside. He'd
been obstructing passage while he stared. He sidestepped
nearer the carrousel.

The caravan master made a final check of the assembled
carrousel, cast a knowing eye upon the freshly stoked
steam-donkey. All was in readiness for the day, at least
such readiness as might be possible with two of his roust-
abouts jailed for thieving and another run off the week past
after some foolish girl in a town they'd passed through,
leaving him shorthandedly trying to do the work of several.
Boards creaked under his boots. The sections of wooden
planking which made up the carrousel's floor were held
together more by hope than by any craft. Did this contrap-
tion but last out this summer's travel, he'd be properly
amazed. Greasings and wirings and creative if unorthodox
carpentries could do but so much—the machine was ancient and falling to ruin. It had seen too many years of
weather, as had he. Well, let it just last the summer, let
him but turn a decent profit, and he'd have the entire winter to work up a new attraction. A board worked loose be-

...ne stamped it firmly back into place. His side hi... longed for a beer to soothe it.

ac... was as ready as it would ever be. Jumping down inside the center of the wheel, the caravan master yanked at a great iron lever. With a squeal and a clashing only partly masked by the calliope, the wooden horses sprang forward.

He hadn't yet noted the youth dressed raggedly and somewhat oddly in gray homespun and road dust, who leaped back affrightedly when the horses rose on their poles. But much later, as the hours boringly crept by and the coins in the till remained depressingly few, the master marked him at last, standing gawking as if he'd done so all day and might happily continue so into the night. What have we here? The master wondered. The village idiot?

He wasn't watching the girl who fingered the keys of the calliope, either, though that would have been expected. Kirsten was a comely thing, well worth looking at, and her cheap costume showed a lot of leg. But no, it was the horses he watched.

The caravan master shoved his cashbox farther out of sight with one boot-toe, as he reached to collect a penny from a scruffy looking child. The watching lad looked a bit ineffectual for a footpad, but one never knew. Best not to tempt vagabonds.

The carrousel screeched into life again, and the vagabond in question scanned the circular herd, searching. The music picked up for a moment as the horses went around, now flying up, now sinking down, oddly sedate despite the wild pace of the music.

His eyes touched a black stallion in the outer ring, second behind a badly realized and greatly fantasized unicorn. Many times his gaze had found this horse, questioning, testing.

All the horses were in poor repair, their peeling paint showing many layers of color. They were decorated with knife cuts and old burns, their stirrups were mostly gone, their leather reins replaced with fraying rope. Among them, the black stood out.

He was no less filthy than the rest. But his painted skin was whole, under the dirt, and his carving was subtly fine,

different from the others. His ey...
and flashed it back proudly.

Somehow, no one had ridden him that day, or ...g sun
others, no matter how once-crowded the ride in its better
days, how eager its patrons. Had every other horse been
double-mounted, his back would still have been empty.

The stallion plunged beside a dappled gray showing
traces of red beneath many chippings. Another stride, one
more leap, and the black's bared teeth would catch the
gray, those silver-rimmed hooves rip and tear his wooden
flesh. The chips of red paint looked like old wounds.

The music faltered, stumbled. The horses obediently
lurched to a stop, some of them listing badly on their poles.
The black was now close to the watcher in gray, bright
pinpoint constellations burning in its eyes. With a last
flicker, the sun dipped behind the hills, and darkness fell.
The black's eyes stayed alight a shade longer than they
should have.

The caravan master climbed out of the circle, setting the
horses rocking gently into each other and their poles. He
crooked a finger at the calliope player, beckoning her to
join him for ale and supper before the evening's trade
brought an unlikely rush of custom. Off ahead, one of his
strolling players had begun a fire-swallowing act and another was doing less showy but equally exacting work as a
cutpurse.

Tristan, left alone and forgotten, peeped out from behind
the donkey-engine and looked unflinchingly into the universe within the black stallion's eyes. New suns burned and
matured there, blazed and then died in old age. Rivers
crawled under the black satin skin, forests of flowers grew.
The clash of fighting armies was faintly heard.

Tristan's gaze never wavered. Now he was sure, at last.
"Valadan," he said.

# Release

IT WAS LATE—or very early. The third, fourth hour of the morning, and the moon was down. A few stars still glittered fitfully. Under them and under rotting canvas and wagons, the caravan slept.

The shadows beside the carrousel stirred, ever so slightly. There were creakings, soft footsteps. The carrousel tilted imperceptibly, and a figure clad in tattered gray stood before the black stallion.

"Valadan," Tristan said, again.

There was no answering sound. The other steeds were frozen, leaping and prancing in midair, impaled with brass.

"Valadan, I have sought you long. Long—" Tristan stopped, seemed to consider. "— and I need your help."

He paused again, swallowing. Travel was still dusty in his throat. He'd never journeyed so far, not in all his life. The past days whirled, a nightmare of roads, seeking, hunger, and confusion. Then he steadied.

"I know you've never served one not of royal blood. I know you may kill me where I stand, if you choose. But I have to release you—not only for Allaire, even though I need you to help me find her. You should never have been prisoned, not . . . like this. Even if I didn't need your help, I could never leave you here."

The stallion's crystal eyes flashed. His bared teeth glowed in the starlight.

"I don't blame you. I would be angry, too, and filled with hate, after all this time." Tristan opened the grimoire, found the proper page and ran a finger down it, though the darkness was such that he couldn't see either the finger or the spell it stopped at.

He spoke the first word of power.

Valadan's satin skin shivered. Deep in his eyes, new light sparked. Rainbow colored lightnings flashed and

18

trembled. A night breeze blew up.... was stirred by it, too slightly to be seen.

"Valadan, I seek Allaire of the Nine Rings. ...ane help me?" Tristan asked formally. "For the old days, the old times, to be brought back again? Not for myself. I have no right to ask that of you."

He stood, looking into Valadan's eyes.

"Please." A longer moment passed.

Tristan felt a tugging at his mind, a hesitant tickle. It brushed him lightly, then passed on. He had a sudden memory of summer rains, and wild flights of autumn leaves.

*Yes.*

It came into his mind, but Tristan knew it was not his own thought. Numbly, he fitted his left foot into the stirrup and mounted. The horse vibrated like one of Blais' strange mechanical creations. Tristan put his arms out past the brass pole and took up the crimson leather reins.

He spoke the final words.

Under him, the world tilted. The brass pole shimmered, dissolved. Valadan moved on star-colored hooves, supple and easy as water flowing. He took one step, then another. He sprang effortlessly from the carrousel and danced over the flinty ground, wind whipping around him.

He trotted, feeling out this strange half-forgotten surface, caressing clover plants, touching gingerly at shadow-hidden grass and moss.

He grew more sure, and they first trotted, then galloped out across the lea. Crushed herbs scented the air about them, perfumes moist and dark.

Tristan was exhilarated. It had worked! Valadan was free! Pride in his success began to swell in him until he thought he might burst in another moment. Can you see me, Blais? See what I did? Me, who could never learn a proper rain-spell, or do a decent wart charm! I didn't fail you. Valadan runs free!

Valadan galloped, and the shadows that were trees and bushes in the daylight flowed ever more swiftly by. Feeling his stored strength, he quickened his pace. Tristan gaily urged him on. Valadan realized the truth of his freedom at last—no more running circled mile after tedious mile, tied

He could run as he was bred to, as he had seldom permitted himself to do. Dirt gave way to soft turf. Grass and pebbles flew from under his hooves. It mattered not.

Bruised grass smells were flung back in Tristan's face, then there was only the chill freshness of the air itself. Yet Valadan ran faster.

Too fast. Tristan was suddenly and forcefully reminded that he'd never been on a horse before. The realization shook him badly, to match the bumping he was already getting. He could keep no proper grip on the saddle, tossed about as he was. The leather felt as slippery as buttered glass. Every leap that Valadan gave threatened to make him part company with the saddle, yet he felt Valadan gather himself again, to level out and run still faster.

Tristan sawed on the reins, sought to tangle his fingers in the black mane, but there was no response. Valadan's neck was iron, immovable. He was drunk with running and he would never stop, no, not until he outran the earth and raced alongside the morning star.

That thought was not Tristan's. And he knew that he could no longer hold on or hope to control what he'd released. He lost both stirrups at one leap and lost the reins on the next. He fell.

The ground hit him hard. He rolled over twice, helplessly, and saw Valadan's hooves flashing, already far away. His failure was bitter and stunning in its swiftness.

*So I found him. What does that matter, when I couldn't even ride him? And what happens to the quest now, ended before it could begin? Valadan is more lost that ever!*

He heard a far-off wailing, which might have been himself, or just his ears ringing.

He didn't even think he could get home now—Blais' spell had utterly fled his mind or else gone on with Valadan. It didn't matter anyway. When he'd so utterly failed, what was the use of going home?

The darkness offered comfort, and Tristan fell back and let it claim him.

# The Quest Begins

TRISTAN WAS COLD, and wet.

Confused, he opened his eyes and saw trees and a blur of orange which focussed into a hawkweed flower hanging over his face. Something warm touched his cheek.

It was Valadan's breath.

Tristan found himself lying in dew-soaked grass spangled with thistles. One of them was under his back now, prickling. His head hurt badly, no doubt from its abrupt contact with the stony ground. Valadan stood over him, scuffing the grass anxiously with his forehooves and exhaling into Tristan's face. His breath smelled of hay.

Tristan could feel the horse's sorrow. Valadan had not intended him to fall. He was sorry. He'd been carried away by sudden freedom, had not meant to run so fast. It would not happen again.

Tristan sat up and instantly regretted it. He was sick, also instantly, in the grass. When he finally managed a dizzy look at the sky, he saw to his vast relief that the sun was still low. He'd been lying here no more than a couple of hours, then—it wasn't much past dawn. A wind was blowing, cold as Darkenkeep.

He sat a long time, his head on his knees and both hands on his head, in case it might decide to try rolling off his shoulders. He half wished it would anyway. Then maybe the pain would stop.

Valadan's nose shoved at him.

*It is not safe here. Is there somewhere we can go? Where were you intending to go?*

He focussed on Valadan's eyes, only inches away. His

...es reflected there were dark and hurt-looking, ...rdly their usual green. Valadan blinked, extinguishing them. Tristan blinked reflexively. When he looked again, his eyes seemed clearer, and the pain in his head was appreciably less.

"I had a place. We'll go there—if I can get us there. I'm not sure . . ." His voice trailed away.

Tristan got uncertainly to his feet, swaying. Nothing felt broken, anyway. Valadan's back loomed dismayingly high above him. He seemed to have forgotten just how one got up there. His head throbbed sharply.

Then the stallion was kneeling, waiting. Tristan scrambled awkwardly into the saddle, and the stallion arose gracefully, without the slightest jolt. He took a few steps.

*Which way?*

"Just walk. Slowly."

Could that have been the ghost of a laugh? Tristan reached into his pouch, found the carved wooden box that held his magical equipment. He selected certain stones and a rain-gray feather. Fingering the last, he began to speak, then stopped.

His mind had gone appallingly blank. No least wisp of Blais' spell seemed to remain, and he hadn't the faintest idea as to what use he'd expected to put the stones and feathers he'd selected.

Valadan pawed at the grass, as if sensing his distress. Then Tristan felt that probing and teasing at his mind again, briefly painful. He swayed a little in the saddle, caught at the pommel hastily.

*An interesting spell,* Valadan commented.

Think about something else, Tristan ordered himself desperately. Maybe then the spell would come sneaking around behind him, the way solutions came when he had stopped worrying about the problem. Valadan moved gently forward under him, and again there was that pricking at his mind. He seemed almost able to see something beyond—but he lost it.

One of the stones in his hand felt warm, and his fingers moved to stroke it in certain ways. Then Tristan found himself speaking, or rather chanting, as Valadan walked him into Blais' sorcery.

The chant shifted and grew as they walked, and the

world began to change around them. It took a long time.
Certain places, there were no landmarks at all, and Tristan
had to feel their way by instinct, by his fierce longing for
home. One false step would lose them forever; he knew
that too. It was hard to move at all with that fear bearing
down blackly, but Valadan seemed unworried. In some
places, the very stars were strange and disturbed Tristan so
that he could hardly look at them. They walked on.

It was dark by the time he became aware that they were
on the path to the cottage—indeed, that the shadow at the
end of the path was the cottage. The welcoming light Blais
had always left for him when he was benighted on some
errand was gone, and there was no moon now. Time was
different on the road, it seemed; he had no idea what hour
it was. Tristan slid awkwardly out of the saddle.

He led Valadan into the lean-to, unsaddled him and
rubbed him down with a hay-wisp. He hunted out a small
bag of good dry oats with which someone had paid off a
love-philtre and fed the grain to the horse out of the palms
of his hands. There was no proper manger. After the third
handful, Valadan lifted his head.

*Enough. That was not hard travel for me.*

Tristan drew water from the spring and carried the
bucket into the stable. He left Valadan drinking and stumbled on into the cottage.

He meant to light the fire and put the kettle on, to brew
up something that would ease his bruises and make the last
of his headache vanish. But just sitting down did both those
things, nearly enough, and he felt sleep creeping up on him
before his hands were halfway through the first sign. He
never made the second one. He wrapped up in his cloak,
and toppled over into a heap.

Morning sun streaming through the open window hit
him full in the face. He sat back out of it, rubbing his eyes,
until twinges prompted a quick check of his bruises. Nothing seemed irreparably damaged. But the thought of the
journey he'd just made and the shape he'd been in when he
made it scared Tristan badly. Anything might have happened. Anything covered a lot of possibilities, all of them
nasty. He was lucky to be back.

As the last power of Blais' spell evaporated, a sort of
dazed wonder replaced it. The very strangeness of the

place to which he'd been overwhelmed him. Without the spell's help he could never have functioned there. He had a sense of incredible distance, of years as well as miles, of having travelled farther than he could properly comprehend without Blais' help.

Tristan ducked his whole head into the fish-pond and felt much better for it. He dried off with a corner of his cloak, which was spattered with mud from that far-off place, tossed the whole mess in through the cottage door, and went to the stable to make sure he hadn't dreamed it all.

He hadn't. Valadan was busily eating the bedding straw and an old mouse-nibbled apple.

Tristan turned him out into the orchard, watching with delight as the horse took a long roll in the grass, his feet waving in the air as he gave great pleasureful grunts.

They'd never had a horse about before. Blais never made that much silver with his water-witching and his match-making. Tristan had never really seen a horse that wasn't galloping by with some great lord on its back, or pulling a vegetable cart to market. Certainly he'd never seen one behave in such ordinary and charming fashion. Valadan scrambled up, stretching out his head and shaking it so that dust flew and his mane slapped his neck.

The stallion was less than impressive, though, by daylight. Tristan was no proper judge, but Valadan really semed quite small, for a horse. His body was heavily built, though, promising power and speed. But he had seemed so much larger, finer drawn, in the night. He had no special style, Tristan thought, knowing horses mostly through the illuminations in Blais' hero-books, though his tail was undeniably long and silken. His main virtues lay in his speed and his courage. Still, Tristan could appreciate the finely chiselled bones of his face and the small ears whose tips pointed so delicately inward at each other when he stood at attention.

He had been sired by the swift west wind, so the legend ran, on a bay mare belonging to some long-dead Duke of Esdragon. She was the Duke's favorite, though too wild to be ridden, and would have no part of any earthly stallion. She outran them all, until some great wizard whose very name was now lost charmed down the wild wind for her

mate. She had lived only a few days after an understand-
ably difficult foaling, but the colt himself thrived and became an even greater favorite of the Duke than his mother
had been. All the Dukes, in fact. He carried them all into
battle, in their turns, for he never grew old, being bred by
magic and stamped more by his sire than by his earthly
dam. His wisdom was beyond that of many humans, it was
said. He had served nobly until the last Duke lay dying by
the side of his King, the swords they'd slain each other
with fallen from their cold hands. And Nímir drove Valadan away before him—

The stallion daintily nibbled a dandelion, then discovered
a windfallen apple. White teeth made short work of it.

Time Tristan was getting started. He had a lot to do.

He swept the ashes from the hearth, shook the mud off
the rugs, bolted the shutters down. No sense letting the
weather in—he might just get back someday. He stacked
the shelf-overflowing books as neatly as possible and
checked to be sure that all the jars of medicines and dried
herbs were tightly covered.

Valadan put his head in over the half-door, amused at
all the preparations, all that work. A magician ought to
have spells to do his chores for him.

Tristan did—but the last time he'd used one, he'd re-
moved the ashes from the fireplace and somehow deposited
them all over the mayor of Dunehollow's new surcoat. Fortunately the mayor had been in Dunehollow at the time,
and Tristan had only learned much later what had become
of those ashes. But he was wary yet of domestic spellcraft.

He heard a snort and caught a blur of motion over the
doorsill. There was a soft plop of cat-paws at his feet.

"Hello, Thomas. What's that, a mouse for my breakfast?"

The mouse was still very much alive, though terrified
into immobility. Its eyes were the size of swollen privet berries as Tristan lifted it up, settling it in the palm of his left
hand while his right forefinger stroked its nose. He smiled
at it, clucked encouragingly at it, got no response, and
turned to the cat.

Thomas regarded him impassively. The mouse finally
squirmed a little, and Tristan put it on the mantelpiece.

Instantly it vanished into a chink between the stones, even its snaky tail.

Thomas stood up and stretched, swishing his own tail and fanning his whiskers. Despite his years of living with a wizard, he could act like any other cat, when he chose.

"If you expect to eat mice, you should know better than to bring them to me first."

*Softheart. Do you seriously imagine that I enjoy eating mice? Or that I even do? I bring them to you because you enjoy letting them go. Why's the cream pitcher empty? And where were you yesterday?*

Tristan picked up the cat and walked to the table.

"I'm sorry. My oversight—I sent the cow away. I don't suppose you'll want any of this bread—it's very stale."

So, his whole trek in search of Valadan had occupied only one day here. He hadn't been sure how the spell would operate, though from the condition of the cottage he'd begun to suspect that he hadn't been gone so long as he'd supposed at first—unless perhaps Valadan had selected time as well as place while he searched Tristan's mind for Tristan's home.

He laid the loaf aside to be put into his pack—travel couldn't possibly ruin it further—and poured the last of their milk out for Thomas. There were still a couple of barley bannocks left from his last trip to the baker's, and he perched on the table's edge, eating one and looking down at the cat.

"Oh, Thomas, how did I ever get into this? It all makes as little sense to me as Blais teaching me magic in the first place." Events were beginning to seem overwhelming, now that he thought clearly about the things Blais had ordered him to attempt. "I've never been any good at it—why not just give up on me? Surely a wizard isn't honor-bound to apprentice any child left in his orchard on Midwinter's Night?" He didn't wonder if Thomas knew what he was talking about—cats make it their business to know everything. Thomas was sure to know at least as much as Tristan himself did about everything that had transpired here.

He'd begun speaking lightly enough, but he remembered suddenly what had become of Blais, and finished by stifling a sob.

"I wonder what happened, if he—" Tristan shook his

head. "Well, that goes nowhere. I'll never know." And he never even said goodbye to me, Tristan thought sickly, choosing self-pity in place of terror at his new aloneness. He slid onto a chair, and laid his head on the knife- and burn-scarred table that had served them for experimenting and teaching and concocting and eating for his whole life so far. Strange that a mere table should remain, a dead piece of wood, and Blais should be gone.

Thomas gave vent to an impatient mew.

"What? You're still hungry?" Tristan blinked away tears. "Here, then. It will probably do you more good than it will me." He took a second bite of bannock himself, chewing reflectively. He rubbed at one knee, which was bruised and aching.

"I'm so inept, Thomas. Blais has been gone—what, two days?—and I've already half killed myself. I feel like something you'd fling out on the rubbish heap. It's all very well for Blais to leave a spell to guide me to the place where he found Valadan and teach me how to release him and say that the quest is mine to finish. But now I'm on my own! How am I ever going to convince Polassar to throw in his lot with me, just for starters? He's a warrior, he's used to having his own way, and he's rich. What does he want with a crazy wizard? And even you must admit that I don't look like much, not to inspire the confidence of someone like that." The cat was watching him unwinkingly. "You want to come with me, Thomas?"

Thomas scraped himself against Tristan's ankles. Tristan sighed.

"You must be demented. *I* don't even want to come with me. But you've got cat-magic, and cat-sense which is better, and I shall be glad of your company."

He looked at his pack, waiting to be filled. Well, it might be interesting to travel, have adventures. Hadn't he always longed to? "Come and meet Valadan properly."

*We've met,* Thomas said, but followed along.

Valadan glanced up from his grazing as Tristan approached with cat and saddle.

"This is Thomas, my familiar."

He smiled, remembering the joking way Blais had always used the term—which was best used loosely where it concerned Thomas.

*I am not your familiar,* Thomas responded. *No true cat would ever be party to such a demeaning arrangement, as well you should know. I've tried hard enough to educate you, undeserving though you are.*

"My good friend, then." He looked at Thomas. "Yes?" He turned back to Valadan.

"He's agreed to help us with the quest. He's a mighty warrior in his own way, a very terror to rats and mice." Valadan gravely sniffed the cat, his breath ruffling soft tabby fur. Thomas bore the snuffly greeting well— Valadan after all being no ordinary horse.

Of course, ordinary cats didn't speak either, even subvocally. And either Thomas was a most special cat—as he always hotly insisted—or Tristan was more adept at listening than most, for the cat had been talking to him ever since that fateful day when a kitten had followed a lonely boy back from Dunehollow. No use blaming magic for this thing, Tristan supposed. Thomas spoke, and that was that. Maybe some travelling mage had witched his mother. Thomas wasn't saying, or maybe not admitting that he knew no more of his origins than Tristan did of his own. Maybe Tristan's unknown mother had been witched, since he could hear Thomas—and now Valadan, also.

Tristan readied Valadan with great care, combing out the rippling silk of the stallion's mane and tail, smoothing the wondrously soft skin of the thick neck. On Valadan's broad back, and again on the belly, the hair grew in circular whorls about the size of Tristan's palm, at the spots where the carrousel pole had passed. Tristan brushed the stallion's coat most carefully, gingerly avoiding those spots.

The saddling itself took much longer. He'd never saddled a horse, or even seen it done, and the multiple straps and bits of webbing were confusing. He wished he'd been more alert when he'd taken the stuff off the night before. Thomas sat on a fence post and offered pungent commentary, but little real help.

*"Fennel!"* Tristan said furiously, having caught his fingers in the same buckle for the third time. Valadan swiveled his head about, ears pricked curiously. The flashing colors of his eyes were dimmer this morning, but there for the looking.

"I'm sorry," Tristan said. "It's just that I've never done this before. I wasn't hurting you, was I?"

Valadan tossed his head. *No. The girths must be much tighter, or the saddle will slip and you will fall. I will let my breath out while you pull.*

Tristan only pulled timidly at first, until Valadan said, *Harder.* Then the buckle's tang slid into the proper hole with ease. Valadan dipped his head, pleased.

The mysteries of the bridle were more easily unravelled, with Valadan's help. Tristan held the silver bit, its ends shaped into falcon's heads, between his palms, breathing on it to take the chill off the metal. Valadan whinneyed gratefully, mouthing the bit as Tristan buckled the headstall behind his ears.

He led Valadan to the door, finally, and tied the reins to the boar's-head knocker. Thomas sprang to the saddle and perched there, purring in the sunlight.

Tristan dressed himself for travel as best he could. It was a shame his sweater and breeches were so patched, but at least they were clean and warm in the cool morning air. And the silver unicorn that formed his belt buckle did add a certain note of errantry to the ensemble. He took a quick look at himself in Blais' tall glass, which hung opposite the fire.

What he saw there never failed to surprise him, since he'd never felt quite so thin as the mirror showed. And surely his nose wasn't really that long—but he'd never been able to prove a flaw in the glass. The only thing that looked right to him was the bruise and scrape over his left eyebrow, and that only because he'd been painfully aware of it ever since he'd wakened that morning.

Toadstools! Why did his hair always look so in need of cutting? He shoved the shadow-dark strands impatiently back from his eyes. It looked as if he'd cut it himself with a very dull knife—and he smiled, remembering that he had. They hadn't earned enough coppers to have the barber stop by last month. The weather had been rough, and the young maids of Dunehollow-by-the-Sea had had no need of love charms to keep their sea-roving men at home.

He turned away from the glass and began packing essentials: his box of stones, of course, some few herbs and medicines that might be useful, his brass table-knife, Blais' gri-moire. A pot, a spoon, bread, a bit of cheese. Everything went into a shapeless leather bag, which unfortunately was neither magic nor bottomless. Fishhooks, wire for a rabbit snare. Instinct told him that he should travel light—and possessions only tended to get lost anyway. Wizards were supposed to rely on their powers for creature comforts. His own comforts would be few indeed, in that case.

His magic-kit he knew well. All the pebbles and feathers in it were worn with use or attempted use.

There was his firestone, and a bit of star-white crystal, a smooth gray stone and a puff of down, white as a snow-flake. A gray feather tipped with white and a smaller feather the color of rain. A stone that was flat and round-edged like a coin, dead black and smooth as night. A flake that shimmered and sparkled and might be used for catch-ing sunbeams. A crow's feather, should he ever want to play with thunderstorms.

A few things he regretted leaving behind. He might need any of Blais' books—but which? There was no room for them all, so he must depend on what he could keep in his head. What he hadn't learned by now, he must do without. And he'd surely miss the glow of that fat yellow candle, and long for the comfort of its burnt vanilla scent. But what possible use would it be? Likewise, the oddly shaped red and blue stone Blais had insisted had no power, but was merely an old friend and a good paperweight. And those dried weeds in the jar by the door—he remembered so clearly the bright day last fall when he'd gathered them. If he could take just one along, he felt he could have the warmth and color of the day always.

It was no use wishing. He didn't even have room for an extra blanket. He would take the whole cottage with him if he could. Tristan sighed, then smiled at his weary, mir-rored self, and fastened his heavy cloak about his neck. No sense taking chances. The sky was clear, but there were clouds on the horizon, and his rain-spell probably wouldn't work again.

His sword hung by the hearth, half hidden in shadow. Tristan reached it down and unsheathed it slowly.

No uncanny light ran down the blade, and there were no runes in gold etched along it. It was blackened past all hope of polishing, and badly notched near the guard. The hilt was in slightly better shape, being leather inlaid with silver wire, all smoothly worn, but once very fine. That silver, suitably spelled by Blais, protected his sword-hand better than any glove could have done.

It had made no singing response as he unsheathed it, and there was no magic thrill of power running up his arm as he held it, no eagerness in it to be used. But it balanced perfectly in his hand and it moved at his bidding, swift and sure as a part of his arm. Even Blais had allowed that he fenced well, and Blais was fit to be a master in that art, as well as in magic.

He belted the sword on and became belatedly aware of a bird singing. It bubbled happily on as he crossed to the cage that hung by the window.

"Ah, Minstrel, my troubador, did you think I'd forgotten you?" In truth, he nearly had. Luckily another spell of Blais' kept seed and water continually available to the bird. He opened the cage's wire door and brought the canary out on his first finger, still singing.

"You're happy today. Did you miss me?" Tristan gently stroked the gray and white feathers, then the golden wings. Minstrel pressed against his hand. "I have to go away again for a while, and what shall I do with you this time?" Tiny rough feet gripped his finger tightly.

Tristan thought a moment, mentally thumbing over spells, cataloguing their reliability in respect to himself.

"I'll send you to a lady, the daughter of some great lord, and she shall love you almost as dearly as I do. You can live in a cage of pure gold and bathe in a silver dish." Minstrel squeaked. "Yes, you'd like that. And you shall dine on honey-cakes and strawberries."

Tristan lifted his hand, fingers held at strange angles as he began to make a pass. This wasn't really difficult, he promised himself—his magic was working pretty well today, which was to say he hadn't tried any yet, hence no disasters—and Blais had often used Minstrel so, as a messenger. The lady in question was an old customer, familiar to Minstrel. The bird probably knew the spell himself.

He shut his eyes the better to concentrate, then opened them instantly in surprise.

Minstrel had left his finger, after dealing it a nip that

drew a drop of blood. He circled Tristan's head once, beating at it with his wings, then settled on Tristan's shoulder, chirping angrily.

"What? Oh, no, Minstrel, you can't come with me! We'll be going into terrible danger, not to mention discomfort. It will be frightfully cold, and—"

Minstrel continued to scold, dancing from one foot to the other. He caught a loose thread on Tristan's cloak, and tugged fiercely.

"Minstrel, I—"

*Let him come. The little one has a great heart.*

Tristan threw Valadan a startled look. Close to the stallion's, he saw Thomas' unwinking eyes. *Bring him,* Thomas advised. *He'll die of loneliness, else.*

He looked at them both, then slid his eyes around to where Minstrel sat. Bright black eyes looked boldly back, as Minstrel deftly husked a millet seed, dropping the bits down Tristan's neck.

"What can I say?" He shrugged in helpless fashion, and the canary took a tighter hold on his cloak. Tristan sighed and tucked a packet of seed into the last space among the other articles in his pack. The cottage looked very forlorn now, worse than the empty birdcage with its door swinging open.

Tristan took a last puzzled look round, lingering. He wasn't taking that much with him—how could the place look so desolate?

*We should not tarry here.*

Valadan had pulled his head back from the door and was sniffing the air, sifting smells. *Something seeks us.*

Tristan stiffened. The sun had suddenly dipped behind a cloud, and he felt chilled, as if an icicle had brushed his spine. And Valadan was right. A something, a searching sniffling something, was very close. Tristan stepped toward the door.

"Let's get out of here."

They rode, the canary on his shoulder still, and the cat perched on the saddlebow. Tristan reined in at the first turn of the path—or rather Valadan paused there, sensing Tristan's need in spite of his desire for haste. Tristan sat quietly a moment, then urged the horse swiftly on. It took all his strength to turn his back on the cottage, and he

forced himself not to look a second time. This might be the
last time he would ever see his home.

At that moment, that seemed certain.

Looking ahead, he didn't see the cottage door breathe
open slightly, as if something had stealthily entered. Inside,
the crystal ball glimmered fitfully, and papers stirred.

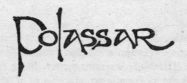

# Polassar

THE ROAD to Lassair Castle was like all the roads in Calandra—long, winding, rutted deeply. They went crosscoun-
try at every opportunity, to save time and jolting. It turned
out that Valadan knew the way quite well.

He cantered slowly at first, while Tristan accustomed
himself to riding. Fortunately he was young, adaptable, and
learned quickly. The pace picked up, and they flew over
moor and woodland, pausing only to ford streams. Even
mounted, Tristan found running water unsettling. They
used nothing like Valadan's full speed, of course.

Despite travelling as a bird might, direct and unde-
toured, they saw few people. Incessant warring of years
past had taken its toll of the population, and the harsh winters which had been the norm since Nímir took an interest
in Calandra made farming difficult here in the north. Folk
lived off the sea where they could, and hugged coasts and
roads. It had not always been thus—they passed many ruined cottages, sometimes whole hamlets slowly disappearing into the sparse forests. And once the stone bulk of a
castle hove up to their right, still secure behind its reedy
moat, its tower windows blind as empty eyes.

Tristan was curious and sent Valadan closer. There were
no castles near Dunehollow; he knew them only from the
drawings in Blais' books. This one was fair to look at, but
when they rode round to its far side they found the walls
blasted and crumbling, the whole like a windfallen pear
eaten out from the back by wasps. Magic had been needed
to end a siege with destruction on that scale. Tristan was

impressed, awed, and yet more curious, but Valadan was reluctant to stay, and Thomas seconded him.

*Beware your long nose leading you into trouble, Blais always said.*

"But this might have been Rynarin's work, or Powell-lynd's," Tristan pleaded, wanting a much closer look. The study of the remains of magical work was proper to an apprentice, at any time.

*So? They're long dead, and so's this place. And I don't like it. Valadan doesn't either—he says he knew it in times past, and it saddens him.*

That was that. Tristan felt himself definitely outvoted in the matter, and let Valadan trot away without further comment. Was he never to see firsthand any of the works of the Nine Mages he'd read about so often?

They reached Lassair just at nightfall. For the past hour the ground had been growing steadily more desolate. Wars had stripped it barer than was usual, and the fighting here had been more recent. Polassar held claim to a poor land now, though once it had been fruitful.

His castle reared itself up from a stony outcrop that long ago had been forested. Scrawny stumps were all that remained of the trees near the rough red walls. There was a fire-blackened gap in the south wall, and a gang of men were busy around it, carrying bricks and mortar.

Tristan looked them over from a distance, then rode unhesitatingly up to a red-haired man who wore a sky blue cloak bordered with red lions. He was shouting at a brick carrier, who scuttled away barely in time to avoid a blow. Bricks went everywhere. There was considerable confusion, and the man in blue swore louder, then turned half away, stamping his feet.

"My lord Polassar."

"Ha! Who calls?" The man turned on Tristan, and half bared his teeth. One hand went to the hilt of his longsword, as much by deep habit as current prudence.

The light from the setting sun flared back hotly blue from the man's eyes. Tristan realized that he must be practically invisible against the brightness behind him—a looming shadow on a shadow-steed. Polassar might well have thought him a ghost or an assassin. The man didn't look as if he particularly feared either possibility, but he was wary.

"I am called Tristan. May we talk? Without—that?" Tristan gestured at the sword. "I assure you, I'm no enemy of yours."

"So you say. Yet you know my name?" Polassar squinted at him.

"Friends as well as enemies know names. And all men know the rightful King of Calandra." Careful, not too thickly at first! Tristan was inwardly marvelling at his own bravery. Being astride Valadan lent him a little courage. He tried to act as a mysterious shadow-wizard should.

Polassar bared his teeth even further, then threw back his head and laughed until great tears streaked his face. He paused, then stroked his moustaches back into place.

"Think you 'twas my friends made yon new gate?" He gestured at the ragged gap in the wall. "Who are you, flatterer?"

"A wizard, of sorts. And as for that—" Tristan also pointed at the wall. "I may offer you a remedy. May we talk?"

"Talk costs me little. And my throat is dry. Join me in a cask of ale, wizard of sorts."

Polassar wore his hair cropped short, for ease under a war-helm, but neither cutting nor being cramped under a cap of steel restrained it very much. It grew to a peak over his forehead and spread back in two wings along the sides of his head, unfurling now as he tugged off the helm. The hairs' deep convolutions might have been chased in copper. In legends, they would have been. A white line across his brow marked where the day's dust and summer's tan stopped. He looked briefly weary.

Tristan's own hair was wind-tangled and overlong. He tried impatiently to brush it clear of his eyes without much success. Polassar eyed him expectantly, waiting for Tristan to state his business.

After his long ride, the room seemed cramped and oddly still, though doubtless this was one of the best Lassair had to offer. It faced on an inner courtyard and thus had avoided battle-damage. And it smelled as if its windows hadn't been unshuttered in a twelvemonth. Tristan frowned and tried to hide his nervousness. He also tried to swallow, but his throat was full of dust, and he only started a coughing fit which refused to be stifled.

Polassar obligingly slapped him on the back—doubtless a gentle blow from him, but it doubled Tristan over until his chest met painfully with the table's edge.

"Aye, well, I did promise you ale." Polassar called then for food and a cask.

Apparently the offer of joining him in a cask had been meant literally. The level of that cask must have dropped very rapidly too, from what Tristan observed. How did the man ever brew enough ale to supply himself—let alone his household and army—in the middle of all this fighting?

The lord of Lassair's table manners would have done little credit to his lowest horseboy. Tristan wondered openmouthed at the amount of food that went into Polassar, and wondered even more that any got in, so haphazard was Polassar about it, drinking and talking and gulping down bread and venison all at once. That his generous moustaches weren't chewed as well was yet another wonder.

For his own part, Tristan ate little. He nearly choked again on the dry bread, which wasn't fresh and hadn't been in some days. The venison was little better. Polassar had been at war and under various attacks for such a long while that he doubtless no longer noticed food's quality so long as it was forthcoming in sufficiently vast quantity. Tristan drank his ale down a shade too quickly and wished he'd brought Thomas along instead of insisting that the cat remain with Valadan. He could have used the cat's suggestions. His right foot ached for the warm feel of the cat leaning against it.

In fact, his legs ached anyway. Horseback riding made lazy muscles protest painfully. He'd been very glad to dismount in the courtyard. He shifted about in his seat, hoping for a little ease, and Polassar caught the movement. His eyes flickered over the edge of his ale-mug.

Tristan set his own mug down firmly.

"I said I could offer you help, Polassar. I have to be honest and say that I've come to ask it of you as well."

"Ha?" Polassar glanced up from the rib-bone he was gnawing clean.

"I seek Allaire of the Silver Rings. And without you I cannot succeed. So the prophecy says. You are the rightful Heir to Calandra's throne."

"But not its only claimant." Polassar gestured at a map on the wall of the chamber, studded with enamelled pins of many bright colors. They signified armies and ringed the drawing of Lassair very closely round.

"No. But your claim is the only one that runs straight and true, without question or taint. You are the one." Tristan explained his quest briefly, and Polassar nodded often as he spoke.

"So the wizard told my father. I should have known. You're not the first to come here on this errand."

"No?" Tristan asked, and cursed the surprised sound of the word.

"No. I recollect once a mage came here when I was a child, begging my father's help, calling him the true Heir. I didn't know what he meant at first. He pleaded well, and told my father all about how Allaire was destined to win Calandra for him."

"So you do know of Allaire?" This might make things easier between them. Though he might have mentioned the fact earlier, and saved a long and mouth-drying speech.

"Oh, aye. Family legend and all that. Very colorful. But what's it to do with me now, other than as a tale to pass long winter nights with the telling? The girl's been dead since time began, or nearly."

"And what did your father do about it?" Tristan asked, not to be distracted into a long evening of reminiscences.

"My father stayed home! He was no fool, wizard!"

Tristan looked away, into the bottom of his mug. Fine time for it to be empty.

"I can't claim that title. I'm not really a wizard. Oh, I didn't lie to you—it's just that my master died before my training was complete. But he did charge me with his quest. What—ah—happened to this other wizard?" Even as he asked it, he wished he hadn't, because he knew only too well what happened to wizards who quested for Allaire. By the legends, death was the most wholesome end one could expect.

Polassar shrugged, and downed a great draught of ale. "Who knows? He never came back. None of them ever do.

Maybe it's nature's way of getting rid of foolish wizards."

"He most likely went to his death," Tristan said, a little stung. "It takes a brave man to set out on a journey, knowing he can never hope to return."

"Or a stupid one." Polassar drained the cask now, lifting it one-handed. "You wizards must all be fools. Do you never tire of your fruitless searches? And aren't you a bit young to be off alone on such an important quest?"

Tristan smiled in what he hoped was a worldly-wise manner.

"Age isn't a consideration on quests," he said. He might have invoked the case of Kewane, who'd discovered the powers of the diamond Sterldrig at the tender age of fourteen, but didn't. Polassar probably wouldn't appreciate the reference anyway. "And I might be older than I look."

Polassar bared his incisors sceptically.

"You cut a better figure on a horse," he said idly. "Took you for Death himself, come to invite me to the Hunt. A sad, gallant end, fit for a saga. And instead you give me legends written in moon-wine by doddering old men who dream of magic."

Tristan felt his face go hot.

"I've told you why I need your help. I also said you need mine. Aren't you curious about that?"

Polassar didn't even trouble to look at him. "Not very."

Tristan stood angrily, the ale buzzing in his head, and flung an arm out toward the window.

"How did that hole get in your wall, anyway? Have you ever wondered why you have so many enemies? Where they all come from? How many more attacks you can beat off, sieges withstand?"

Polassar lurched to his feet.

"See here, wizard—"

"Hear me out!" He was shouting now, impressively enough to override even Polassar. If he were going to be thrown out, he'd at least have his say first. "I don't doubt you can stand them off—so long as they come singly! But how long will it be before it occurs to them to band together? What happens if they all attack at once, every last one of them?"

"What are you getting at? I know my dangers, man."

"Why are they your enemies?"

"They dispute my claim to the throne. They haven't your sense in these high matters."

"Why?" Tristan catechized relentlessly.

"Why? Why—"

"Who puts the thoughts into their heads? Who keeps this feud alive, son after father after father. Who pours evil into men's minds like treacle over porridge? Shall I tell you? Or would you rather I not mention his name? They do say it has the power to invoke him." That wasn't true, but it was impressive.

"No! I catch your meaning, I think." Polassar shook his head slowly, as if that helped thought. "Do you say the Cold One is behind these attacks?"

"Who else? Isn't his hatred for Calandra old and deep? He's worked hard to destroy you, bit by bit—and now he's nearly ready to close his hand. Will you sit passive while he does so? Or will you come with me?"

Tristan thrust out his hand. The moment was crackling with emotion.

Polassar ignored it.

"What makes you so sure your quest will succeed? None other has. And you'd better have a blasted good reason, before I'll put faith in you. You ask a lot on trust alone. I am not fond of wizards. You're just another unnecessary trouble."

Tristan sank back into his chair, staring at his hands. Then he leaned forward suddenly and spoke with intensity.

"Three things are needed to release Allaire," he said. "A mage, the Heir of Calandra, and the warhorse Valadan. Quests have failed because the mage could not convince the current Heir to join him. Some chose the wrong man and failed. But most of all, they were doomed to fail because they forgot to seek for Valadan. It was decided long ago that Nímir had hidden him too well, that he could never be found and the quest must be tried without him, no matter what the prophecies said. Too many mages stopped seeking him, and that was a grave mistake."

"And you have sought?" Polassar's tone was half interest, half insult.

"Better than that. But you saw him," Tristan added smugly.

"What?" Polassar whistled between his teeth, as he realized what Tristan meant. He leaned back, hands behind his head. "I'd never have believed it. Wizard, you must be something more than you look."

He gave Tristan's face a searching glance.

"Was the last Heir to whom you mentioned this crackbrained quest the one who marked your face?"

Tristan fingered his eyebrow, tracing the bruise around it.

"No," he said, very quietly, faintly surprised that Polassar would have thought along those lines. "No. There is only one true Heir. I've come only to you."

Polassar thrust his chair away, and walked to the window. He strode back to the table, seemed about to speak, then moved restlessly back to the window again.

He's not going to do it, Tristan thought. I'm not surprised. Toadstools, I've failed Blais again! And I don't even care. I'm too tired. My head aches—every bone in my body hurts. I doubt I'll be able to walk by morning. I suspect I'm drunk.

There was no use even watching Polassar. When the lord of Lassair decided to throw him out, doubtless he'd be informed. His chin sank onto his chest, as much from sleepiness as depression.

"By the Gates, wizard, I think I'll do it!"

Tristan gave a start.

" 'Tis folly—but a man must seize adventure where it offers. And for sure there's nothing here. Not now. You were right, though, 'tis a pity. One more big attack and 'twill all be over."

Tristan watched him, wide-eyed now. Polassar continued to stride about the room, clanking as he armed himself, speaking loudly of the great feats they would accomplish.

He makes up his mind in a hurry, and no half-way about it, Tristan thought.

Polassar was lacing up his mail-shirt, snapping wide brass armlets onto his wrists. Next the two-handed sword went back on, and a helmet of brightly polished steel, adorned with a snarling bear.

He turned, the bear's face riding just above his own. It was an awesome sight.

"Well, wizard, don't just sit there gaping like a fish! When do you want to leave?"

Tristan got up again, shaking inwardly with excitement and chill, for there was no fire lit on the room's hearth. He crossed to the window. "Moonrise," he said, looking down into the courtyard where Valadan stood tethered. "The road to Darkenkeep is clearest then. And that is the road we must follow."

# Winterwaste

THE WIND HOWLED petulantly, full of snow.

"I thought you said this road was clear!" Polassar was an angry voice, lost somewhere in the blowing snow behind Tristan.

"It is!" The soothing intent of his words was spoiled by the need to shout them. "You just can't see it, my lord. How is your horse standing up?"

"Ha! This mare is ugly, I'll grant you that, but you'll not find her mate in all the known lands. She's twice as mean as she looks and thrice as tough! She'll match your magic horse mile for mile, no fear." Polassar was proud of his boney mount, inordinately so, to Tristan's mind.

The road stretched like a silver ribbon ahead of Tristan, though to Polassar this was nothing more than cold wasteland, trackless and unmarked. No trees even grew here, or else they were buried in the snowdrifts. There were no landmarks, nothing to break the wind's force in any direction until you came to Darkenkeep—or if you were wiser, went back the way you'd come. Tristan wished that Polassar could see the road. Two pair of eyes watching would have been less wearisome.

He also vainly wished that he'd been able to snatch more than an hour's sleep at Lassair. That hour had proved more tiring than refreshing, and he hadn't felt well since.

Their departure couldn't be delayed. He'd read that the road was visible only to wizards and was clearest at the rise of a full moon. This moon would soon begin to wane, and Tristan wanted them to have the best possible start. Especially since he wasn't any too sure how sharp his perception of the road would be.

He and Polassar talked sometimes, when conditions permitted their horses close enough for speech without shouting. It helped keep the strangeness of the Winterwaste at bay.

"This spreads farther every year, despite all the mages do. If Nímir has his way, all Calandra will look like this!" The ribbon gave a sharp twist, and Tristan stopped speaking as he guided Valadan around it.

"How much more?"

"No man knows. None has ever returned to tell of it, except those who crossed the Waste's edge and didn't linger. We shall reach Darkenkeep soon enough. Long before we're ready to do so—or really wish to. The Winterwaste is considered trifling, compared to what lies beyond the Gates."

They'd ridden the whole first night away, and only reached the Winterwaste's nearest edge. Valadan could have covered the distance more swiftly, of course, but there was Polassar's mare to think of. No matter how extraordinary—either in ugliness or virtue—she was still unmagical flesh and blood. And they still moved at a good enough pace.

Polassar had not once seemed to question the wisdom of his sudden decision. Tristan was frankly amazed. His own mind was questioning all the time, as was his now shivering body. He'd huddled beside their small campfire re-reading every word in Blais' grimoire that pertained to Darkenkeep and the Winterwaste while Polassar unimaginatively slept. And he'd only found more possibilities to worry over. He knew he should sleep, but couldn't seem to do so in the daylight, and the wind off the Waste before them chilled him to the marrow.

Sometimes his breath frosted the grimoire's pages. He skimmed over instructions for dealing with cockatrices and changing the color of tulip bulbs. Neither was likely to be useful to him, however fascinating. He did find a formula which set his firestone glowing for a while, but it only burnt his fingers without warming the rest of him.

Snow drifted hard across their path. It reared up like a

live thing, full of menace, choking. The wind wailed and shapes moved in it.

"Wizard, stop! I hear voices—some lost travellers, think you? We must help them from this place!"

"Do not look!" Tristan grabbed Polassar's reins and dragged the other horse forward. "There's nothing alive here but us! You hear a trap, laid for the unwary. My book warned me of such. Once we've passed through it, it will trouble us no more."

Polassar hesitated. This was the first real opposition they'd met, except for the incessant wind, and also the first test of Tristan's authority. As they stood, the voices pleaded the more loudly.

"An enchantment?"

"Yes. And if we stray off the path after it, we'll never find the path again. We can follow those voices till we freeze, and never find them either."

"Aye." The hood of Polassar's cloak might have been empty, so shadowed it was as he stood listening. The moon picked out the fangs of his bear-helm, nothing more. Not even a glitter of eyes. The voices gave a last despairing wail as he kicked his mare into motion.

Tristan felt a heart beating close to his own, and a warm stirring of feathers. Minstrel rode safe, nestled inside his sweater. Thomas was in his pack, well fastened down and very unhappy, though less miserable than he'd have been with ice-crusted fur. An odd fellowship, this. Polassar had been full of mirth when he learned of it. Thomas had not been amused.

The snow had been dry and stinging. It now turned wet, and clung to face and clothes. Its weight increased rapidly. Valadan surged forward with a tremendous effort.

Next moment, ice needles were flaying their faces to bone. Tristan dragged his cloak across as a shield. That left a gap farther down, through which chill air flooded. He heard Polassar give a muffled shout and tried to answer him.

"This too shall pass. Nímir guards his hold well, against all comers." He tried to sound matter-of-fact about it, as if he did this sort of thing every day.

"Aye. This would turn many back." Polassar sounded as if he wished he were among the many.

"There's worse in store," Tristan whispered dismally, to his own ears alone.

The sleet fell away into nothing. The ground snow thinned, and they could move easily. The terrain was very flat, leaving them once more to the wind's tender mercies.

"That must blow for twice a hundred leagues."

*At least.* Valadan had his ears laced back tight against his neck. Next moment, they plunged into a belly-deep drift.

Tristan swallowed snow, breathed it deep through nose and mouth. He nearly lost the saddle, he was choking so hard. They floundered twenty long paces, following a path that was no more than a phosphorescent hint. Tristan ceased to wonder if Polassar was following him. All that mattered was the road and keeping to it. One step off it, and he was sure he'd never find it again.

Follow the path! Nothing else existed. Just keep to the light, the road that only shows under the moon. Tristan heard curses behind him and knew that Polassar was still there.

"Why set a path to follow, if he'll go to such lengths to keep us from following? It makes small sense," Polassar complained irritably. If snow and wind had found ways into his cloak as easily as they had into Tristan's, he could hardly be blamed.

"A challenge. To attract the best of mages and heroes, lure them to their deaths. Thus he weakens Calandra."

"Wizard, I almost wonder what you're leading me into."

Tristan thought perhaps Polassar was laughing, but it was difficult to be sure with the wind howling so.

After a time they had to dismount, struggling waist deep themselves, dragging the horses after them. They began to feel that it should be morning, but no light was seen. No stars, either; there had been none since they entered the Winterwaste. The path looked straight here, but Tristan felt they were twisting and circling, despite that. The sky went white, and there was no shade of difference between it and the ground. They walked within clouds, it seemed. How easy to doze among them, and sleep away into death.

Snow still fell—it struck their faces and melted softly. There was no seeing it. Tristan's feet were numb, his senses dulled. He was somewhere beyond mere cold now.

Then it all stopped. The air was still and barely frosty. The ground was rock now, wind-battered, with little ripples of snow wind-spread across it.

And the path! It spread from their feet straight as a flung dagger, wide as a doorway, to the Gates—and beyond, Darkenkeep. It seemed to bid them welcome.

# Darkenkeep

ITS SHAPE was that of a great fanged mouth, rimmed with teeth of ice. At the sides, the ice formed mighty columns, thick as a man, higher than trees. Icicles hung down from the roof also, dripping watery venom down onto the pitted snow. Wind whistled among them, sounding like mocking laughter, and there came a tinkling from inside, as if part of the vast roof had fallen in.

Ice might quench the fires of Polassar's brows and moustaches, but never the hot blue of his eyes. They stared out, surrounded by spikes of white.

"Come, wizard, what holds us here gawking? Dare we not venture in?"

They led the weary horses and tied them just within the Gates. Tristan tried to lay a small protection around them, that they might not be driven away by fear or come to any harm. Then he unsheathed his sword.

"Follow me. Keep just behind, walk only where I do, touch nothing. There are bound to be traps here, and tricks. Magic," Tristan went on as they crossed the great cavern, skirting hissing pools of unwholesome snow-melt.

"Aye." Polassar's sword hissed free of its scabbard. "Wait here for me, evil-tempered one." Exhausted, his roan mare still had strength enough to bite at him as he left her.

Valadan watched them out of sight before bending his head to the oats they'd left and bidding the mare do the same.

Within, the ice pillars continued for some way, in double rows, only their varying thicknesses ruining their semblance to a king's throne hall. The baleful chill emanating from them prompted Tristan to pull his cloak tighter about his neck. He wished they'd brought torches, which would have been more reassuring than this icy werelight.

Thomas soft-footed behind, stepping fastidiously. His long fur brushed the snow, leaving curious patterns in his wake. If he felt cramped by his long cold ride, he said nothing of it.

"Is there no guardian for these halls, wizard?"

Thomas leaped two feet straight to the left and landed spitting, as Polassar's idea of a respectful whisper shook down six icicles from the roof behind them.

"There's a Guardian," Tristan said into the silence that followed. "A dragon, some say."

"A worthy adversary for my blade."

"Then pray we don't meet it! We've no time to waste tackling something of that size."

"Well, do your books suggest what other perils we've to face?"

"Not by name." Tristan stepped gingerly over an improbably steaming rivulet. How could steam possibly give off cold rather than heat? How could water thus chilled not freeze, as all around it did? "This isn't a place travellers frequent." He smiled wanly, hoping Polassar wouldn't think the jest amusing enough to warrant another of his walloping back-slaps.

Polassar was preoccupied. He stared at the strange water, but remembered Tristan's admonitions about touching anything here. He was making a sign against evil with three of his left-hand fingers when Thomas leaped over the stream and walked scornfully past.

"How do we discover this lady, now? Will this glowing trail you claim we're following lead to her?"

Tristan hated to admit his uncertainty, especially when he was in the midst of creating a good impression. It wouldn't inspire confidence.

"It may," he said, settling for a hopeful truth. "It makes as good a way as any to start, and it's led us this far."

The light of the road was still with them, but it cast little more than a reflected glow on the walls and ceiling. Few details were visible, but the place seemed to be a warren of tunnels and archways. They sensed many doorways, some quite large, none very small, opening off the main way. Icy blasts issued from them, and sometimes ghastly smells.

After perhaps half a mile of this, they came to a branching. The path bent left, past a great column of clear ice. Another path, fainter, ran through a hole on the right.

"Which way, wizard?"

The path was plain enough. "Left." Tristan wondered what strange magic it was that left the path visible to none save wizards—and of those, only such ones as took up the quest. Some chivalry of Nímir's, contradictory as that was? He wondered how the spell was worked. Then suddenly he stood rooted, staring at the wall.

Polassar collided with him roughly and called an angry question.

The ice was clear as Blais' glass. Within it, like a fly trapped forever in an amber drop, was a man.

He was clad in silver armor chased with moon crescents and stars and rainbows, and there was a bursting sun picked out in gold upon his sable cape. Remarkable, but it was not his clothing Tristan stared at.

His face was high-boned and noble, his brows level and strong and, like his beard, spun of the finest gold. He held an opal-hilted sword before him in the first guard position, warding off some unseen terror.

"I've never seen a look of such fear." Tristan's voice seemed loath to cross his lips.

"He died hard, that's sure. But he's safe out of it now. Just a bit of window-dressing, to take the heart out of us."

"I wonder who he was?" One of the warrior-wizards the old songs spoke of? Perhaps a very great one? Hadn't the sunburst been Maxon's badge? Tristan shivered, wondering how they'd come unmolested so far.

They moved left. The path dipped down, not rapidly, but steadily, and it wound upon itself. Tristan grew nervous. Darkenkeep was renowned as a place of peril. How had they penetrated this far undisturbed? He expected to plunge into a pit of powder-snow at any moment and be stung into excruciating death by the apple-sized spiders lurking there.

The path led them on, sometimes straight for long stretches, then rising to cross slender bridges of ice. The bridges spanned chasms toothed with spear-tall icicles, and Tristan was certain that the bridges intended to give way just as they crossed. He hesitated.

*Coward,* Thomas said, and walked across with great disdain and deliberation, leading them.

It was tempting to let him continue doing so, if he could have. But Tristan alone could see the path, so he was soon in command again, with all its attendant strains. Whether Thomas couldn't see the path or didn't choose to was impossible to say. He shouldn't have been able to, but should-haves meant nothing, Tristan had found, where Thomas was concerned.

They walked a weary way, mostly in silence. The roof was low now, and the walls drew close. The floor was treacherous, its surface slushy, its base unyielding ice. It seemed designed for promoting nasty falls, since the walls were close enough to bruise oneself against effortlessly but were too smooth to offer handholds. Polassar swore petulantly. Thomas merely sat down and waited for Tristan to carry him.

"This hardly seems fair," Tristan murmured, as he scooped the cat up.

*I am not heavy. I keep myself trim. And you know I hate wetting my feet, as proper a wizard's cat should.*

"Of course."

Polassar looked miserable. Tristan sympathized; his own boots were soaked through too, and his feet likewise numb.

"When we hit a dry spot, we can make a fire. A rest would be sensible."

"How far to go?" Polassar slogged doggedly behind him. Tristan gave a mental shrug.

"There's no way to tell. There's no doubt we're on the trail. We just have to follow it to its logical——"

There was a pile of human bones in the middle of the slush. Something slithered through the pile and out of sight as they stared.

*Well, at least someone else has come this way.*

Polassar's fingers were moving again. And Tristan's would have been, if they hadn't been full of cat.

*There are bound to be more, you know. Six thousand and forty-three, plus assorted heroes?*

Tristan noticed a very queer taste in his mouth.

Eventually they were able to dry their boots, but not to rest, though they tried. Since there was nothing but ice to sit on, and that colder than ordinary ice, there was no point in trying to get comfortable. After a few mouthfuls of dried meat, they moved on.

Talk would have passed the time more pleasantly, but Polassar seemed averse to it. Tristan suspected that he was about to be accused of misleading them. He wished he could be sure that he wasn't doing just that.

He was also beginning to hear things.

Partly it was nerves, again. He kept expecting to hear things, as heralds of catastrophe if not warnings. Ears have a way of producing expected sounds within themselves, if no external sounds are forthcoming, so he ignored the things he thought he heard, or passed them off as ice settling and creaking.

"What was that?"

Tristan thought he'd never force his heart to start beating again, Polassar scared him so badly. And Polassar hadn't even shouted, though it had seemed so. He should have been able to hear quite well while his heart was still, but he wasn't thinking about his ears then.

He started to make a protection sign and joggled Thomas in doing so. The noise stopped. Tristan half completed the protection, then broke off to stare at the cat.

Thomas snuggled against his chest, then yawned.

*I was only purring. You're comfortable.*

"Probably just ice falling somewhere," Tristan finally answered Polassar, and walked on.

Ice began to build up under their feet after that, as if a stream had been frozen in the full course of its flow.

Rounding a bend, they saw its cause. Where a stream had once burst from an opening in a glacial wall, a great waterfall of ice now glistened. White ice, shading away to near transparency, glowing blue and cream in spots. It rose to what seemed an impossible height, up into the shadows. It glowed dimly, and at the top was a greater radiance, filling the man's height of space between the ice and the roof.

Between the glow and themselves lay a hundred feet of sheer, slippery ice. Tristan gulped.

"Well, there lies our trail."

*Lovely,* Thomas said. *I think I'll have a nap now.*

Tristan took out the grimoire and paged through it hastily. He didn't want to try to melt the thing. Could he turn it into a stairway, maybe?

He selected a spell and made preparations for it. He fetched out a couple of his magic stones, some herbs and some powders and arranged them as the book set out. Polassar watched him with mild curiosity, then turned back to studying the slope.

The spell involved many hand passes before the chant was to be begun. Tristan's fingers wove nimbly as he spun out the spell. He smiled, thinking that he was doing very well. He completed the last pass easily and bent to pick up the herb bag.

As he did so, a carrot-sized icicle dropped from the roof, shattering itself smartly on the top of Tristan's head.

He yelped and jumped, scattering the herbs and stones hopelessly out of their neat patterns. Tristan stood rubbing his head and looking sadly down at the wreckage. It really had been going so well—

"Let's try the ropes," Tristan said as briskly as he could manage at that moment.

Polassar already had the ropes ready.

"Nothing like a bit of magic to smooth the way, eh?" he asked. "What's the mess do—keep evil spirits away?"

"Yes," Tristan snapped, uncoiling his rope.

They began the climb at once, before the sight of the slope could daunt them, but the ropes proved to be of little use. There was nothing on which to anchor them; though many casts were tried, the rope always slid free and fell back into Polassar's hands. They finally essayed to climb without it. Tristan groaned at even the thought, especially as Thomas was clinging needle-clawed to his shoulder as he climbed.

The slope was deceptive, growing both slicker and steeper as they neared its top. Progress was slow, as they paused to hack out shallow handholds with their daggers, then somehow had to fit their feet into those same holds as their hands clawed higher. They dared not even stay roped to each other, for fear of both falling.

Tristan's hold gave out unexpectedly under his boots, and he found himself dangling by his fingers on a level with Polassar. Polassar could not move upward without dislodging him, and his grip looked to be weakening.

"Have a care, wizard, you'll bring us both down!"

Tristan tried to get a better hold on the melting ice with one hand, freeing the other to use the dagger. It was not to be done. His feet scrabbled for a new hold, but it had to be done slowly, so as not to throw him farther down. There! Almost he had it—

He glanced back at his chilled fingers, having peripherally caught some flicker of movement there. Not an inch from his face was a small ice-lizard, the poison sac at its throat winking like an immense ruby. It was three inches long, from white nose to ivory tail—and had fangs the length of Tristan's fingernail.

He had to force himself not to jerk back—any move at all might provoke a fatal strike, not to mention the fact that he'd certainly fall. It might not be poisonous—but the odds against anything living in Darkenkeep being harmless were not of the sort he'd care to wager on.

"Wizard, we can't hang here all day! Slide down and try again, if you're stuck!"

The lizard's tongue flicked out swiftly at the sound, as if tasting it. Little claws scraped off minute ice-shavings. Tristan could see its burrow, a blue hole no bigger than his fingertip—which was just now quite near it, as it happened—in the vertical face of the ice.

"I can't." Tristan permitted himself only the smallest of whispers, in place of the scream he felt growing in his lungs. "Look."

He heard the hiss of Polassar's breath. So did the lizard, which answered it evilly. It writhed, coiling itself snakelike, ready to strike.

Something flashed past Tristan's ear.

Thomas' weight left his shoulder, and Tristan's balance passed the point of no return. He lost what little was left of his hold and fell, trying his best to slide, rather than dropping straight down fifty feet. He had only fair success.

Ice cut at his grasping hands. He was skidding faster than he liked, despite digging his boot toes in, hoping to slow himself.

He hit bottom and a large lump of ice, both at once. His unicorn buckle punched him hard in the stomach. He slid to a halt, finally, rolling over, and lay there winded.

Polassar's laughter floated down.

"I know you bade me stay close behind you, wizard, but I doubt any could follow that performance! Are you hurt?" The inquiry was offhand.

Tristan considered the point, while his head and stomach settled back to normal. He sat up. More bruises, but nothing worse, he hoped. Thomas came mincing down the slope, the lizard white and red and limp in his mouth. He laid it at Tristan's feet.

"The oddest mouse you've ever brought me, my friend. Thank you." Never were thanks more heartfelt. His knees felt loose as an old bowstring. He lifted the cat back to his shoulder, and looked searchingly upslope.

"You're within ten feet of the top now, Polassar. If you could tie the rope to something and throw it down? It will save time."

Polassar obeyed, still chuckling.

When the rope was secure, Tristan climbed and soon stood on the ledge beside Polassar. The path was before them, running downward again.

It grew dark, impossible to see far ahead. They began stumbling into walls that remained unseen until the last moment. Polassar cursed inventively, and Tristan grunted, caught between the discovered wall and Polassar's chest.

"Happen we're off the track?"

Please, Tristan thought, don't let us have to backtrack down that waterfall! Anything but that.

"No. The more difficult the going gets, the closer we are to our goal." He hoped the words were true, as he spoke them.

He peered closely at the ground and was reassured. The path was bright enough, so there was something in the air itself which clouded their sight and made the place seem so dark. Puzzling. By paying the closest attention to the ground, they were able to proceed. They just proceeded slowly.

They came abruptly to a large chamber, lit by a great radiance at its far end.

"There, wizard! Yon light! Can it be?"

Could it—already? But where were all the hazards? The promised perils? The tricks and traps?

*You should have kept your thoughts shut.*

There came a slithering sound and, as they stood wondering, a dragging that ground the very rocks beneath Darkenkeep. It was a sound such as a glacier might make in moving, but thrice a hundred times faster. A blur of movement came out of the light.

"A dragon!" Polassar sounded delighted.

"The Guardian!"

The thing lumbered forward, indistinct and huge. Tristan lifted his sword in the half-light and knew that Polassar did the same. He wished they had more light to fight by— if they could stand the sight of the thing they fought.

The dragon took another step, lifted its head, and roared. A small hissing answered it from near Tristan's feet. He looked down at Thomas, who stood ready to do battle with his own small swords, five to each paw. All were unsheathed.

As the dragon drew closer, more details were revealed. They studied them during that curious leisure which danger brings, when eternity may be contained in an instant, or an instant be stretched to an eternity.

Ice hung from the dragon's head, dropping off onto the floor with each movement the beast made, and its gray scales were heavily frosted with white. On the belly, the frost thickened to ice-armor. Wings that seemed made of the blizzards of many winters covered the mighty back. The cave was too small to allow those wings to unfold fully.

Why do they call it a dragon? Tristan wondered. It didn't look much like the illustrations in any of Blais' books. It looked a lot bigger than he'd expected, and less . . . finished, somehow.

The dragon opened its fanged mouth. Its teeth were unmeltable icicles. Tristan stepped forward, sword ready. He semed to have gone beyond fear with the movement. It was impossible that they should kill this vast beast with only swords, so of course it made perfect sense that they must try.

Instantly it was night. The blackest, coldest night of the longest of all winters, a winter that had never really ended since the world began. Every memory of light and heat leaked out of Tristan. It began to snow, even though they were indoors, and the weight of the snow's accumulation smote him down. Light had never been. Heat never existed. The sun went out, not with a blaze, but only a small sizzle. The dark filled his every pore, and it had always been, would always be.

He remembered the word to make fire. He spoke it— without voice, ultimately without belief. The word whirled from his mind and had never been there. In another moment, it was the same with his own name. Or had he ever possessed one?

There was light. He knew that, even as it faded from his sight. All this blackness was within him, but that was where it really mattered. It was night without moon or stars, it was a doorless pit in the earth's bowels, it was forever. He felt black ice growing, blooming in his veins. One last sharp feeling was left to him—the bitter taste of failure. Then that went too. All was nothing.

Cold and everlasting night, and an everlasting laughter that was older and colder than the stars he would never see again. His heart squirmed wildly in his chest, seeking an escape that was denied it. Laughter like a glacier came again, rolling and crushing all else before it.

# Minstrel's Song

A BIRD SANG.

It was liquid joy, bubbling, growing, leaves shooting from rich soil, flowers exploding into color. It rose and fell, was sunrise and blazing noon. It trilled, and was sweet water rippling out of a spring from which Tristan drank, filling his belly with the song. It was the melting of ice, and each falling drop a bright diamond bursting into a butterfly. It was peace, strawberries, green grass, a sweet kiss from the red lips of a woman. It was hope. It was life.

It was Minstrel, perched on Tristan's shoulder.

Tristan opened his eyes, and saw the tiny throat feathers swelling with song. Warmth poured down his arms, spilled into his clenched fingers. The sword moved in his hand.

Minstrel took wing, still singing. Throwing notes before him like missiles, letting them drop after like raindrops, he circled the cavern.

The dragon roared and snapped its jaws at him. Tristan chose the moment to leap to battle. His sword arced up, then down, biting deep. A cold wing nearly smothered him with its beating. He sliced again, as he leaped back.

A bellow near at hand rivalled the dragon's. Polassar's blade whirled and struck. He and the dragon closed in a shower of ice.

If the dragon possessed blood, then they were simply unable to draw any. Their blades made little impression on that frost-steel hide. Sparks flew, and chips of ice, but they were beaten steadily back. The edges of Tristan's sight began to darken, as the spell took hold again. This wasn't the way to fight the beast . . .

"Think of the sun!" he shouted to Polassar. "Think of the brightest, most summery thing you can remember! Drive it back!"

He forced his mind to fill with flowers, blazing white against green. It seemed a carpet of them spread from wall to wall, becoming spangled with yellow-hearted daisies. Grasses spiked up. Deliberately, remembering Minstrel's song, he added chicory's flaming blue, hawkweed's orange, and a sky the color of Polassar's eyes. Sweet winds blew, stirring the flowerheads.

The dragon was gone.

Tristan relaxed and nearly fell, as the meadow-carpet faded away. All that lay at his feet was a yellow feather, settling gently down.

TRISTAN PICKED it up, feeling gritty tears in his eyes. A spot of red dappled the feather. Another glistened on the white floor. Any excitement he might have felt at his success against the dragon spilled out of him.

"Minstrel—" His voice broke. That tiny body, so fragile, so full of energy, so alive—Why did I let him come? Why didn't I have the sense to leave him safe at home? He felt colder even than when under the dragon's spell, empty and ill.

Thomas reared himself against Tristan's leg, licking concernedly at his dangling fingers.

"He's gone, Thomas—" Oddly, this hit him harder than Blais' death had. Tristan fell to his knees. Somehow, Minstrel had seemed too insubstantial to be mortal.

The fellowship was broken already, though scarce begun. They'd be lucky—beyond lucky—to escape with only one death among themselves, Tristan told himself, but the truth held no comfort. His face felt stiff with grief.

"He didn't know," he whispered. "He didn't know about anything except flying and singing and begging for treats. I was supposed to be taking care of *him*—"

"There, wizard! Yon light!" Polassar laid hands on him, spun him to his feet. Unwillingly, Tristan looked in the direction he was pointed, and forgot Minstrel.

The light centered about a table of crystal; on it lay a maiden, robed in white. White? Clothed in the light itself! The light came from her hands, streaming up in nine rays.

They ran to her, stumbling as if they were drunken men, careless of traps or obstacles. And she lay at last at their feet, wrapped in her magic light, clothed in a white rainbow.

Her face was like a snowdrop, flawlessly white over sculptured bones, and her hair was the silk of new-husked corn. It was wound about her perfect head many times, coiled in intricate braids. Loose, it would fall to her ankles. And on every matchless finger, save for one, was a silver ring of strange device.

Two bore summer-sky colored stones. One was set with pearl shell, rippling and iridescent. Another of metal shone like water running over marble, while a tear-shaped crystal hung from a thin band on her left thumb. Moons, stars, hearts and strange curves marked the others. Light rippled out from them all, save the third finger of her right hand.

"Allaire," whispered Tristan, and felt his heart leave his keeping.

"We must awaken her!" Polassar was awestruck, almost unto silence. Thomas crept closer for a better look.

Tristan, greatly daring, took one of her hands in his and wondered at its smallness. The rings were cool against his palm.

And how shall I awaken her? Blais never told me. Did he not think we'd come so far? Have any, ever? Or did he truly not know? For an instant, Tristan could see nothing but silver, as if the rings left her fingers and flowed through his skin, glowing in their own light, moving of themselves as they would on her fingers, working their magic. Through the silver blaze he saw her closed eyelids, veined and delicate as hepatica petals.

There was something he was supposed to be trying to do. It eluded him just then. No rose was ever the color and texture of her slightly smiling lips. No winter stars ever blazed so brightly as her hands, so light and smooth in his own, yet so curiously heavy for their size. He'd forgotten something. Maybe many things.

Among them was the necessity to breathe. Allaire did not, or he might have been reminded of it sometime before his lungs became painfully insistent. His lungs expanded, drew in air, expelled it, and Tristan blinked. He felt as if he were wearing someone else's face—indeed someone else's body.

He looked around him and discovered eyes watching him. Two were green, with slitted pupils. Two were blue, with tiny black dots. Thomas was truly watching him, but Polassar was as mesmerized as Tristan had been, and as unaware of time passing.

He heard a birdsong, and looked absently about for Minstrel. The cavern was shadowed and empty beyond the rings' light, and within the light were only himself and Thomas, with Polassar kneeling beside Allaire's bier. Of course, he thought, stricken afresh, mistrusting his ears. This was a place of trickery. The air was utterly still, scarcely stirred by their combined breaths, certainly not by any music. Far off, ice tinkled; but that had not been what he'd heard, and the notes were still clear-cut in his mind.

Clear as a summer morning . . . and at last he knew what Minstrel's song had been trying to teach him. Tristan bent eagerly back to his work.

He made the field of flowers in his mind again for her. It was all he could think of to do, and surely if it had worked against the dragon . . . He closed his eyes to shut away the sweet distraction of her face. He let summer wash over him.

He needed a call of summer so strong that no fell magic could resist it. A summer with no trace at all of cold, or winter, or death, or Nímir. He needed a *magic*, and he'd long suspected that he had none—just a few tricks he'd practiced so often that they were mostly reliable. But he had Minstrel's song in his mind, and Blais' misplaced confidence behind him, and memories of Calandra's sometimes summers . . .

The silence, so lonely and isolating at first, became now his friend and tool, a summer afternoon's stillness, the hush born of small continual noises, the world turning and breezes blowing, leaves rustling and whispering the air's secrets to the earth, flowers opening to overhear.

He began feeling drained with the work of envisioning, yet she did not stir, so he mixed in the scent of roses, ones deep and soft as silk, almost the color of her lips. Still no response. Where was the one thing that might call her back to the sunlight, back to full life? He thought of clouds shaped like elephants and lambs and hippogryphs, and let them be. Still no answering spark, no parting of her lips.

He bent his will still further, until he was near to fainting. The field he'd made had shape, dimension, smell and touch and taste. The walls blurred, so that the field seemed to run right through them, in all directions. There were carpets of moss, fat and soft as caterpillers. Milkweed down, sailing the wind, and the cry of a trumpeting swan. Wild strawberries, beaded with dew.

His head spun. A lake appeared, filled with silver fish and emerald frogs. Its bottom was carpeted with gold, and sunlight spread through the water, to be captured by waving cresses.

A kingfisher leaped into that water, lilies-of-the-valley bloomed beside it. Bees hummed in fragrant mint. Pussy-willows grew fat fur. Windflowers nodded. He mixed spring and summer together, indiscriminately, to make a paradise.

A deer leaped, a hawk soared. Sunflowers followed their love across the sky with their faces. A ladybug crept its way up a grass stalk.

Allaire's eyes opened.

They were the color of chicory and kingfisher down. They were deep like pools, dark as violets in the shade.

Tristan sank down onto the floor. All the flowers fell away again, save for those in Allaire's eyes. His head ached fit to burst asunder. Thomas rubbed against his knee, purring, proud.

Allaire raised herself from her couch. She held out a hand. It reached right past Tristan's face—and up.

"My rescuer," she said to Polassar, and put the hand in

his. Her voice was the ringing of midsummer bells, the shimmer of finest crystal.

"Nay, lady." Polassar's voice was rough with gentleness. He was looking deep into her incomparable eyes. "I deserve no credit—here's he who woke you. Wizard, are you all right?"

Tristan saw, as if outside himself still, how Polassar looked at Allaire. And how she looked at Polassar. He saw himself—dirty and ragged and hollow-eyed, feeling like soured milk. Polassar's armor glittered magnificently.

"Yes," he finally said, faintly. "That was—harder than I expected." He got up from his knees, somewhat stiffly. Polassar helped Allaire to her feet. They were tiny, of course, shod in white doeskin.

She took several steps, still gripping his hand, and her smile, if possible, was more radiant than before.

"Oh, if you could know how fine that feels—It has been so long. But tell me, who are you? Surely you have not come alone?"

Polassar introduced himself, most gallantly.

"But if you are alone, then we must make haste to flee! The Guardian will return—" Fear flicked across her eyes, until she blinked it away.

"We should not linger here then, wizard."

Tristan seemed not to hear. "Thomas, did you mark where Minstrel fell? He saved us all—he should not lie in this place." *I can at least bury him someplace warm,* Tristan thought.

"Wizard?"

They walked toward the spot, Tristan sorrowing, ashamed that he could have forgotten his friend, even for so little a time, even for so important a reason. There were no feathers, though, save the one Tristan had tucked into his pouch before.

"Thomas, are you sure? He must be here. The dragon carried nothing off—" He could feel the tears in his throat again, as the sorrow hit him afresh. Minstrel was such a little thing—almost nothing, just air and feathers and love and song—

"Wizard, we've no time to waste! Say a charm, or light him some incense. But let us be gone now!"

There was a soft fluttering, just as Tristan was about to

spit angry impolitic words at Polassar. A flurry of wings and something like a caress brushed Tristan's cheek. Minstrel briefly settled on his left shoulder. Many feathers were missing from his tail; as he took to the air he seemed to need to learn flight all over again; but he was singing softly to himself.

# Cold Iron

MINSTREL'S WHITE FEATHERS BLOOMED in the light of Allaire's rings, and the gray patches on his head and body gleamed silver blue. He completed a circle of the group and settled back to Tristan's shoulder, busily preening.

"How lovely," Allaire said in her voice that was like ferns uncurling their leaves in a cool-shaded forest. She stretched out a silver-clad finger to him. Minstrel's throat began to swell again, and Tristan's blood beat in tempo with it. Close to, she was the loveliest woman that ever breathed, and her hand was nearly touching his shoulder. The light from her rings dazzled his eyes so that he saw her through a haze. It was enough to make him forget his amazement at Minstrel's safe return.

"Lovely——"

Polassar coughed, as delicately as he was able to manage.

"Should we not be going?"

Thomas helpfully dug a few claws into Tristan's right calf.

"Uhhh—yes, let's get out of here!" He tried hastily to regroup his wits. "Stay behind me again, the same as before, and keep your sword ready. Expect trouble. We must be on our guard more than ever."

Turning, he saw that the path was gone, save for their footprints, which were dully glowing. One by one, the glows began to wink out.

Tristan felt all his blood drain into his feet. His mouth opened. They'd never get out! Darkenkeep was as mazy as one of Duriron's unfathomable weather spells. Without the path, their situation was desperate enough; but in darkness—why hadn't he had wit to bring a torch?

He mastered himself and stepped forward. There was a magic for light—there was a magic for almost everything, he supposed. And he had in his pouch a certain bit of crystal which should serve him well. An act of the will alone could light it. No need for complex preparations.

The stone was rough in his fingers and cold on the surface, but warm within. It flickered feebly when he spoke to it and dwindled to a firefly's light. Tristan swore and began again. The room seemed darker than when he'd begun.

"Wait, wizard. Her rings, might they not help?"

"Yes!" Allaire spread her hands out before her, and the glow lit them all. She took a step toward Tristan, and the rings too dimmed and went out. They were left in utter darkness.

"Oh!"

"Can't you light them again, my lady?" Polassar must have found his way to her side; his voice came from nearly the same spot.

Tristan could feel her consternation, before she even attempted it.

"No, Polassar. She has no control over them, not yet, without the tenth ring. I'll have to try again. And pray it works better this time. Or else we grope our way out of here." He suspected they'd more likely die here in the blackness. No glorious, crushing defeat for their audacious enterprise. Just a futile death of starvation, possibly hastened by broken limbs gotten from falling into a handy chasm. The Guardian wouldn't even need to finish them personally. Time would prove an apt executioner. He rubbed his fingers sadly over the crystal.

What an end to all their hopes! But he'd never thought much about their succeeding anyway, or he'd have given more thought to an escape plan.

Never before had he been so tired. Weariness spread from his bones into his mind, sapping his will; he could hardly remember the words with which to bespeak the crystal. Some new trick? Yet another trap? Just enough to finish them. With light, the way out of here would be as clear as the path to Blais' cottage; without it they would wander in circles till they froze or died some other way. How exquisitely simple. If he could just light the stone! Once done right, it would hold the spell of itself, if he could just manage to start it. Sweat pricked out on his back.

Light. Light! The stone should have split in half by now, he was concentrating on it so hard.

Too hard, that was the trouble. He must relax, let the spell out. Slowly, as naturally as a flower opening. How many times had Blais told him that? He had understood what Blais meant—how he might manage it was the continual puzzle.

Steady! The power needed a channel to flow through—a clear channel. The wrong kind of effort could block it off, stop it up. Maybe he hadn't anything left; he felt completely drained. Fighting the dragon had used more strength than he'd thought he possessed, and waking Allaire had been still harder. But this might take only a little out of him; he should rest and gather his strength, and then—

His shoulder was on fire, pierced through with flame—ten points of it.

The crystal burst into light.

Tristan stared at it, glowing between his thumb and forefinger, then at Thomas, who was singlemindedly washing his face. The crystal's light winked off the tips of hastily sheathed claws.

"Well done, wizard! That was quick work. Now we can be on our way."

Minstrel had mistaken the darkness for night, and gone to sleep. He woke now, with a shaking and fluffing of feathers. Tristan clucked soothingly to him. He straightened slowly.

"Closed spaces make you nervous?" he asked lightly. "You're anxious to leave this lovely place?" He even managed a small tired smile. In fact, he was vastly pleased that the crystal-lighting had worked.

Polassar clapped him across the back. Minstrel scolded at him.

"You read me aright, I mislike this place. As we should, no doubt. 'Tis most unwholesome. Let's be quit of it now. My lady?"

Allaire gave Polassar her arm.

Tristan held the crystal high, and the cavern enlarged and shrank with the movement. Thomas arose, hoisted his tail, and trotted straight away from them. He led unerringly, turn after turn after twist.

"Hark, yon cat knows our way better than you, wizard."

He probably does, Tristan mentally acknowledged. I should have thought of him before this. Cats have a perfect sense of direction; Blais always said so. Did I never listen to anything he said?

The way back to the icefall seemed long. Despite his confidence in Thomas, Tristan grew sure that this was not the way they had come in. The cat still moved with complete assurance, sometimes so quickly that they were hard pressed to follow.

Thomas apparently was taking no chances on pursuit. He hesitated for nothing, staying always just at the forward edge of the pool of crystal light, a bounding shadow. Tristan wanted to call out to him, begging for more caution or at least a pause for breath-catching, but it didn't seem a good idea just then. There was an unspoken realization of their need for silence.

They flitted after Thomas, sometimes slipping, sometimes floundering into soft snow, but mostly surprisingly unhindered. Only once did they need to climb, when their trail ended at an ice wall. Thomas sat down at its base, staring fixedly up into the shadows. Tristan raised the crystal. Six feet above was a triangular patch of blackness.

"Through there?" Tristan whispered. Thomas meowed and lashed his tail frenziedly, all the while looking upward. He tensed himself to jump, though the opening was far outside his range.

Polassar's rope flicked past him, snagging firmly on the stump of an ice-pillar. He pulled himself up easily, even with Allaire tucked within the circle of one arm. Next he hauled up the rope, Tristan, and Thomas all at once, coiled the rope away into his pack, and made a sweeping gesture with one large hand.

"Lead on, Sir Cat."

Thomas gravely did so.

*I could have found an easier way,* he admitted to Tristan

as they hastened on. *But now at least he feels useful, since he's flexed his muscles.*

Tristan still had no idea how far they were from safety. Less idea than ever, really—Thomas' twistings and turnings had him totally baffled. His eyes were strained from peering into the dark, tired enough to make him see false lights and glows before them.

A man appeared in their path. Allaire shrieked and Polassar's sword screamed free of its scabbard as he thrust her behind him. Tristan marked how Thomas ran straight on, and did likewise, extending his hands. His fingers brushed the smooth coldness of ice. He relaxed happily.

He recognized the frozen wizard, glimpsed in what seemed three-quarters of his lifetime previously. Polassar apparently did likewise, as he explained something rapidly to Allaire and put his sword away.

*Any idea where we are yet?* Thomas asked.

Tristan bent down to him.

"I think so. Did you miss the icefall on purpose?"

*On consideration. Though as you found, it's easier to go down it than up.*

"My bruises thank you. Can we rest here?" He'd noticed that Allaire was leaning visibly against Polassar.

*We'd be better off resting while the horses run. But if you'd like to carry me again, I won't object.*

Tristan sighed, and waved the others on.


Valadan neighed them a greeting long before they were in sight of the horses. Then they had reached the Gates, and still there was no sign of trouble. Tristan permitted himself to draw a free breath.

"Valadan can best carry two, I think. He's bigger than your mare—" He made a wide detour around her head as he said this, marking the evil look the roan gave him. "If my lady will mount first—"

"Tarry a moment, wizard."

Tristan turned in surprise, stirrup still in hand. Polassar had not followed him to the horses.

"What? I thought you were so anxious to be away." He felt a thrill of fear. What was Polassar about? Had Darkenkeep preyed on his mind to the extent of plottings already?

His voice had held no hint of danger; it merely sounded distracted, and peremptory.

"I saw something. Bring light."

Tristan advanced cautiously, the crystal held before him. Polassar had dropped back a few feet, into a small tunnel mouth. The light was thrown back out of it a thousandfold.

"Wizard, look at this! Gold!" Polassar was gesturing excitedly with both hands, even the bear-helm's eyes glittering avidly.

This had to be a trap, Tristan's mind screamed. All the treasures that had trickled into Darkenkeep, gathered so neatly and conveniently together? A trap, certainly, though not necessarily for them.

"I'm looking. Leave it, Polassar. No good will come of any of this lot. Dead men's gold, all of it, and it would only weight us down."

"Jewels, then? No?" Polassar's brows rose toward his helm.

"No."

"Then let us be practical." He cast a look back at Allaire. "M'lady needs a cloak. 'Tis cold without."

"You really can't stand to leave all this behind, can you? Have to take something? Find a cloak then, but hurry." He supposed he could afford to be generous.

Tristan's elation at their accomplishment outweighed any nagging awareness of their vulnerability. They were nearly safe, his mind insisted, proudly turning events over for better examination. He was trembling with a happiness that had nothing to do with the treasure before him.

Allaire was standing beside him. Spring scents tickled Tristan's nose, and he shut his eyes rapturously.

The sight of the gold and jewels might have dazzled him too, if he'd thought about them, but he'd seen—and needed—so little of riches in his lifetime that they didn't matter much now. Allaire was another sort of treasure indeed. Tristan was very glad that it seemed they weren't going to die in Darkenkeep. Still, he was having a great deal of trouble adjusting to the idea.

Neither of them had thought to bring warm clothes for their chief treasure, however, so maybe Polassar made good sense with his searching. How was Tristan to be sure? Just so it didn't delay their joyful leavetaking. Let the man amuse himself.

Polassar threw open a great chest and withdrew heaps of green and gold silk, until at last he came to a sable cape. The skins were very fine.

"This may do." He looked to Allaire, who nodded. Being a princess, she wasn't overly impressed by finery, but she had a woman's love of luxurious, soft furs. "And a knife— she may need it. 'Tis no idle pleasure journey we go on." He longingly fingered a double-pointed bejeweled sword, then set it back to select another. Doing so, he peered behind the chests, and snapped his fingers.

"Not to forget you, wizard! Here's the very thing. You may have need of this—sure to, with the fighting we'll be doing! And look you, 'tis made to your pattern. Perfect fit."

The object in question was a suit of armor, wonderfully chased with a design of spider webs, picked out in gold. On the left gauntlet lurked the spider, carved from a diamond.

"Polassar, wizards don't wear armor. Cold iron is not comfortable for us." Tristan smiled indulgently, or wistfully, depending on the observer's point of view. Cold iron indeed, lying here in this ice-pit.

"Are arrows, sticking out of your flesh? 'Tis not even heavy—doubtless magic smithwork. Fitting that you should have it. And if I have my enemies, as you so boldly told me, then you share them now, master wizard. Put it on."

It was easier not to argue, so that they might be the quicker gone on their way. One touch told Tristan that the armor was not ensorcelled—no danger of being drawn back here against his will by it. It was only loot, like all the rest of this precious heap, with no trap involved. And it did fit him perfectly. He drew it on over his clothes, feeling the strangeness of its touch. The intricate straps and buckles seemed to fasten of themselves.

*Oh, very nice,* Thomas said, crouching on Valadan's saddle as Tristan jingled toward him. *The perfect steel popinjay. Why didn't you look for a black robe covered with moons and stars, while you were at it?*

Minstrel was not pleased with Tristan's new costume either. His feet skidded across it as he tried to land, and he wound up clinging to the shoulder seam for dear life, cheeping plaintively until Tristan tucked him gently into the warmth of his sweater.

Tristan stroked him tenderly, trying to forget the hurt Thomas' words had inflicted.

"At least it will keep the wind out, eh?" Minstrel looked no happier, though he quieted.

Valadan knelt to Allaire then, regal as any prince, and she was helped onto his back, Tristan scrambling up after. The armor somewhat hampered free movement.

Polassar also mounted swiftly, and they rode away, Tristan still half expecting the icicle jaws of the Gates to snap shut before them.

It was only then, as they left Darkenkeep behind, that Tristan realized that Polassar had never seemed to covet any of the treasure for himself. Gold and jewels would have been of greatest use to him, providing much-needed income for his army, but he'd never even argued it. Could it be that Polassar simply liked giving presents to people?

For all its fine fit, the armor weighed on Tristan greatly as they rode across the Waste. This is not me, he thought, looking down at the metal armpieces that hid his sleeves. There's not a patch or a dent on it anywhere. A king might wear such. Small wonder I don't look myself in it.

Maybe armor was not such a bad idea at that. He might manage to cut a dashing figure in it, and he was very conscious of Allaire, nestled sideways in front of him on the saddle.

It seemed he hardly knew how weary he was, what with everything altogether, until they had eventually gotten out of the Winterwaste—Valadan's work, that—and were splashing fast along a muddy cow-track. The sun was nearly down, and it must have been raining all week, by the depth of the mud. Somehow it had become autumn—magic again. They had been only hours in Darkenkeep, but hours there were not as hours in the world. It must be late in the year, or perhaps not. Winters began sooner, ended later and had grown more severe as Nímir's power waxed.

In any case, it was growing dark—time to make some sort of a camp, and lie low in case of pursuit. There was no knowing what might be sent after them. Polassar found them a sheltered spot some way off the road and at last pronounced it good enough. No use trying to press on to Lassair in the dark.

Tristan dismounted wearily. Coltsfoot, but this armor was heavy after all! His legs barely held him up. Fortunately, Allaire noticed nothing as he handed her down from the horse.

They began to gather wood, but what they found was too wet to take the sparks Polassar's steel made. The sticks smoked and sizzled, but were barely scorched before the flames went out.

"Wizard, perhaps you might lend a hand! If it wouldn't be asking too much—"

Polassar sounded angry that the wizard hadn't jumped to do so already, and Tristan dragged himself up from the spot where he'd just sat himself down. This wouldn't take too long, he promised his aching bones mentally. Only a little spell, which he'd never failed with. One quick little fire kindling. His firestone felt smooth and ready.

He lifted one hand, said the words, and sketched the passes.

Flame leaped from his hand. There was a tremendous crash, and all the lights went out.

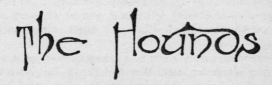

# The Hounds

WHEN HE OPENED HIS EYES, everything was mostly dark, but he could see Allaire's face as she bent over him. They had stripped the armor off him—he could tell by the new lightness of his mind. The pain remained.

"I think I know now why the wizards don't wear armor—" That weak voice must belong to someone else, it couldn't possibly be his own. But Allaire's lips had not yet moved.

"Is there aught we can do to ease you?" Her voice was full of sweet concern.

"In my pack—" Tristan gasped. "A silver box shaped

like a butterfly—take what you find in it. A salve. Rub it
on, as little as you can manage—"

She drew the box out, and began smearing the ointment
on his wrists and throat, everywhere the metal had touched
unprotected skin. The salve took the pain of the burns
away at once, and he slept.

The sleep was badly broken, full of troubled dreams of
danger and pursuit. Once he woke half on his feet, shouting, and felt Polassar grab at him. He was shoved down
and wrapped tightly in his cloak again, ordered to sleep.

Tristan opened his eyes, and it was light. The morning
was mist and gray sky. Polassar squatted beside him.

"By the Cold One's icicled nose, wizard, that was some
fire you lit! I thought the whole wood would go, before I
could beat it out! How do you feel now?"

Tristan sat up experimentally.

"All right." His wrists only hurt a little, though they'd
been cruelly burned, and the other injuries and indignities
of the past few days were old friends by now. He was
rather stiff. If Polassar hadn't been shouting so in his ear
he'd have felt even better and could have scratched a headache from his list of ailments.

"Are you able to handle things alone for a bit?"

Tristan winced.

"I suppose so. Why?"

"Have you thought what we're to do next? I see not, by
your blank face. I've found sign of an army about, so we
dare not make for Lassair as I'd hoped to. Like as not,
we'd find her under siege! We need to stay quiet a while.
We need food and a horse for m'lady. I'm going to steal
both; my herd is pastured somewhere near here, if I recollect properly and if it hasn't been run off."

"What do we need another horse for?" He must still be
half sleeping; nothing was registering.

"Too risky, riding double. Not comfortable for m'lady
either, if it come to that." He stood up and took a few steps
away from Tristan. "When I get back, we'll find a safer
place than this to talk things out. We've plans to be laying,
wizard!"

He was gone.

After a minute, Tristan got up and walked over to their
small fire, shivering and blinking because the morning air

was unexpectedly chill. Allaire sat close by the coals, holding Thomas on her lap. He was permitting her to stroke his fur. She smiled as Tristan approached, and the day grew measurably brighter.

She leaned close, her face showing just a lovely hint of a concerned frown.

"Are you all right? That explosion last night was terrible. The armor was red-hot when Polassar took it off you—I can't think how you weren't worse burned."

Tristan looked at his wrists and felt of his neck, but Blais' salve had done its work with customary thoroughness. The skin was still tender, but unmarked and not painful.

"I'm fine," he said. "Really. What did Polassar do with the armor?" It seemed his nerves were wakeful too, since he was worrying again.

"Oh, he pitched it straight into that stream! There was a tremendous sizzle and clouds of steam. I think you'd fainted by then."

Tristan nodded absently. By its noise, the stream ran fast, though it didn't look large. As long as the armor was hidden in running water, there was no danger of anything out of Darkenkeep scenting it and hunting them down. He'd been crazy not to consider that when he'd let Polassar force the armor on him. Tristan relaxed fractionally and decided he was hungry.

He took a hunk of bread and toasted it as best he could. It tasted awful, but there probably wasn't much else. They'd eaten all of his provisions in Darkenkeep, and the only food Polassar had thought to bring had been two jugs of wine. Those had been broken in the midst of the Winterwaste, when the wine froze and burst them.

His cook-pot was on the fire, with bits of what looked like rabbit in it, along with lots of water. He dipped the bread into it—at least it might be warming.

"I'm afraid I'm small use as a cook," Allaire apologized.

Tristan looked up in surprise.

"No one really expects you to—" He broke off from confusion and shyness.

"To know how to do such a simple thing?" She shrugged, and looked away. "We were talking last night, while you slept. About what we should do now."

They sat silent a while.

"I never hear Polassar call you anything but wizard. Don't wizards have names anymore? Or can't you give yours?" Her eyes were flower innocent.

"We do. I can. Mine is Tristan."

"A sad name. But a wizard's name. We have a kinship in magic."

It was his turn to shrug.

"Properly speaking, I'm not a wizard." He forced the difficult words out. Something in her seemed to demand it. "I was apprenticed for it, yes, but I never made much progress. Oh yes," he went on, as she raised an eyebrow at him. "It's true. I was the worst student you can imagine. Then my master was killed, and all this started. If I were really a wizard, I'd have known better than to try any sort of spell with cold iron touching me. I'd have remembered how iron affects magic. I know better now, but that doesn't make me a wizard."

*Very nice light-show,* Thomas said. *I meant to mention it.*

Allaire said nothing. She was looking a bit uncomfortable.

I make more of a fool of myself every time I open my mouth, Tristan berated himself dismally. I can't be brave or heroic—can't even do magic properly—and then I have to rub it in her face when she's only trying to be polite. She'll never look at me the way she looks at Polassar—and why should she?

She was lovely. Even unlettered in her power as she obviously was, her face lent a touch of springtime to the almost-winter clearing. One expected violets to spring up from her footsteps.

Tristan got up abruptly, while she was engrossed in pretending to play with the cat, trying to conceal the longing in his face. It would never do for her to see how he felt; that would be too humiliating. He found his pack, with the packet of birdseed within, and spread some atop a fallen log.

Minstrel dove down at once, before he could be summoned, jauntily informing Tristan that he'd roosted in a tree the night before—a marvel he'd never done before in all his sheltered life! He seemed proud, and spoke of a great feathered monster that sailed the night with hooting cries. It had not frightened the intrepid Minstrel, he assured Tristan.

Tristan stroked the white and gray head-feathers.

"You are truly brave, little one. More than you know." Minstrel turned his head sideways, looked at him, and ran a foot through his left wing.

Thomas announced that he was hungry, too. It was hard work, hunting in this wild place; he ought to share in the results, now that they were cooked. And looking after incompetent wizards was no easy work either.

"I'm sorry there's no milk for you," Tristan apologized. "For all I care, you can lick out the soup pot—it wouldn't be the first time we've shared a dish. But m'lady might be more particular."

She looked up.

"You can use my name. Surely friends need not stand on ceremony, and what else should we be after sharing such an adventure? I have your name and make you a gift of mine. Come here, little cat, you shall eat too. You might have done so before this, had your manners permitted you to mention the matter to me."

Thomas lapped daintily, meowed his thanks and prowled off, no doubt in search of luncheon.

After that, they sat in silence for a very long time. Casual conversation seemed impossible—what exactly did one say to the most magical and beautiful woman in the world? Tristan couldn't think of a single appropriate subject.

They might have broken through this barrier sooner, had they not each been lost in private thoughts. Tristan's mind wandered and roamed hundreds of leagues, effortlessly. He sat so still so long that Minstrel chose to nap on his finger, and was undisturbed for hours. The time wasn't lost—there was plenty for Tristan to think about. Polassar wouldn't catch him unawares again.

The light had taken on a definite afternoon slant when Allaire spoke. "Polassar seems to think we'll see fighting."

Her voice did not startle him, since he'd been thinking about her quite a lot. Yet Tristan found himself studying his feet, as if his boots were greatly fascinating. Kinship in magic or not, he was finding it difficult to look on her face without losing control.

"He's probably right. I'm surprised we got this far without trouble—Nímir won't let you go easily."

Allaire began to fiddle with the belt-knife Polassar had found for her. "Tristan—is swordplay very difficult—to learn, I mean? Is there some great secret to it?"

That drew a smile out of him.

"Only practice. A lot of it, and if you work hard at it, sometimes it looks like magic—after you've mastered it. A sweaty magic."

"Will you teach me?"

He was more than ready to leave off thinking. He'd arrived at the fretting stage, anyway.

"If you like. Let me see—"

He examined her knife, which was certainly long for a lady—or a man either, he saw as he held it.

"I fear Polassar judges arms by his own size, and not that of us ordinary folk. This is a child's sword, not a knife. But for our purpose, it will do very well. You hold it so—" He drew his own blade, demonstrating the proper grip, adjusting her fingers where they required it. Allaire looked seriously into his eyes. "And try to stand so—the idea is to keep the edge of your body facing your enemy—a smaller target. Also in this stance you're well balanced, which is important for both attack and defense."

One thing—magic had made him a good fencer. Most passes and gestures used in spellcrafting strained the fingers unmercifully, as tensions were set up between muscles and tendons were stretched in undreamed of ways. Tristan's fingers were thin, and long, and very strong, besides possessing a suppleness most folk would have found remarkable. His wrists were tough as sword-steel, but as flexible. His grip on a sword was thus firm but light, easily shifting as chance demanded. He would have highly recommended the Arts Magical, whatever their other drawbacks, as a peerless training aid to any swordmaster.

"What an odd sword that is." She touched it as timidly as she might have touched Minstrel.

Tristan blushed, embarrassed for his sword's lack of style and grace.

"It's very old. I'm not sure why Blais—he was my master—even kept it. Except that he used to say whoever left me with him left the sword too, and he was hard put to tell which was the worse bargain!" His eyes misted over. "Joking, of course. But he taught me with it, and since I've grown taller, it—feels right, that's all. Like part of me. And it has a good edge, for all it won't take a polish."

"Show me what to do next." She had the grip right already, and her face was avid.

Tristan gave her a few quick moves, weaving a net of steel, feints and mock thrusts about her, until she gasped.

"That was beautiful! I never would have believed it possible, looking at—"

He forestalled her before she could say which had impressed her least, his sword or himself. He rather feared the latter might be true.

"You have good hands for this. Supple, strong, quick. You can accomplish more by quickness than by strength. Don't slash; that will be too hard for you to control, because of the blade's weight. Lunge with the point, so—" He showed her how to place her feet, how to attack and parry and attack again.

They circled around the fire. Tristan let her force him back while he called instructions, to give her the feel of it, then pressed her with his own attack, before she could grow complacent. Metal rang on metal.

Allaire caught on very quickly. Twice he barely beat the blade back in time. She was really attacking, assuming him enough of a swordsman to hold her off. What magnificent spirit she had!

Eventually she did get through his guard, either by luck or his own carelessness. He was still weary, more so than he'd thought, and bruised, and not as agile as he might normally have been. There was a flick of pain, and his wrist reddened. He barely felt the cut, and kept on with his parrying, but Allaire shrieked and flung down her sword.

"I've wounded you! Oh, Tristan, forgive me, is it bad? Let me see!"

"Allaire, it's only a scratch. No, really. Look. I swear it doesn't even hurt. Blais used to give me worse just to teach me to stay awake. I—"

"You make enough noise to be heard a league off! A dozen armies could have found this place by now—what did you think you were doing?"

Polassar stood on the bank above them, sword in hand,

feet planted wide apart, the sinking sun bloody behind him. His hair was standing on end with his anger, and it was a sight to inspire awe—abject terror, even. Allaire tried to speak, and seemed to have lost her voice for a moment.

"I asked Tristan to teach me the use of a sword." Her words crept out like timid little mice. "Did I do wrong?"

"He should have known better! Didn't you think it would attract any attention?" He was glaring at Tristan, not seeing Allaire. "Or didn't you think at all?"

Tristan felt the blood rush to his face, until he knew it was of a shade to match Polassar's moustaches. He held onto his temper somehow, handing Allaire her sword and sheathing his own before he dared speak. Better not to say anything with sword in hand.

"As for that, Valadan would have warned me long since if anyone but you approached. Did you get the things you went for?"

"Aye, I—See here, wizard, don't use that tone with me! You forget to whom you speak, sirrah!"

"And you forget to whom *you* speak!" Tristan flared. "I am no vassal of yours. And you are not crowned yet."

Polassar's sword hand was twitching. What do I do if he draws steel on me? Tristan wondered desperately. I'm no match for him, certainly not when he's angered. How did I get myself into this?

Allaire thrust between them.

"Stop this! I'm hungry."

They looked at her, then at each other. Polassar bared his teeth, then began unexpectedly to laugh.

"I can respect a man with spirit, wizard! You've more of that than I figured, for sure—"

Valadan gave a shrill neigh. Tristan spun toward him, staring, though the horse could not even be seen through the trees.

"Something's coming."

"There, wizard, I told you—" Polassar was delighted at getting vindication.

"Not human," Tristan interrupted, careless of courtesies. Valadan's message was staggering. "Something else. It scents us by magic, and there was enough here last night to draw it! We've got to get out of here. *Now!*"

Polassar chose not to argue. They broke camp instantly,

there being little to do except douse the fire. Allaire made to mount the horse Polassar had brought for her, but gasped in dismay at the sight of the saddle, which would not accommodate her skirts. Polassar had not thought, or had not been able to locate a woman's saddle. Riding astride would be more difficult in a skirt than riding before Tristan had been.

"If my lady will permit—" Tristan drew his belt knife. Flushing slightly, he slit her skirts front and back. She smiled thanks swiftly as Polassar swung her up onto the mare. They rode.

After a mile, Tristan reined in sharply.

"This is where we separate. We're leaving too wide a trail."

"What are you going to do?"

"Cover for you. Keep riding as long as the light holds, and take Minstrel with you. When you've made camp, send him back for me. Valadan can catch up quickly."

"Aye. Right. But go carefully, wizard."

Now what did that mean? Tristan wondered, watching them around a bend and out of sight. A moment ago the man was ready to kill me. Then he shrugged and set himself to wait for the coming menace.

It would not be the dragon again. The Guardian would not leave the Gates, even if it were finished sulking over the hurts done it. It was too large and heavy, and the source of its power lay in Darkenkeep, in the evernight that lurked there. It would not venture so far away. It must be something else.

Tales told of the Hounds of Nímir, though it was never said they were truly dogs. They were questing and dauntless, but they certainly had nothing so normal and wholesome as tails. And what was it that he'd felt before, leaving the cottage, and sometimes after? That sense of something moving through the door, though he knew he'd locked it firm? That chill, those eyes in his back? It occurred to him that he'd hardly felt unwatched since.

He chose a stone from his box, a green-black oval, smooth and featureless. He lifted his right hand, beginning the required pass. His index finger was cocked back, while all the others strained forward. He felt the tension of muscle against muscle as he spoke the counter-chant, drawing his thumb toward his palm. Now his elbow ached too, as did the burns on his wrist. His bone-ends creaked against each other.

He knew he was straining and that if he snapped a ligament he'd pay dearly for it. But there was no other course open—he needed this spell.

The stone looked blank now, open and receptive. It was blank, utterly blank, and so must his mind be. Not a trace of magic must enter his thoughts from here on. Let the blankness spread to the landscape too.

Dust blew back into the hoofprints on the path. Magic came trickling in, from the ground, the air, the campsite. It soaked into the stone, was lost beneath its surface.

Tristan felt himself beginning to skin over with it. In a few moments he and Valadan were outwardly no different from any other horse and rider. Their peculiar natures were hidden within them, as was the magic in the stone. Let the Hounds come.

Something cold touched his leg, then circled around and pressed against his cheek. He and Valadan stood stark still. Whatever it was stayed behind Tristan, just out of reach of side-sight.

It examined every inch and scrap of skin and leather, with many tiny prickings. A centipede of ice crawled up Tristan's spine. The Hounds hovered around him, waiting. One crack in the shield, and—best give that no thought.

They went as suddenly as they had come, in a howl of wind. It was a disappointed sound. It diminished away to the south, and that was good. Let them go a thousand leagues south! Tristan knew that Polassar had ridden into the sunset. He'd fooled them, somehow.

Again he was amazed—he'd been unsure he could really protect against the Hounds with the few spells at his command. And of those few, how many could he be sure would work? He'd chosen this one by instinct.

Valadan moved swiftly over a landscape stained red by sunset, and Tristan tried, this once, to hold onto the unfamiliar idea that he'd really succeeded.

# Fortress Radak

THE FIRELIGHT FLASHED back green from Tristan's eyes. He poked a boot into the embers, stirring until sparks flew up unto the night.

"We can't just have her try on every ring in Calandra—no, I stand corrected, we only need her to try every *silver* ring! That should narrow the field considerably! It would work, of course, eventually, or maybe right away, if we were amazingly lucky. And *if* the ring is still in Calandra. But it would be impossible to hide our purpose, and there lies the danger."

"Any man who interferes with her will answer to my blade." Polassar rapped his sword hilt with his fist for emphasis.

"All of them?" Tristan cocked an eyebrow. "You're missing my point. A woman with her hands already aglow with rings, asking after every bit of silver in sight—a child could tell you what was up! We'd have more trouble than even *your* blade could handle."

"Just so," Polassar said, with an air of great wisdom. " 'Tis why I spoke with the lord of Radak, on my way back to you today."

Tristan stared at him.

"You told Galan of Radak about Allaire?"

"Aye, but don't burst yourself, wizard. I did not tell him where we were, and I took care not to be followed. I told you we would take council, and we are doing so. Will you hear my plan now? Or perhaps you've one of your own?"

"No." Tristan looked off into the night. "I must bow to your experience in these matters, Polassar. I'm no strategist. What did you say to Galan?" He was vastly troubled at the thought of letting outsiders in on their quest. The complications could be endless.

"That we need his help. 'Tis true enough. He's agreed to shelter us in his hold, while we go about the search. We can trust him; I've had dealings with him before and found him honest enough. If you're agreeable, we'll go to Radak at first light."

"And once there, what?" Tristan asked bleakly.

"Plan. We haven't time for that here; you said yourself we were close pursued. And Lassair is besieged again. Galan confirmed the rumors I'd heard. We're surrounded by armies now. We can't hope to get through."

"If we just had some clue as to the nature of this ring! Once we're mewed up in Radak, how do we go about seeking it? Can you tell me that? It may become impossible to slip out without attracting notice."

"It has become impossible to stay here. I feel a need for walls around us. And how can you expect m'lady to continue sleeping on the hard ground, living out of a packbag?"

"Perhaps the ring is a wedding ring."

Allaire sat by the fire, perched on her saddle. "I can remember it being told to me that for the power to come, I—I need to be in love! So that the power could never be misused, or abused. That must be why Nímir never sought the Ring. It was of no use to him, and he could never have forced me to use it for him." Her eyes burned ice-blue, into theirs. "Couldn't that be it?"

"If we search not for the ring but for the bridegroom, no need to look far." Polassar stretched out a hand to Allaire, but she was looking at the fire again, and failed to see. "It was written that you would marry the King of Calandra."

"I wish I could think," she faltered. "There's something lacking—" She broke off agitatedly.

Tristan dared touch two fingers on the white sleeve of her gown.

"It's all right." He smiled comfortingly. "I have the same sort of trouble myself sometimes, remembering formulae. Magic's such a complicated art—"

She hadn't even been listening.

Tristan gave the embers another fierce kick. They'd been at this discussion for hours, accomplishing nothing save to increase Tristan's desire to have nothing whatsoever to do with Radak. Polassar spoke again.

"These thoughts about wedding rings are easily proved. And the sooner, the better."

"The legends say she weds the King," Tristan pointed out.

"When we're wed, I'll *be* the King. Is that not so?"

There was something wrong with that logic, Tristan thought. Or am I only objecting to the idea of her wedding him, now or anytime?

"Polassar, does it never strike you that *any* man she weds will become King, by the power of her rings? Even if she can't use them. There's still tradition to be reckoned with. There lies our chief danger, and if we go to Radak tomorrow, I'll not answer for the consequences."

"And how should you?"

Tristan looked up from the flames sharply, as Polassar went on: "You've admitted you took no thought beyond releasing this lady from her prisoning. You've done your job. You say the old books and tales promise her to me. I presume you've no privy objection to that?"

Tristan shook his head in furious denial of the barely voiced accusation. He had no right to object—

"Then why do you dispute with me?" Polassar thundered. Minstrel jerked awake, cheeping plaintively, and Thomas had a hiss startled out of him.

Polassar continued more softly, but no less dangerously for that. " 'Tis most impolite of you. Who do you conceit yourself to be, wizard?"

Even Allaire seemed taken aback.

"I've followed you this far because we found her—" Polassar stabbed a finger at Allaire. "—where you said we would, crazy as it sounded. And I'll admit, you handled things very well, for a while. I trusted you, but you're obstinate now, and it makes no sense. There's nothing wrong with sheltering in Radak."

Tristan started to speak, but Polassar wasn't finished.

"I trusted you. But I'll follow no madman, and no jumped-up wizard either. You can follow me now, or take yourself home!"

Now Allaire did protest, fluttering her hands like the wings of agitated white doves, while Minstrel flapped his own wings, and Thomas' fur stood straight out from his body. But no sound came from Allaire's lips, as if she felt she wouldn't be heard. And Tristan didn't move at all.

He sat huddled under his threadbare cloak, knowing the truth, however unkind, in Polassar's words and thoughts. He was mentally kicking himself far harder than he'd kicked the logs.

Polassar was unused to having his will questioned. They were a fellowship only so long as they needed each other, and why did Polassar need him now? He'd served his purpose. And not to see Allaire again, ever—

It was unthinkable. He had to smooth this over somehow. Yet his eyes stayed locked with Polassar's. Even Thomas might have been forced to look away from that stare.

They still needed him to find the ring. He couldn't go home now, even if he did prefer playing the coward and keeping what was left of his bleeding heart. Blais' quest was far from done.

Maybe I deserved the rough side of his tongue, Tristan thought, for not knowing my place and keeping to it. But toadstools, what I wouldn't give for one impressive, reliable spell to put him in his!

Unfortunately, he had nothing like that at his command. So he broke the eye contact and said, with as much grace as he could manage, "I'm tired, and I want to sleep. Call me for my watch."

He rolled himself up in his cloak, his back to the fire, and shut his eyes; but of course there was no sleep for him. He felt tears starting, and squeezed his eyes tighter shut.

Why must you always play the fool? he questioned himself angrily. It's plain obvious that she's as in love with him as he is with her—or will be, soon. And it's right she should be. He's a prince of the blood, a mighty fighter; he deserves to be king, and he deserves her. What are you, but a nameless foundling an old magician had the good heart and poor sense to foster? Will you beat yourself against a stone wall until your head splits? Is that the only way to stop these thoughts? But she is so very lovely, and I can't look at her without . . . without . . .

"Tristan?"

He opened his eyes and saw her by moon and firelight,

her braids coming undone and streaming about her face like all her silver rings melting.

"Tristan? It will be all right when we reach Radak, you'll see. I'm sure Polassar's right. Please don't be worried for my sake. I know I'm safe so long as you both are with me. It will be all right, it really will."

He could not move, for surprise, and she must have thought him asleep already, in the shadows, for she had spoken very softly. She melted away, and then he did sleep.

If he could just carry the thought of her with him— Surely she had looked at him with tenderness, surely he could read some comfort into her words—imagine that she cared. But the only things that stayed in his mind as sleep claimed it were her silver rings, gleaming softly by moonlight.

Polassar woke him to stand watch, and he used the time to pack up, then quietly groomed Valadan. Thomas crouched on that saddle, looking at him strangely.

"What's the matter with you?" Tristan asked roughly. "It's not my fault there aren't any mice about. What's wrong?"

*Quit breaking your heart,* Thomas said.

They rode to Radak in the rain.

Three hours riding saw them at the gates of Fortress Radak. They were all chilled and wet and thoroughly miserable by then, Tristan most of all. It had rained the whole way; and try as he might, no spell he could devise would keep the rain and mud off them. The rain had crept through Tristan's clothes and into his bones. The bones resented this and were beginning to creak. Tristan winced at every long stride that Valadan took, both from the discomfort and from the knowledge that the strides brought them closer to Radak.

He was trying to sort out feelings the like of which he'd never experienced in his life. Even through the drizzle, Allaire shone like moonbeams—seen through smoked glass, but moonbeams still. He could hardly keep his eyes away from her. He forgot his rain spell, didn't even remember to duck his head out of the worst gusts, and so wind and water found unobstructed ways into his clothing.

He'd long since run out of comparisons for her beauty.

She brought to mind's ear every heroic ballad and saga he'd ever heard or read. There'd never been anything in his life like her.

It hadn't occurred to him yet that she was the only young woman he'd been around for any length of time.

Blais had hired no woman to keep his cottage neat—none could have stood that hopeless task at yet more hopeless wages. And the young girls of Dunehollow-by-the-Sea had never been terribly impressed by Blais' threadbare apprentice. Sorcery might be said to lend a man a certain glamor, but none had ever rubbed off on Tristan.

But Allaire! Allaire had smiled at him, and spoken kindly, and listened—sometimes—when he spoke. And who'd ever done that before? She'd even thanked him when he'd handed her a bowl of porridge that morning. Between the thanking and the silken touch of her fingers brushing his, he'd nearly spilled the porridge all over her. He'd felt his face go hot, but she'd graciously not even noticed.

She and Polassar were talking as they rode. Tristan was only a little way behind them, but the wind carried their words away, and he heard only snatches of conversation. Tristan wished Polassar would bespeak him occasionally—even if in anger—anything to reassure him that he wasn't to be ordered home after all.

He had to content himself with the sight of Allaire's slender back—compensation enough for almost any hurt—and glimpses sometimes of her silver hair when the wind lifted her cloak's hood. One tendril had escaped her braids now; he told himself that it looked fine as spider silk.

The sight was doing odd things to his insides. He had only to look at her, and his blood pounded uncertainly in his ears. His breath got short. He felt as if he'd eaten something that was not going to agree with him. But he'd breakfasted on porridge as they all had, and he wasn't so poor a cook as to ruin porridge.

Polassar's shout roused him. Tristan looked up—or rather, focussed his eyes; he found he'd already been looking ahead blindly. There was Radak on the horizon.

Radak looked the part of a hold that had never been taken and never would be, save by treachery from within. Its wall stones were thick and well cut, needing little mortar, and they rose high. To Tristan, they seemed to block out what little sun the day offered, darkening the whole sky.

The fortress was built into the side of a rocky bluff, its walls unscalably sheer. Overhangs at the tops of the walls made doubly sure of that. Radak's stonework was famed throughout the land, and justly so, Tristan saw firsthand.

Radak was overawing, though it wasn't as if he'd never seen a castle before. There were those ruins he'd passed on his ride to Lassair and Lassair's own crumbly walls; and even Dunehollow had *some* fortifications. He and Blais had lived remotely but not in isolation.

But Radak's immense pile of artfully dressed stone was so vast that Tristan wondered that the very earth did not groan at its weight.

No simple stone work for Galan's hold! His ancestors had built with a craft long since forgotten. Radak's base-stones were monoliths taller than Tristan on horseback, so close set that, though they were mortarless, a feather could not have been passed between them. Above, mortar had been used, but the patterns in which the smaller blocks were set spoke of strength and, just possibly, magic. A hard strength, stern and with nothing in it of beauty, but what mattered that? Radak had stood unconquered for nine hundred years.

Polassar shouted to the guard, and the drawbridge clanked down. The way was narrow, admirably defensible, forcing them to ride single file. Tristan went first, having been closest to the bridge when it dropped. He rode into the outer court and looked curiously around, despite his weariness. Was everything in this place made of gray stone? Galan did not allow even blades of grass to creep among his stonework.

Someone was coming down a broad stone stair. Servants and men-at-arms flanked him. A collar of gold was bright about his throat, so this was almost certainly Radak's master. Tristan saw that his hair and eyes were dark, his lips red and full. A face passion could easily rule. Perhaps he knew no other master. Tristan only sensed that, but with an arcane certainty.

Tristan stared at him, and it was as if a great light burst into his mind. He felt, abruptly, more alert than he had all that day. The dream mists vanished from his head, leaving it aching but clear. His sight sharpened on Galan's face, blurred on all else, as if he scanned its inmost thoughts and instincts as well as the passing scene. An alarm bell rang somewhere just behind his eyes, stridently insistent.

Danger here? But he couldn't quite make out how . . . Valadan shifted restlessly between his knees, snorting. Something Blais had once said, in reference to Galan's policy of rule? They hadn't studied Radak much, except in passing. The guards? There were no more—or not many more—than were normal in a well-run hold. And these weren't heavily armed. Yet the very air seemed thick with warnings, portents—only he couldn't quite hear them.

Then everything crystallized in Tristan's mind—

He spun Valadan around sharply, blocking the bridge with the stallion's body. Polassar's roan bit at him, but he grabbed her bridle and forced her to a halt.

"Wizard, have you taken leave of your senses?"

Polassar controlled the mare's plunging savagely, jerking her head away from Tristan's hands.

"Have you? What in heaven's name made you think we'd be safe here?" His thoughts and fears spilled out before he could hope to make sense of them. "What makes you think a man like Galan will be noble enough to refuse a chance to grab power like Allaire's? And even without the rings, can he look at her and not want her? Once we come inside his walls, we'll never get out alive! We've got to go now, while we still can!"

"Tristan!" His name was a shocked gasp from Allaire's lips.

"Wizard, you're embarrassing me." That dangerous quietness was in Polassar's voice again. Tristan didn't heed it.

"To Darkenkeep with that! Don't you see this is just another trap? This may be our last chance to—"

Polassar hit him.

He saw the blow coming. Valadan screamed, and that was all.

# PRISONER

COOLNESS FELL on his cheek, then went away. A sore something on the side of his face began to throb.

Allaire was seated on the bed beside him, dipping a cloth into a basin. She leaned forward to lay the cloth on his forehead, and he felt water run down into his hair.

"Polassar is very sorry," she said softly. "He didn't mean to hit you so hard, but you made him angry."

"Allaire?" A pain flickered behind his eyes like heat-lightning. Tristan waited for it to come again, his body uselessly tensed against it, but there was nothing, at least for that moment.

"Allaire?" Maybe it wasn't too late yet. His mind was fuzzily insistent on the point that she was in deadly danger somehow.

"Yes?" She dipped the cloth again. "Galan is feasting us tonight, but I don't think you're well enough yet."

He struggled to sit up, rather heedless of the pain in his face. His hand captured one of hers, blindly, gripped it.

"*Allaire!* Don't go. Don't let Galan set eyes on you," he said urgently. "Maybe we can still get away, before—"

She laughed.

"That would be most impolite, to refuse to see him after two days of such splendid hospitality. And he's gone to such trouble to plan this banquet specially—Galan's really quite a charming man. I can't think why you took such an instant dislike to him before you'd even properly met."

"Two days—" He felt disoriented, not without cause.

Allaire helped him to lie down once more, and plied the cool cloth again. She fussed gently with his pillow.

"Poor Tristan. It's been nearer three, by now. You've been very ill. I wasn't sure you knew how long we'd been here. This has all been a terrible strain for you, hasn't it? All that riding—I'm still sore myself—and the magic—and Polassar told me about the dragon, too. I didn't know—"

She let her eyes grow great with wonder, very prettily. "You needed a good rest."

All he could do was lie there staring at her, too light-headed to think properly.

A servingmaid crept in, bearing a towel-covered bowl. When she whisked the towel away, rich scents swirled about the room, tickling Tristan's nose.

"Ah, this will make you feel better. They've wonderful cooks here." Allaire signed the maid to leave with a wave of her hand, and the door hangings sighed softly closed.

"Can you sit up? Otherwise, we'll have this all over the sheets." She was quite casual about it, but her every least touch made his skin tingle, where it was not too bruised to bear even her delicate touching. She arranged his pillows carefully, and sat close by him, the better to feed him. The soup was barley and mutton. She spooned it up for him, and he hardly tasted it, for his eyes were tasting her. By the time the bowl was nearly emptied, his belly and heart were both contentedly warm and full.

If only that nagging inside his head would leave him alone. It had damped down to unease, but it refused to vanish utterly.

"Allaire," he asked, licking a last drop of broth from his lip, "what's Polassar doing about the ring? Has he made any inquiries? Or asked Galan to make inquiries?"

"No, I don't think so. He was talking about taking some troops to lift the siege his castle's under—"

Tristan's eyes snapped wide open.

"But Lassair has nothing to do with the ring! You don't mean he was just going to leave you here, while he went off fighting?"

Allaire raised one silvery brow at him.

"Well, why not? It's his castle. We can't expect him to abandon it to his enemies, just because of me. It's all he has."

"If he has you, he has something a lot more valuable than that burnt-out shell he calls a fortress," Tristan said angrily. "He was really just going to run off, without a word to me, without talking about the quest, or the ring— leave you at Galan's mercy—"

"Shhh. Galan promised to look after me. I'll be quite safe. And Polassar won't be gone long—he's sure his enemies will turn and run, if he moves upon them with an army. And Galan will give him one. Don't upset yourself any more, you're looking quite ill again."

"Never mind that," Tristan said. "Allaire, you've got to listen to me, if Polassar won't. We've got to—"

"Yes, of course," she said soothingly, and reached for the basin again. "But later. Lie still, you'll bring on a fever if you aren't careful."

"But the quest! He's forgetting all about it. We've got to find the ring before Nímir catches up to us, or we're helpless against him! And we can't find it if we stay here, if Galan—"

"Hush now—"

He grabbed at the rag, thrusting it away from his face and taking hold of her hand. The rings felt like cold fire under his fingers. She's in danger, his mind shrieked. Danger, and she doesn't even know it.

"Allaire—"

Her fingers whisked out of his grasp, and she backed uneasily away. Her skirts rustled loudly.

"Tristan, stop this!"

He stared at her.

"I won't have any more of this!" she went on, her voice rising. "Less than a week I've been with you and Polassar, and you're driving me to despair! You quarrel over me, and what's to be done with me like two dogs at a bone— but dogs would have let it lie by now. You can't treat me so. I'm not a chattel, I have a say in this, too!" She was trembling, her soft lips white.

"Allaire, don't you understand?" he asked urgently. "It's all for the freedom of choice you want. Every argument has been over that. We have to get away from here before it's too late."

"You're starting again! I won't have this!" Her voice was shrill, tightly stretched by nerves.

"You and your rings are the key to Calandra," Tristan explained with a great attempt at patience. "All Calandra, not just Radak, or Lassair. We've got to make Polassar see that. If we're not careful—if you're not careful—you'll be married off to Galan, or the man strong enough to take you from him. And you'll have no say at all in that. Our one chance is to stay free, stay to ourselves until we find

the ring. Nímir twists minds too easily for us to be child-
ishly trusting!"

"Stop it! Don't you listen to anyone? Get off this! We're
not going, we're staying, and that's all there is to it!" She
was almost weeping.

The soupbowl had shattered on the floor, somehow, and
she looked at it a moment, drawing little sobbing breaths.
Then the hangings swung wildly again, and she was gone.

After a time, Tristan stood up hesitantly, shaking with
reaction and a fear that had nothing to do with himself. He
brought the blanket with him, seeing the servingmaid on
her knees by the door. She gathered the bits of broken
crockery carefully. Bits of greasy meat were staining her
skirt.

"Where are my clothes?" Doubtless his sudden realization that he was completely naked under his blankets had
been responsible at least in part for his loss of control during the argument. He'd behaved badly, he knew, but Allaire had been no better—what had put her nerves so on
sword's-edge?

"Being cleaned, sir. And mended. Please don't try to
leave, it isn't—you're not well enough yet."

"You mean to say it isn't permitted," he corrected. "I
only want to see to my horse."

"He's well-stabled," the girl informed him helpfully.

"I pity the man who touches him."

"Lord Galan gave orders that you're not to leave this
room. There are guards on the stair," she told him pleasantly, and pointed at the door hangings. "He thinks you're
dangerously mad. He told the lady Allaire not to see you."

But she did come. Why? Not to nurse him; something in
the girl's tone made him suspect that Allaire hadn't been to
see him before today. Why had she come? To tell him to
give up his hopeless love? Did she even know of it? And if
she did, she need never have seen him again, it seemed.
Why, and again why?

"And you're not well enough yet." The girl had turned
back to her work now, but her voice held a curious authority. Tristan looked at her a minute, then shrugged. She
gathered up the last of the debris and left him.

He sat back down on the bed, putting a hand out to
either side to steady himself. So, Allaire's not a prisoner—

but I am. I hope Valadan isn't kicking the stable apart
trying to find out what happened to me.

*He isn't.*

Tristan jumped. The servingmaid was gone. He was
alone in the room—

Thomas crawled out from under the bed.

*I told Valadan the moment you woke.* He sprang to the
bed, pushed his face against Tristan's limp hand.

"Oh." Tristan felt ill with relief, though what menace
he'd expected was anyone's guess.

*He would have fought for you, but you might have been
trampled. Serve you right. That was a poor place for second thoughts.*

"Where's Minstrel?" Tristan asked, touching his face
gingerly for the first time. He flinched away from his own
fingers, and swore violently.

*The want-wit is in the stable, romancing a barn swallow.
Has no more sense than his master. You should have paid
more attention when Blais was teaching the personal protection spell. Since I did, shall I lesson you?*

"No," Tristan said irritably, and more sharply than he'd
intended.

*Did you want Minstrel to come sing your headache
away?*

"No. I just wondered. Thomas, did you happen to see
where they took my clothes?"

*To clean, first. Then in that chest. And Galan's master
of magic charmed the lock himself.*

"They put them in there while you watched? The master
magician can't be very bright. Why bother to lock it at all?"

*Who minds what a cat sees? You're the only one here
who believes in cat magic. Which is probably why I stay
with you, in spite of your all-too-human stupidity. And
they all think you're mad.*

"So I gather."

Thomas returned to washing his paws.

"How's the hunting, Thomas?" Tristan asked, trying belatedly to be cordial.

*Poor. Galan runs a tight ship, no rats worth bothering
about. Though I might teach his overweening dogs a thing
or three. What are you thinking of doing?* He arranged his
tail carefully about his feet.

"Getting dressed, for a start, I think I mind being naked more than I mind being a prisoner."

*He put a strong spell on that lock.*

Tristan sighed. He would have.

"But my sword is in there. It's got strong ties to me—I've had it all my life. Maybe that will help. Anyway, I have to try." Even the smallest control over his situation would be welcome.

Tristan knelt by the chest and put an ear to the lock, trying to catch a last whisper of the spell. It might help him to unravel it. The lock was brass, of course, as were all the chest's fittings.

"They took all my stones, too. I hope they're in here. I was a long time collecting them. Unless that master magician took them away to examine?"

*He didn't. Matter of fact, he laughed when he saw them—called them children's toys.*

The lock seemed to melt before Tristan's eyes, in a flash of anger. What exquisite, final humiliation! It was not enough that he'd been knocked senseless, stripped naked and penned up here, but the scorn of his peers must be added as well? Children's toys!

A wizard's stones were sacred to him, beyond mockery. One used whatever worked, however humble or exalted . . . Why, Tristan had once seen Blais invoke a thunderstorm using nothing more than a flung waterdrop and a flash from a mirror! And any fool knew that certain nondescript stones could be possessed of more power than the largest ruby. I'll show him toys, Tristan raged.

The lock flew open under his fingers. His stones lay scattered about inside the chest, still glowing with power, hot to his touch. The wood about the lock was scorched.

"Did he really say that, Thomas?" Tristan asked softly, fighting for calm. "Or did you just want to make me angry?" It was irritating, to have been so easily manipulated by a cat.

*You needed to be. You were too depressed to accomplish anything without a good jolt of wizardly wrath. And what difference does it make, as long as it worked?*

"You're too good to me, Thomas." Tristan let a little sarcasm creep into his voice, but the cat did not deign to notice.

He dressed himself then, feeling better as each familiar thing slipped on. Even his boots seemed to hug him, glad of his return.

"Those breeches are worn almost past mending."

He jerked to his feet, before recognizing the voice. Only the servingmaid, with basin and razor. Tristan fastened the unicorn buckle with great care.

"I'm to be permitted something that sharp?" he inquired acidly. "Or is Galan perhaps hoping I'll kill myself in my despair, and save him the trouble? Couldn't I just fall on my sword?"

The girl said nothing.

He felt ashamed almost at once for his rudeness. The savageness of his tone, so unfamiliar to his ears, seemed to linger in the room. And none of this was her fault.

Feeling sorry, he looked her over more closely. She'd scared him, coming in quietly like that. Small wonder he was startled. And in this place everything was a danger, until proved otherwise.

She was dressed in rough homespun, as he was, except that her clothes looked a lot newer and fitted her much better. Her dark hair, falling in curls to her shoulders, was woven through with great drops of crystal, as if rain ran through it. And her eyes were gray, silver-gray. They seemed to shine. Was she going to cry, because he'd spoken roughly to her? No doubt she would be well used to such treatment. Galan had not looked the man to be gentle with women not sharing his bed.

"What's your name?" he asked, very politely, trying to make amends.

"Elisena." She turned to go, crystals singing softly to one another.

"Elisena, wait. I'm sorry. Do you know where my friends are?"

"They dine with Lord Galan. Shall I shave you now?" Her eyes were expressionless.

"No, I think I can manage. Thank you."

He had supposed she would go then, when she'd handed him the basin and shaving things; but she did not, staying to hold the mirror for him, despite his churlishness.

It was awkward, trying to shave with her watching. He

could even swear that her eyes grew sympathetically wide as his own did when he first caught sight of his face.

Every one of Polassar's knuckles had left its own separate mark, but they merged into one huge bruise down the swollen left side of his face, purple and green at the edges. It was too sore to bear more than a cursory touch of the razor. Even the warm water he dabbed on the wound stung.

"I have herbs that will help that." Her voice was very gentle. "I've used some, but you could do with another dose."

"I have my own." He fetched out the butterfly box, and dabbed the ointment sparingly on. Not much of it was left now. His face burned till his eyes watered, but felt better soon after.

Elisena lifted up the box, sniffing.

"What's in this?"

He was busy with his wrists, rubbing leftover salve on the almost healed burns, as well as on the lump above his eyebrow, which had finally receded to something like normal proportions, though it was still tender. An incredible assortment of bumps and scrapes, he thought, totalling them up. Her question finally soaked through to his brain.

"The salve? I'm not really sure. My master made it, and I was never quite able to learn the formula. He said it was special for me, because as a child I was always falling down and hurting—" He found unaccountably that he was looking deeply into her eyes, a finger's length away, and she into his. "—myself." His voice had dropped almost to a whisper.

"He loved you," she said. "That would give it a power that none could duplicate."

She had melted away from him somehow and was folding the halves of the mirror in on themselves, gathering up the razor and basin.

I wonder where Galan stole her from?

Tristan stood watching the hangings swing, after she had disappeared through them. That girl had never been born a servant, he was sure.

# Reynaud

HE WAS sitting on the bed, thinking about that, when he sensed soft footsteps approaching. He almost spoke her name. The hangings opened.

A man stood before the gently swaying curtain. He was tall, somewhat stern of expression, robed all in black. He took another step into the room, and the robes swirled apart, revealing bright scarlet and gold magic signs underneath.

His age was indeterminate, as age sometimes was with wizards. Between thirty and fifty years, perhaps. His hair was still dark, but his skin had seen a lot of weather. Until the hair and beard went white and marked him as aged, there would be no further information to be gained from them.

The beard was small and elegantly pointed, and the rest of his face was likewise small and sharp, all intelligent angles. Excepting his eyes, that was. Tristan couldn't make them out at all, because the candle threw such shadows into the deep eye sockets. He could almost have sworn there were no eyes there at all, and unaccountably his heart began racing, and his blood went swiftly cold.

"I see my spell presented you no difficulties." The man's long fingers brushed the clothes chest negligently, tapping the ruined lock. "Merely a small test of your abilities. I confess I did not believe what Polassar claimed for you, at first. I could not credit it. Would a mage who had the power to brave Darkenkeep and wake Allaire of the Nine Rings allow himself to be taken so easily? So ridiculously easily? No, I could not give credence to it. I am Reynaud." He inclined his head slightly. "Galan's master of magic." He hardly needed to add that. He could have been no one else.

Tristan said nothing, but his mind ran wildly. He in-

tended me to break his spell. Else he'd have used an iron
chest, and locked it with a key. He's been watching—

"Why do you look at me so? Like a hawk, whose broken
wing I was once trying to mend. It savaged my finger. I
hope you will not be so foolish." He flicked a glance at the
sword lying by Tristan's side. "But perhaps you are not yet
feeling yourself. That was a grievous blow; Polassar might
have cracked your skull like an egg, without intending it. I
feared at first that the damage he'd done might yet be
greater than my skill at healing, when you were such a
long time waking." He shrugged delicately. "Have you no
tongue? You spoke boldly enough to Polassar—though perhaps not wisely—and to the Lady Allaire a short while ago.
And you were right—Galan will take her from Polassar.
That cannot be helped."

Tristan knew he probably should try to make some sort
of answer. The mage's words were friendly enough, and
there might be some advantage to conversation. Reynaud
would understand things no one else did, and wizards were
supposedly all brothers. But those eyes—where had Tristan
seen that look before? In Thomas' eyes, when the cat was
at an especially promising mousehole? What does he want
with me? Tristan asked himself frantically.

Reynaud came closer, still searching Tristan's eyes, as if
for fever—but perhaps also for something more? He put a
hand out to Tristan's cheek, and frowned as Tristan
flinched back, unable to help himself.

"Why do you start so? I'll not harm you." The fingers
probed with professional skill. "Hmm, a pity, but I think
that's going to mark you. He came close to smashing the
bone. Of course, a discreetly placed scar does sometimes
intrigue the ladies."

Tristan watched him coldly. Were those magic signs
really embroidered on his clothes, which must then be very
tightly fitted? Or were they perhaps his very skin?

"I had hoped we might talk. I burn to know how an
apprentice, who can barely handle stones of small power,
has been able to accomplish what you have. It's a considerable achievement. You must be more than you appear, or
else you have some powerful friends, which Polassar
swears you don't. You interest me very much, wizardling."

"Why?" Safety to the winds, he had to know.

"It speaks after all! A vast improvement."

"I'm of no use to you," Tristan was quick to point out. "I am what you say—half-trained, unskilled, friendless. Nothing, to a mage of your stature."

"Then you deny waking Allaire of the Nine Rings?" A raised brow, followed by a knowing shake of the head. "No, I thought not. And you're right to be proud of that work. Never fear to admit to it. Perhaps we may work together one day. There is much I could learn from you. You're altogether too modest about your—talents."

Those talents don't run to mind-reading, Tristan thought. What's he really after? Why the flattery? He can't think I'm some one of importance. He gives nothing away. Tristan was suddenly intensely aware of Thomas, lying hidden behind a heap of bedclothes. The tip of the cat's tail was twitching rapidly, but never so fast as Tristan's heart was beating.

"Yes, we really must talk. There is so much I would hear. Polassar has been remarkably close-mouthed for him, one gathers. No doubt he does not wish to speak of deeds of valor that would cause his own deeds to appear petty and commonplace. He has mentioned something about a dragon—the Guardian of the Gates, no less! And they tell me your master perished before he could finish training you? By the Powers, what may we yet expect of you?"

Tristan felt his head spinning. He needed a distraction, before he lost his sense of perspective entirely. He sought about for a topic, found none, and so kept silent.

One of the candles was beginning to gutter, its wick spitting noisily. Reynaud noted it offhandedly and jabbed a finger at it. The flame rose, steadied, and remained bright.

"So," he continued, "Allaire of the Nine Rings is found, and Valadan as well. After so much time, one had almost forgotten how to hope. And the world is very changed. I thought there were no real wizards left in Calandra. But I don't wish to tire you."

For all that, he made no move to leave. Rather, he seated himself on the high-backed chair by the hearth, and seemed to be waiting for Tristan to speak, to be tempted by his words, to beg for more of them.

The world was changed, Reynaud had just said. But what did he know about the beginnings of all this? More than Tristan, who'd had all of Blais' years of research to draw upon? Tristan rather thought that he did.

Over such a vast span of time, much had been lost and destroyed. Blais' information had had many tantalizing gaps scattered through it.

And this man might just have the missing answers.

Tristan could feel that Reynaud wore his knowledge wrapped all about himself, like a cloak, though he'd have liked for it to be called mystery. In the end, it meant one thing. He knew.

He knew who—or what—Allaire was, other than an impossible goal to be longed for over centuries. His mysteries stretched back to the beginnings of it all . . .

When Tristan had sat silent for a long while, not betraying his curiosity at all, Reynaud began to speak again.

At first he might have been addressing the flames on the hearth, for he spoke softly and kept his eyes on them; they leaped and tumbled with his words, as if in response to them.

"Yes, so long ago, and so much lost. Calandra and Esdragon were once one land—you'll have surely noted there's not even a river to divide them—under the Maristan kings." His tone suggested that all this must be long familiar to Tristan, which it mostly was. "Then Nímir came down out of his fastness in the Mountains of Channadran, and made Darkenkeep, and began to sow discord, and there was war. Of course, men being what they are, it didn't need a heavy touch to start trouble. Just a word whispered for the right ears to overhear. It would take a hundred years of study to unravel the politics alone, disregarding various changes of coat and outright betrayals. And fully half the records we once possessed are no more!

"Then the High Mage finally acted and forged the rings and bestowed them on the daughter of Esdragon's Duke. I don't know why she should have been chosen over all others, since she was quite young and virtually untrained, but that line was old in magic, and there came a prophecy that she would inherit a mighty power and be a shield to her people. Allaire was to wed Calandra's King, and thus unite the warring houses. Nímir's power could have been broken, even then, had Calandra and Esdragon stood together. But there was some treachery—doubtless inspired

by Nímir—and she was stolen away before she could be
either schooled or married. The final ring, which was Calandra's surety in the marriage-bargain, was never put on
her finger. Calandra and Esdragon went to war again, both
King and Duke were slain along with most of the men of
fighting age, and Valadan the Mighty was lost. Things
have never been right here since. Nímir's power has grown
from that day, for there's none to oppose him. Now we
may see it broken at last!"

"With the last ring, of course," Tristan added quietly.

Reynaud looked delighted at his response.

"Yes. And between us, it may just be found. Galan is
ruthless, but if we have a King again, we'll have protection
for the search. No more need our best mages die in a fruitless quest. We'll have better uses for them."

Tristan found himself still with nothing safe to say. His
face must have shown it.

"But you must be weary. Forgive my eagerness, I see I
have tired you. Also, I assure you, I will speak with Galan
at once, and have you released. No need to lock you up;
you're not mad, as Polassar said. How little these common
warriors understand the ways of wizards!" He smiled
smoothly. "Galan will listen to me. You'll be freed."

"My thanks."

"No need. Of course I shouldn't try to go anywhere just
now, if I were you. It might be taken as a sign of bad
faith." Reynaud sketched a handsign Tristan did not recognize, tossed a spell into the room and left as silently as he
had come.

Tristan discovered that he was shivering. I don't understand him. Or what he wants, really wants. Why come in
here and make a long speech repeating things that we both
know perfectly well, and which don't matter at this point
anyway? He doesn't know a thing about the last ring. Does
he think I do? He's as easy to catch hold of as smoke. That
is a very dangerous man.

Thomas hissed beside him. *I suppose you've never heard
how one mage will feed off another, to bolster his own
power? You must look like a feast to him, since you can't
even protect yourself from mere physical force.*

Restless, unnerved, Tristan walked to the arrow-slit that
served the room for a window, as much to escape Thomas'

gloom as to see what was going on, and watched Galan's
guard march the walls until it grew very dark. Torches
wove about like fireflies, so many steps this way, turn
about, so many steps more. The monotony made him
sleepy, and he laid himself down on the bed, with his
sword close beside him and his box of stones tight in his
hand, this time. They would not be spirited off again while
he slept. Thomas curled up tightly by him and began to
purr a lullaby as Tristan stroked his tabby fur.

Yet of course he couldn't sleep. Tristan's eyelids kept
flying up just when they should have been heaviest, and he
was seeing frightful things in the shadows that choked the
room's corners. The more he wooed sleep, the less sure he
felt of finding it. Eventually, he gave up any pretense, sat
up, and began to study his surroundings.

It wasn't a bad little room he'd been put in. Small, of
course, and unfurnished save for bed, chest and chair, but
it had a window, though the arrow-slit was small and set
uncomfortably high. It was also too narrow to be escaped
through. The blankets on his bed were clean and thick,
scented with herbs. He sniffed, recognizing lavender and
fleabane, not without some nostalgia at their familiarity.

Now that the backwash of anger and fear had left him,
he began to feel his hurts again. His face ached, a steady,
pulsing pain that made him long for sleep's oblivion while
keeping him wakefully away from it. He ran his fingers
over his cheek, in the irresistible way one probes the cavity
left by a drawn tooth. Tristan decided he was indeed very
lucky there weren't bones broken. A shade lower and he'd
have lost teeth as well.

His eyes burned; he'd been staring at the candle without
realizing it. The rest of the room seemed triply dark.

Whatever was going to become of Allaire and Polassar,
Tristan conceded that he was mostly wondering what
would become of himself. If Thomas was right about Reynaud, there was not much question about his fate, he
thought, despair thick around him.

Thomas kneaded his arm with all four of his paws. From
a cat, that was meant as a comforting gesture, uncomfortable and uncomforting as it was for Tristan.

*Sleep*, Thomas hissed sternly. *Ssssleep. Never mind that
carrion crow, he won't be back tonight.*

Tristan supposed that if he weren't going to sleep, he ought to try to calmly assess his situation. Getting the facts straight might bring him ease.

He wasn't locked in, or chained to the bed; that was a plus; but with guards on the stair outside the door, he might just as well have been trussed hand and foot. Tristan was under no illusions. He wasn't going anywhere.

He felt fit enough now, except for his cheek aching, and that was nothing. He had his clothes, and his sword, and Valadan waiting for him. But Valadan was too far away, even if Tristan had any foolish thoughts of finding the stables quickly. No, he was stuck here.

And there was no one who cared about that.

He could stay here for the rest of his life—doubtless a short one—and no one would ever miss him. Polassar would be glad to get rid of him—no more arguments and embarrassments. Allaire was furious with him momentarily and would easily forget he'd ever existed. And Blais was dead.

There it was. Not one soul in all the world cared about what became of him, and very few would even wonder. And what about the quest? He'd messed that up beautifully now.

*Well, never mind,* Thomas told him. *You tried. Blais would have understood.*

"My failing?" Tristan's fingers moved absently through Thomas' fur. "Oh yes, he'd have understood that—he'd had lots of practice—"

*Don't get all maudlin. You'll just make your headache worse.*

A fine point I've come to, Tristan thought, as self-pity rose irresistibly in him. The only friend I've got in the whole world is a cat.

*I think,* Thomas interrupted softly, *that I should consider myself insulted.* One paw, claws safely sheathed, patted Tristan's arm. *The friendship of a single cat is to be valued above the love of thousands of mere humans.*

Despite himself, Tristan fell asleep with a smile still on his face.

# Escape

"WIZARD? No, *quiet!*"

There was a hand over his mouth, clasping so tightly that it hurt him. He could scarcely breathe, far less speak. By its size, the hand was Polassar's.

"I never thought to admit you right, but we're getting out of here. Are you awake now?"

Tristan nodded as hard as he was able, being held so.

"What's changed your mind?" he asked, when he could speak again. Polassar had not been overgentle, and he rubbed one hand over his sore mouth. "Last I heard, Galan was your good true friend, and I was only an embarrassment to you."

"Tread softly, wizard! You'll never know how it galls me that you were right."

"What happened?" Tristan asked impatiently.

Polassar's bulky shadow threw a shadow arm toward the corner of the room. Someone was there, weeping—or perhaps, from the next words, panting with fury. It was Allaire's voice, oddly harsh.

"Galan came upon me alone, just before we were to dine. He spoke of being pressed by work and said that he must miss the meal, but hoped to see me later. Later! Then he made so free with his hands, he left me in no doubt of what he meant by it. Speaking fair double-edged words of a guest's duties to her host, all the while—as if I were his to touch—"

Well, what else did you expect? Tristan thought privily.

"So I told Polassar of it."

But she must have had the sense to wait until they were out of the supper room and alone, before doing so. Else the resultant noise of Polassar's wrath would have wakened Tristan and every other sleeper within half a league.

"Wait," Tristan asked puzzledly. "There are guards on

the stairs, aren't there?" Or had they just lied to him about that, assuming he wouldn't check? "How'd you get in here?"

"They sleep," Polassar said. "And would sleep like the dead if not for m'lady's begging mercy for them, despite all. Now will you help us, before they wake and I must slay them?" His sword clinked faintly, as if it had been eased a little in its sheath, then shoved home. Allaire made a little sound of despair.

"He shall not touch you, lady," Polassar said firmly as she began to sob afresh—whether with rage or fear, Tristan couldn't tell. It had a terrible stifled sound to it, whatever. Polassar put one great arm around her, and she swiftly calmed.

Then she said, deadly quiet, "Give me my sword. I will—"

Polassar lifted her to her feet.

"Softly, my lady. The wizard will help us. We'll be away before Galan ever has time to look for you—"

They weren't thinking about him anymore, or the quest, or the ring—only getting away, together. The besotted fools—Tristan's belly churned with resentment. If they could have done so without his help, they'd have been gone from the castle this instant, and he never the wiser that he'd been abandoned.

"Help you how?" he asked, glad of the darkness.

"Weave us a cloak of invisibility! Sing a spell to melt these walls like butter! Put Galan and his men to gentle sleep for a thousand years! Do I need to teach you your craft?"

Someone should, Tristan thought, but didn't dare voice it. They might leave him yet. Aloud he asked, "Is that how you think a magician works?"

"Well—isn't it?" Polassar sounded surprised.

"No. But I'll try something." Could he use the blank stone again, shielding them from all passing eyes until they could get outside the walls? What had Blais always told him, that things were easiest hidden in plain sight? Get them to the stables first for the horses, that was the thing. He drew the stone out, held it tight, and—

"—No!" he cried, feeling his lips tear apart to let the words pass. *No, not this!* his mind screamed on, his heart racing. He was a bird, beating his wings against walls of black glass. He could gain neither hold nor exit. The air felt solid; there was no light to help him find his way. The pain and disorientation of it were appalling. He flung away the stone, and forced his eyes open. His mind felt burnt, smoking. His hands were still twitching.

Polassar and Allaire huddled before him on the floor like children, arms around each other.

"I thought you were having a fit, wizard! What's amiss?"

Thomas mewed concern.

Tristan stayed on his feet somehow, reeling, fighting for breath.

"I—can't. He's walled me in. I can't use my magic. I can't help you—or myself." He said a lot more, none of his words making much sense to the two on the floor.

He could feel a sob forming in his throat, but he was too numb even to sit down. Reynaud must have fenced him with spells while he slept, or perhaps even earlier. Those strange passes he'd stupidly noted before, and forgotten.

I couldn't even light a fire now, if I had a lit taper to do it with, he thought, fighting panic. I'm more helpless than a baby. We'll never get out of here, and it's my fault. I've failed again, and this time it's worse because they're both depending on me. Oh, we could still fight, but we'd never make it. It would take a lot of men to stop Polassar, but Galan has them! And I—I count for nothing in this, and haven't from the start. I should have known.

His stomach ached now too, as well as his head. His mouth tasted metallic. Thomas brought his stone back to him, laid it in his limp hand.

"If you can't help us, then we must trust to our blades," Polassar said resolutely. "Shall we try now, whilst they sleep?"

They probably never do, not the ones at the gate, Tristan thought, and was about to say as much.

"Let them try to stop us—" Polassar lovingly caressed his sword.

Something in Tristan snapped.

"Think with your brains for once, instead of your muscles! How far would we get that way? They'll cut us up into little pieces and take her anyway! We need a better plan than hacking our way out!"

Nevertheless, he belted on his sword and fastened up his cloak, fingers shaking only a little. His nerve-sharpened ears caught a noise, and he spun about.

Had the hangings moved? They must have, for Polassar's blade rasped its way out of its scabbard, throwing sparks into the darkness.

"Wait." Tristan's ears had also heard a light tinkling, as of crystal. He drew the hanging back slowly, and Elisena stepped forward into the room.

" 'Tis Galan's witch-girl!"

"No, she's his daughter." Allaire's rings gleamed as her hands fluttered about her throat, as if for protection. "Did you not hear—"

"I heard him name her changeling, in front of all those in his hall last night! What do you here, girl? Spying for your sire?"

He made to grab her, but Tristan shoved his hand away before he could touch her. The gesture was oddly automatic; he barely noticed himself doing it.

"Elisena," he asked. "What are you doing here?"

He saw then that she was muffled from head to toe in a heavy hooded cape, and that she had something bulky clutched in one hand, half hidden by the cape.

"I will take you to the stables, by a secret way," she said. "All of you. You won't make it *that* way." A small note of contempt crept into her voice, as she turned her hooded face toward Polassar and his sword.

"Wizard, can we trust her?"

Tristan didn't know. This was so unexpected, so magic-sent—

Elisena had crossed to the hearth. She tugged at a stone. As it slid back, a narrow space opened with much grinding, revealing steps spiralling down. The coals of the dying fire lit the topmost three; beyond that was guesswork.

"Follow me." She did not once look back to see if they did so. Beyond the door hangings, a voice called a sleepy question.

Tristan scooped up Thomas with one hand and moved after her without hesitation. It was a tight fit, and his sword hilt rang against the stones, throwing sparks down.

They winked out, and he had to feel his way, fingers on the rough wall. There was no rail. Steps sounded behind him—Polassar had chosen quickly.

He wished he dared make a light, or was able to. The stairs were worn and very shallow. No telling how far you'd fall if you missed one. Elisena moved swiftly ahead of him.

Allaire was close to him too, just behind; he felt her hand brushing his shoulder often, as if she reassured herself that she did not rush into the darkness alone. Polassar must be standing rearguard.

"A secret stair in a prison tower?" Tristan wondered aloud.

"Some secrets are more so than others." Elisena's voice floated back. "*I* chose that room for you. This leads to the stables—but hush, there are chinks between the stones, and ears near us."

Her warning made their softest footsteps seem to echo like cannon shots, their breathing whistle like a rushing wind. Tristan would have held his heart from beating, had he known how.

Very abruptly, there was light. A smoking, dim rush-light, which nonetheless seemed bright as the midday sun, after the dark. The stairs stopped, but Tristan's feet kept blindly stepping down until he stumbled in the deep straw.

Valadan nickered softly. Thomas scratched to be let down, and ran to the horse when he was. The stallion was saddled already, as were the roan and white mares.

"Have you been planning this so long?" Tristan began incredulously, but Elisena held a finger over her lips. She motioned them to lead the horses out.

Minstrel gave a quick chirp and dove down, waiting to be tucked inside Tristan's sweater. Tristan did so almost absently, his eyes on Elisena at the stable door. Her whole body was tense as she searched the yard for intruders, but it must have been clear, for she waved them on.

"The postern will be open this hour," she whispered. "To let the baker in. We must try to slip through, in the shadow of the wall. They will not be watching for anyone from this direction, but the last few paces are well-lit. We must creep as close as we can to the gate, then run."

Tristan was half amazed at his ready acceptance of her

unlikely plan. This reckless snatching at escape struck him as insane. Just because Elisena had an escape route ready—had she been planning to use it herself?—should they be blindly trusting of her? He was worse than Polassar, leaping at shadow-chances. At least Polassar knew he could trust his own sword arm!

Still, Valadan was making no protest. He moved quietly, and when Tristan pressed close to a satin-skinned shoulder, he found it dry. If Valadan wasn't nervous, that surely meant something—

Of course, Valadan had also brought him unquestioningly to Radak in the first place.

He knew his nerves must be pulled snapping tight. His breath wouldn't come, his mouth was so dry he couldn't swallow, and he feared he'd start coughing, giving them all away. How did they know this would work? And if it didn't—

They crept, but the horses' hooves rang with what seemed unnatural loudness, and harness jingled. Polassar was cursing softly.

There were suddenly torches, and armored clashings, and shouts. Galan appeared among his men on the wall. His master mage stood beside him, scarlet and black robes flowing. Metal began to ring in earnest, as men rushed down the stair toward them, and they were surrounded. Not far off, hounds bayed eagerly.

"Wizard, she's played us false! 'Tis a trap!"

Polassar drew his great sword and lunged, but Tristan's blade was there first, blocking. Polassar tended to get carried away by his own swordplay. Tristan couldn't let them be delayed by that. This was neither place nor time for discussion of betrayals.

"*No!* There'll be time for that later." He vaulted to Valadan's back and hauled Elisena up behind him. Already Galan's men were at them.

Valadan quickly cleared the way with teeth and hooves. Faces were reddened by more than the flickering torchlight, and Tristan was hard put to keep his seat as the screaming stallion plunged madly into the soldiers. But the tactics worked, the men scattered.

Polassar's blade was a flashing arc of blue steel. He had Allaire close behind him; as they won to the gate, he swung her from his horse to her own. Tristan laid about him with his own sword, catching glimpses as he did so of Elisena behind him. She clung tight to him with one hand, far from trying to escape, and she'd drawn his belt-knife, flailing out with it in her other hand, protecting his back. Tristan parried an axe-stroke, steel screaming nerve-tweakingly.

Fighting on horseback was vastly different from fencing afoot, as he ought to have expected. Valadan had his own ideas of the best direction to charge; if Tristan carelessly attacked in another line, he was apt to be thrown onto the cobbles of the yard. Only Valadan's long mane saved him from that very fate several times. And he'd never before fought an opponent who was seriously trying to kill him. The dragon aside—after all, it hadn't been human—he'd only fenced with Blais and Blais' friends, who'd coached him and scolded him and whacked him sharply in an advisory way without ever really cutting him. Blais had never hurt him beyond the pain necessary to teach him respect for another's weapon. And he knew only theoretical things of the defense against axe and spear.

Galan's men were brave. Valadan's flinty hooves were taking a terrible toll of their number, and Tristan's most desperate strokes were doing a lot of damage, but they refused to back off even briefly.

*They mean to hold us here till they're reinforced, then overwhelm us,* Valadan said coolly. Tristan heard Galan shouting orders.

They must get closer to Allaire, hem her in before Galan could reach her. He forced Valadan forward. Galan's men were belatedly trying to shut the postern. There were not enough of them at the task yet, and Polassar was riding them down.

Polassar was through. His mare's teeth were red, as were Valadan's, her hooves likewise. The white mare balked at the opening, afraid as much of the wild-eyed roan as the torches, and Valadan careened right into her. He dodged her kick, and all three horses shot through the gate. Like an afterthought, spears whistled by them.

Tristan was sure Valadan's pounding hooves were jolting his teeth out—and then the stallion gave a great bound, and they were racing away so fast that he could no longer see the ground. Valadan bullied the two mares before him, forcing them to speeds they could never have normally met, and they were out of spear's reach.

Tristan glanced back and saw Reynaud on the battlements. His hands were lifted, as if with a spell to draw them back. Tristan wondered frantically if he were free of the spell-net yet, and if he had enough strength to stop whatever Reynaud chose to throw at them. But Reynaud's upraised hands never moved.

THEY GALLOPED for hours, on a twisted course that few trackers could have followed. Valadan let them slow down after a bit, and Tristan was able to begin covering their backtrail. He couldn't ensure that Reynaud would never find them—but he could hope to slow him down, if they were even followed. Tristan had a half-memory, an instant frozen behind his eyelids, that was most disturbing. A glimpse of Galan leaping into the fray, sword in hand, too close for his parry. Tristan's blade had been pointed in altogether the wrong direction. The memory took on sound, with Thomas' high battle-scream, and the sword had gone flying wide as Galan clapped both hands to his eyes. Thomas was still trying to lick his claws clean while keeping his balance on the saddle, and purring over his prowess.

As dawn lightened the sky, Polassar jerked the roan to a stop, pulling her head back. She bucked savagely, as he turned her to face the others, but he took no notice. He dismounted and drew his sword in one swift movement, and placed his point at Elisena's throat.

"Now, witch, I think you will explain some matters. The which being why you led us from our rooms into the hands of armed guards!"

Elisena neither flinched nor looked at the sword. She locked her silver eyes with Polassar's, holding her little chin high. Tristan was impressed, for it was more than he could have managed himself. Life with Galan apparently taught courage.

"Sometimes risks need to be taken, or there's no hope of winning," she answered composedly. "I gambled that we'd take the guards enough by surprise to make it out. And we did."

Tristan stared sidelong at her. It was all very well to speak of necessary risks, and in abstract principle he quite agreed with the sense of it. But when his own life was one of the things being gambled with—

"But why should you aid us?" Polassar was asking, mystified, his brow furrowing. "What gain seek you?"

"You accepted my help without question," Elisena replied. "Accept the reason for it in the same spirit."

Polassar began to open his mouth, but before he could speak Tristan had reached out and shoved the sword away. He'd never have dared do such a thing twice in one day had he not been lightheaded with exhaustion.

"Toadstools, what does it matter why she helped?" he snapped. "You might try being grateful that she did."

*I suppose you're not curious either?* Thomas asked as they rode on. *It's a most illogical thing for her to have done, leaving her home for three strangers on a mad errand. Unless she intended to leave anyway?*

"I'm too tired to be curious, Thomas."

*Of course, I've never understood why you humans do the things you do, anyway.*

And Tristan, thinking of Allaire again, looking at her slim white back and her high-piled silver hair, decided that he didn't know either.

They rode another couple of hours, and he still didn't know. But something else had occurred to him. Tristan tugged at the reins, and Valadan halted.

"Wizard, what are you about? We've no time for this—" Polassar had halted a hundred feet off, turning back impatiently.

Tristan was fetching out his box of stones, searching through it hastily. He settled on a blue-gray feather and a smooth gray stone. Climbing down from Valadan, he knelt swiftly in the long grass.

"Let him be," Allaire ordered unexpectedly. "He knows what he does."

Tristan held the stone cupped in the palm of one hand, the feather resting between thumb and forefinger. Softly, he began stroking the feather with his other hand. How was it, now, that Blais had said this was done? This place ought to be receptive; the ground was squishy-wet. His clothes were soaking already.

He had his hands close to his face, and his breath warmed the feather, was caught and held by it, in a little ball of mist. He continued stroking, letting his mind go blank, feeling nothing but the warmth between his palms, lighter and softer even than Minstrel.

When he looked about the mist was spreading, curling in wet tendrils about his feet. The grass was soaked with it, the sun was beginning to disappear, and he cast no shadow when he stood.

"We can go now."

He shivered a bit, surprised at the spell's working so well. It was a little unnerving.

They hastened on once more, until Valadan said that the white mare was beginning to tire. He recommended not running her to exhaustion; they might need to move again that night. Tristan called a halt by a grove of beech trees. He was pleased to see a stream close at hand—besides being convenient, it would help foil any magical searches, added to the other defenses and barriers he would try to set up.

They left Valadan standing watch on the hillside, and entered the wood. Allaire flung herself down at once in a pile of fallen leaves, too weary to speak. Polassar quickly knelt beside her, drawing her cloak closer about her shoulders, offering his own cloak as well.

Tristan hobbled the mares and rubbed them down with twisted handfuls of dry grass. The roan showed her teeth to him until he threatened her with a baldness spell, but the white mare only stood, trembling all over. Her head hung limply between her forelegs. Tristan worked on their coats until both horses were cooled and showing interest in the sparse grass beneath the trees.

He must make an effort to shield them. The stream might help, if he could work up the energy needed to use it, or think of a spell that would be effective. He was longing to flop down in the grass himself and lie there till it grew over him. The mist had ceased to dog them, and that spell probably wouldn't work again.

In the end, he was forced to content himself with drawing lock-runes in the sand on both sides of the water. For the rest, he would simply have to depend on Valadan. The stallion seemed to be grazing, but Tristan sensed that he was as alert as the finest of watch-hounds. Tristan unsaddled him, but of course the stallion wasn't sweating, or even breathing hard. Like Minstrel, he always looked morning-fresh.

Tristan rejöined the others. Elisena was just returning from the stream with a pan of water. She had already collected wood and laid a fire, made small so as to avoid revealing smoke. Tristan stole a glance at Allaire, as he knelt to light the wood. She was rebraiding her silver hair, rings moving like a weaver's shuttle. Her face wore an incredibly contented expression.

Of course, Tristan thought, as he surveyed their orderly camp. She has a servant now. Or perhaps two? And why is that thought suddenly so bitter? To serve her in the slightest way is joy past counting. He began scraping piles of leaves together, to serve them for beds.

Elisena dropped herbs into the pot and brewed them a strengthening draught. They had only two cups among them all, so they shared as best they could. The herbs were pleasantly bitter, clearing minds and relieving weariness. Tristan's tongue picked out milfoil and nettles, and cailon flowers, picked and dried just as the buds opened.

There was also bread and cold meat, which Elisena must have thought to bring. Tristan made sure that Thomas and Minstrel both ate, and both were soon sleeping, the one on his lap and the other high in a beech tree. Night had fallen some while ago.

"Well, wizard, have you thought what we're to do now? Seeing you were so all-fired anxious to get us on the road again." Polassar lounged comfortably against a fallen log, propping one great hand against his knee.

Elisena was offering her mug to Tristan again, and he took a long sip before answering. The question, the tone of it anyway, was manifestly unfair, but he had an answer ready. The meal had revived him fractionally, and his mind was clear.

"I've thought. Most of the way here, in fact. We must find that last ring—the sooner the better. That takes priority over all else. Only we don't quite know how to go about it, and our time is fast running out."

"Galan will be hot after us now, and my other foes with him. So what do we do—visit every jewelmaker in Calandra? Or hold a quick wedding?" Polassar reached out for Allaire's beringed hand.

"I think we must prepare for a very long journey," Tristan said crisply. "We must learn what we can of the ring, and we can't do that safely here. Not now. A quiet search isn't among our options anymore. If the information is even here, which I more and more doubt. And Galan's sure to pursue us, or his men will."

Allaire shivered. Polassar put his arm about her, whilst still keeping hold of her hand.

"Then where shall we go?"

Tristan stroked Thomas' fur.

"I was thinking of Kôvelir. The Library there is said to be very complete. All the mages go there to study, if they can. Surely someone there will help us."

"That's a long journey indeed, wizard. And all our enemies between, to cap the mess. Could we not lie low for a bit, search softly?"

"If we're lying low, we can't be searching. Besides, Galan will be looking for us. We'd have to hide, and that would make any kind of organized search impossible."

"We'll need to ride the length of Calandra to reach Kôvelir," Polassar pleaded. "I doubt it can be done. If 'twere anyone other than Galan—" He broke off and glared suspiciously at Elisena, who looked noncommitally back and said nothing.

"What if we crossed the Est?" Tristan asked.

"You have to cross the Est. Kôvelir is on the other side." Polassar spoke his explanation as if to a simpleton, around the bit of meat he was chewing at.

"I meant here," Tristan said, with the same sort of obvious patience. "What sort of country could we expect?"

"Rough. Mountains, or the feet of 'em. There's a bit of flat ground near the river. Barren—the Est scours her floodplain clean. There'll be no forest. 'Tis said to be passable. But no one crosses the Est here at this time of year, wizard. It's in flood." That patronizing tone was again in his voice.

"Then Galan couldn't follow us?" Tristan asked thoughtfully.

"Not if we drowned, no!"

"If we get across, we simply have to follow the river down to Kôvelir. And no need to worry about pursuit. This begins to sound better and better to me." It did, and presented totally new prospects and hopes. There might just be a way out of this after all. "Could we find game there, do you think? We've got almost nothing left to eat."

"Wizard, I will find us food anywhere we go, but we cannot cross the Est in flood. 'Tis folly."

"But passing good strategy." Tristan smiled crookedly. "And what other hope do we have? I'd rather face a river than an army."

"That's only because you've never seen the Est, wizard," Polassar insisted.

"We don't dare try to reach Kôvelir down this side of the river. We could ferry across at Est-mouth, but Galan would long since have caught up with us, so that's no good."

"I fared across the Est once," Polassar said reminiscently. "When Danac of Westif attacked treacherously, and I had to run for it. There was hard work retaking Lassair, I can tell you, lady."

Allaire's eyes grew big as she listened. Tristan merely wished Polassar would get back to whatever point he was trying to make, or stick to the subject under discussion.

"We were driven nearly to Kôvelir," Polassar went on, just as Tristan was about to prod him.

"So you *have* crossed the Est?" Tristan said pointedly.

"Aye. And half the men with me were drowned, or swept so far away we never found 'em. And that was during a dry summer. The Est is not a river I'd sanely tackle again, given choice."

"But you aren't," Tristan pointed out.

"Better to drown, than be taken by Galan's men," Allaire said. It was almost the first time she'd spoken since they'd left Radak.

"Are you determined on this course?"

Maybe only because it was all he could think of at the

moment. And Polassar *did* expect him to come up with something. That seemed to be his job now. Tristan looked Polassar in the eye and nodded.

"Then we'll try it."

Tristan looked amazed, which he was.

"My own choices have not gone so well that I should say nay to yours," Polassar admitted. "It's a wizard's business to lead quests anyway."

Shape-shift me into a mouse! Tristan thought. Maybe he deserves to be king after all. Just when you've begun to doubt, he throws you a colossal surprise.

Polassar tossed the bone he'd been gnawing into the fire.

"Just one question, wizard. Can you swim?"

Tristan smiled sadly and shook his head.

"Wizards fear running water worse than cats do, I've heard it said. Yet you urge us straight to the biggest river of them all. Madness must be a requirement for wizardry."

"No. Just for undertaking quests. And let's hope the horses will be able to do most of the swimming." Tristan shivered in spite of himself and tried to cover it with a yawn. "It's late. And we should make an early start."

They all lay close to the fire. Polassar certainly slept, and Allaire might have done so. Tristan did not. He was tired enough, and then some, but his mind was active, refusing to stop planning. And now dreading also. What would he do, when it came time to cross the river? Suppose he couldn't? He'd never been near a true river, certainly not a mighty one like the Est. And he'd never even considered that prickly fact, when this great plan popped into his head. No one knew why wizards had such trouble with running water. They just did.

Little streams gave him twinges of discomfort, varying in severity with the swiftness of the water. They made him uneasy. What would happen when he came to the big river? Suppose he couldn't cross? He tossed about restlessly, and Thomas mewed a protest.

"Don't be trapped into thinking we'll be safe in Kôvelir."

The soft voice made him start farther away from sleep's edge. Elisena must be just behind him. No one else appeared to be either awake or listening.

"You're right in thinking it will be hard for the Hounds to find us, in the midst of so much magic." Her voice came cold and quiet as moonlight. "But the Cold One has many servants. We must be always on our guard, for we will be sought after as much as we seek."

Her words finished the work his nerves had started, and left him wide-eyed and wakeful for hours. In the morning he was cold, stiff, and developing a headache from lack of sleep. Their course must take them south for several hours, for there were said to be rapids in these reaches of the Est. Half a day's riding would take them to a crossing place with enough daylight left to attempt that crossing. Tristan's mouth had an odd taste to it again.

They ate dry bread and broke camp quickly, before it was fairly light. Tristan was trying to will his headache away.

The land undulated away from them in shades of gray accented with rust-colored dry weeds. Good country for galloping over, which they soon did. A cold drizzle began to fall.

Tristan wanted very much to ask Elisena what she'd meant by the things she'd said the night before, but she remained utterly silent, giving him no opening, and he felt unable to make one. She looked as innocent as if she'd never spoken. Were the Hounds really still on their track? They'd surely have caught up by now. And what would she know about them anyway? He was afraid to ask, lest she might answer. He had enough problems.

He became conscious of a dull roaring sound, which seemed to have been growing steadily louder for some moments. The horses cantered to the top of a gentle rise.

At once Tristan saw why the Est was sometimes known as the Snake-Rolling-at-the-Foot-of-the-Mountains. They could see miles of the river as it rolled toward them out of low hills, gleaming in the dull light.

It flowed below the hill they stood on, almost at their feet, it seemed by some trick of perspective. The water's surface was a dark and choppy gray, much broken with branches and often whole trees being carried downstream by the flood.

The rumbling was much louder now, fuller sounding. The river raged and tore at its banks, sending crumbling sections crashing into its waters every minute. The Est was plainly in the process of carving itself yet another twisting channel.

"She's carrying boulders in her belly, wizard, the better to gnaw us with. Still sure?" Polassar's teeth flashed whitely.

Tristan found himself trembling and mortifyingly unable to stop. He was wet through with the cold rain, but he felt sweat starting out all over his body. He fervently hoped that he was merely chilled, even sickening with something, and not really so frightened as he felt. The saddle leather was slippery between his knees.

He tried to study the river less in terror and more with an eye to the best place for a crossing. Somewhere without rocks—but there was no telling what might be hidden under that deep water. He wondered briefly about monsters, though he'd never heard of any in the Est. They stuck to the open sea, mostly; no doubt it was quieter there.

Polassar was watching the water too.

"Wizard, no need to say I mislike this. The autumn rains have swollen her sore, and even in the best weather she's so wide it properly needs a boat to cross."

"Is there a better place to ford? Farther south?"

"Not likely. There's little to choose between one stretch and another for leagues downstream. And sourceward's no better—'tis narrower, but wilder. If you're set to cross, this is as good a place as may be. But I still do not recommend it."

Tristan nodded stiffly.

"You're sure? 'Tis a strange choice for a wizard who can't swim and is chary of wetting his feet."

Tristan thought Polassar was trying to smile at him, and he made an effort to return the kindness. "I'm wet through anyway. And I don't think much of our chances of slipping past Galan's men now. They've had time a-plenty to nurse their anger."

He looked at the gray water again. It rolled and rolled, ever new, ever different, and yet its appearance never changed. Was that its secret and the source of the fear it inspired?

"I think we'd best rope ourselves together, with Allaire in the middle. Valadan is the strongest. We'll have to lead."

His heart sank as he thought what that meant. The stallion shook his head fiercely, snorting as if to lend him courage.

*The waters are high, but it can be done.*

He could trust Valadan to pick their crossing place and do the real work of guiding them across. But first—

He whistled, and Minstrel swooped down onto his shoulder.

"Fly across now, Light-Bones, and wait for us in the bushes. But be careful, there may be hawks about." Minstrel rubbed his cheek gently once, and was away.

*This is the first time*, Thomas remarked acidly, *that I have ever wished to be a bird. It would be useful.*

Tristan tended to him next. He fussed with his cloak until he had formed a sling with it across his chest, and settled Thomas in it.

"There. I doubt you'll stay dry, but at least you won't drown."

*Unless you do.* Thomas squeezed his eyes tightly shut.

Polassar had already roped the mares together, as closely as he dared while still giving them room to swim. He fashioned a harness for Valadan now, and fastened it about him. Valadan arched his neck and called a challenge to the river.

They slithered down the steep bank, like three beads on a string. Tristan twisted half around to look at Elisena. She was clinging tight to him.

"All right? Have you got a good hold?" He thought she looked pale.

She nodded at him. Her face was impassive, her eyes enormous, great drops of silver spiked round with ebony. For a startled moment he almost forgot the river, now filling all the air with its sound.

He looked past her, at the others. The white mare was shying, jerking hard at the rope as Allaire strove to control her, but the roan seemed to be holding her end well. Allaire had a fine color in her cheeks, though her lips were tightly compressed. Her gaze was resolute.

"Ready?" Tristan called, and Valadan plunged into the Est.

# The Crossing of The Est

TWO STEPS, and the water was over his boot tops. One more, and he felt Valadan's movements change, as he left the bottom behind and began to swim. The mares had no choice but to follow, bobbing after like corks. Behind him, Tristan heard Allaire give a little shriek as the cold water touched her.

He soon saw that they would make little headway. The current dragged them downstream much faster than he'd expected. By the time they won across they would likely be miles closer to Kôvelir, which might be good or ill, depending on the condition of the opposite bank at the time they tried to climb it.

Valadan was now swimming strongly, his head well forward and his ears tight back on his neck to keep the water out. He was very low in the water, though, with his double load, and they were in trouble almost as soon as the main current hit them.

Tristan was hardly aware of it. All his eyes registered was water, gray water, on every side and surely about to close over his head. His fingers were knotted as tightly in Valadan's mane as if they had frozen there.

He knew that he ought to be fending off the floating branches with his sword before they could crash into the horses. But they looked so much like hands—of a black, clutching kind—that he shut his eyes. Not for long—the dizziness and disorientation that closed eyes produced were worse than anything he might see with them open. Thomas' escape was not for him.

This was many times stronger than the discomforts he'd felt crossing the cottage brook—about as many times worse as the Est was larger than the brook. It was hardly even comparable.

The nausea, the achings deep within his muscles, even the flashes of excruciating pain, so brief that they were over the instant his brain registered them—over and cropping up somewhere else—those were almost nothing compared to the terror overwhelming him.

What was he doing in the middle of so much magic-baffling water? It felt as if they'd been at this for hours, and he was too dazed to remember how they'd gotten there.

Valadan's breathing grew labored. Tristan heard it even through his own agony. They were still a great way from the shore, but it did seem to be drawing closer. Could they make it? Rain lashed them; the sky had gone dark.

Polassar was cursing the river in very creative terms. He damned its wetness, its coldness, its length and its breadth, and all the plaguey lands and rivers that drained into it, as well as every drop of rain that fell on those lands. Most fervently of all, he cursed the drowned pig the river flung down at him. The river, like the pig, took no notice.

They hit a pocket of calm water, most welcome and unexpected. After a few seconds of unhindered swimming, the shore seemed within their reach. The bank was high, but Valadan's hooves scraped rock, and he moved more quickly as he found a foothold once more.

Elisena screamed.

There wasn't time to turn his head. Tristan only saw the streamswept tree out of the corner of his eye, and then its groping roots hit them, with all the force of the floodwaters behind them.

The impact knocked them both out of the saddle. Tristan felt gray Est-water rolling over his head in earnest now, a lot of it going into his surprised mouth. Then somehow he was clinging to a stirrup with one hand and Elisena with the other and Valadan was dragging them all up the bank together. The ground was giving way beneath them, but the stallion never hesitated, not even when the white mare nearly pulled them all back in with her fighting, and missed Tristan with her feet by only inches.

Tristan felt grass under his boots. He fell to his knees,

heavily, and then flopped flat down on his face. Thomas squirmed hastily free of the sling. Somewhere far off Tristan could hear excited voices, and Minstrel's wild squeaking, and someone asking if he were all right, and another voice answering that of course he was. He didn't much care.

The next thing he knew, it was night, and he was sitting beside a smoking fire that seemed determined to give off no heat at all. His soggy cloak was wrapped about him. He had a mug of something in his hands, but he was trembling so that he couldn't get it to his lips to drink from it.

Elisena took the cup away from him, but still he went on shivering like a sick dog. It seemed impossible to stop doing so.

Her hands came back, filled with a powder of dried herbs well crushed. Gill-go-over-the-ground, his nose dispassionately noticed. He was ordered to breathe deeply.

When he did, the resultant sneeze would have sent him right over backwards, if Elisena hadn't been quick to grab his shoulders. She made him inhale more of the powder, then left him for a moment. His brain was numb.

Elisena returned with something wrapped in rags that had been part of her under-robe. The something was a rock heated in the fire, and she put it at his feet, ordering him to lie down. Tristan did what he was told, and slept. Just before he lost awareness, he realized they'd crossed the Est.

## Kôvelir

HE WOKE SO STIFF that he was sure he would break if he dared to move. Thomas was lying on his chest, grumbling to no one in particular, and Minstrel was somewhere about too, for he was singing with great abandon. Tristan dislodged Thomas and stood up, creakily. His head felt light as a puffball.

Their fire of the night before was a heap of cold ashes,

past any hope of his reviving it. Tristan looked miserably at it, prodded the ashes with a toe, and sat down again. He felt as if he might be having a rare lucid interval in the midst of fever. If he'd been ill, if he'd delayed them—if Galan's men had crossed the Est after all, or the Hounds—

No, they hadn't been here more than a few hours. His clothes were still damp. Tristan shut his eyes weakly.

Polassar's exasperated voice came out of the darkness. It seemed unnaturally loud, paining Tristan's ears.

"Is he going to be sick again? Witch-woman, we've no time for this. There's no shelter here, and more rain coming."

"Let him be. What he did was harder than you can know. He's lucky even to be alive."

Tristan forced his eyes open. "I'm all right." He tried to stand again, finding that his feet were hopelessly tangled in his cloak. He sat down rather hard and swore as he kicked free of the hampering folds. Elisena shook her head at him, wonderingly.

They seemed to have come through the flood without any major losses, despite having soaked all their gear. It was uncomfortable to ride all day in wet clothes, but that was what they eventually did, after eating what they could salvage from their waterlogged rations.

*Lucky if we don't all die of an ague,* Thomas groused as he settled himself on the saddle. *Couldn't you have contrived to stay on the horse?*

Tristan was heartily sorry he hadn't, impossible as it had been. His wet clothes promised to chafe him raw before they dried. He shifted a little, trying to ease himself, but nothing seemed to help, and he winced in anticipation of worse problems than stiffness that night. He glanced ahead at Allaire, expecting that, as always, the sight of her would cast all lesser matters from his mind.

She was very silent. The country was not conducive to much talking, being bleak and disheartening under the continued rain, but Tristan could not recall her having spoken a single word since they'd entered the Est. He'd not thought of it, but she was as much a mage as he was, even if less trained. Had the running water affected her in some way too, even though her rings as yet had no power? She didn't look really ill, but her white gown had turned to gray tatters, and she was clearly saddle-sore. Even her rings seemed tarnished, leaden dull with no shine at all.

Her taste for adventure seemed to be fast fading. Polassar rode ahead to hunt, and she barely noted his departure. Tristan decided to call a halt early that day, even more for Allaire's sake than out of any consideration for himself.

"Oh, fie on this rain!" Allaire cried, shaking out her dripping hair before their tiny fire. "How I long for summer!" Her fingers were red with wet and cold.

Tristan added twigs sparingly to the fire. He hadn't been able to find much burnable wood. They'd have to be careful if they expected it to last the night and cook whatever supper Polassar brought back. But arranging the fire gave him something to do with his hands, besides lending him a fine excuse for huddling close to the warmth. He couldn't look at her as he spoke.

"I'm afraid this may *be* summer, my lady. Nímir, you see."

"You mean to tell me it's always like this?" she asked, unbelieving.

Tristan spoke a word of encouragement to the flames.

"Well, mostly. The mages can manage a little weather-witching, here and there, but it's terribly tiring, and some of them aren't too reliable, so it's mostly saved to dry things out around harvest time. And in the spring, to help the seeds sprout. The rest of the time, it's like this, except in winter, when it snows."

Allaire stared at him. This, after all, was what she was born and trained to combat, but apparently its scope exceeded her memories.

"Remember," Tristan said gently, hopefully, "this is wild country. No one would waste a spell on it anyway, when there's good farmland that needs the magic more—"

Valadan lifted his head sharply, setting Minstrel flapping between his ears.

*A horse comes.*

After a couple of tense moments, they were able to make out Polassar. A thinly elegant roe stag hung over his mare's rump, brought down with a spear Polassar had makeshifted from his knife and an oak sapling.

"There, wizard," he boomed, once within earshot. "I told

you I'd feed us." He set to work dressing the meat, whistling in a pleased manner.

They dined on venison, which cheered them all a little, but chiefly Polassar, who seemed prepared to expand for hours on the difficulties of hunting deer and his skills therein. It was the first bit of decent food they'd had since fleeing Radak, and Elisena prepared it wonderfully. Tristan cheerfully volunteered to turn the roasting spit, since it gave him another excuse to hug the fire. He was so grateful to be warm at last that Thomas needed to point out several times that his boot toes were smoking and oughtn't he sit just a *little* farther from the flames?

The meal done, Tristan paid scant attention to Polassar's boring recital of tales of this and past hunts. He paged through Blais' grimoire for a while, trying to find some word of comfort or, failing that, a useful charm against mildew.

The grimoire protected itself admirably against water damage, by means of spells ensorcelled into its very parchment and binding. There was an added plus to that— nothing Tristan spilled on it ever stained. Small wonder a wizard's books often outlasted the wizard.

But the flickering firelight made concentration difficult, as did Polassar's tales of glory. And another sound kept intruding.

It seemed to rise and fall with the wind, whisking over the floodplain. The humming tones changed and mingled with each other, like the iridescent colors of oil on water. They possessed an eerie, spine-shivering beauty. The horses shifted restlessly as the wailing rose to a higher pitch. The sound was not quite an animal sound.

Polassar, when questioned, had some idea of what the sounds were, though his explanation of them made little sense to Tristan.

"Windtowers, aye. They pepper the hills with 'em, near Kôvelir. And I saw other signs today that we're near the city, nearer than I'd hoped. With good weather we should reach it by sunfall tomorrow."

"But what *is* a windtower? It makes the strangest sound—like weeping." Allaire shuddered, drawing closer to Polassar as she spoke. He obligingly put an arm about her.

"That I do not know. I have heard little of them save

that they are put on lonely hilltops, and make just such a sound. Mayhap they top grave-mounds."

"Strange I haven't read of them." Blais' educating of him had been rather complete in most areas; if the towers were as common as Polassar indicated, they were an odd omission.

"Not mage work. The way I got it, they're older than Kôvelir." Which was old indeed. "The mages don't even tend 'em. They aren't like shrines. Doubtless we'll see this one we hear tomorrow, and others after. They grow close as toadstools in these hills."

As if in answer to him, the windtower's pitch changed without the least warning, from a hum to a nail-scraping shriek. Allaire clapped her hands to her ears and half sobbed.

*Wonderful. Want to lay odds she's scared of thunderstorms too?* Thomas yawned, and calmly began grooming his back.

Tristan decided that the tower's sound had indeed a proper note of perpetual mourning in it. It was not a pleasant sound to fall asleep to, and he didn't like to think what sort of grave that sort of sound might act as a mourner for.

The windtower was more disquieting when they actually faced it next morning. They rode past its hill, and paused for a look.

None attended the building, as Polassar had said. It stood clean and lonely, without even trees about it to lend it grace, only its own pure lines reaching up to the sky, a trapezoid-shaped thing, higher and wider than it was thick, holed in its middle—a squared-off flute of stone, through which the wind played.

The architecture matched the odd beauty of its voice. Tristan decided then that this might not be a bad thing, a building that sang. Thomas simply reveled in its music, today but a soft murmur, and Tristan dimly remembered the cat answering the tower in the night, at least until Polassar had flung a boot at him.

Valadan dipped his head abruptly in salute as they passed. Whether he honored the tower itself or the grave it guarded, Tristan couldn't have said. He was too busy trying to stay on the stallion's back to ask, for the movement had

taken him by surprise. Valadan's upswinging neck caught
him smartly in the chest, rocking him back and making
him half choke. Elisena's arms tightened around him,
steadying him, but further cutting off his air supply.

*I do wish you'd learn to sit a horse.*

"Sorry," Tristan managed, still gasping for breath and
not liking to waste it apologizing to Thomas for something
that hadn't been his fault in the first place.

"It's all right," Elisena said, mistaking the apology.
"Horses do that sometimes." She reached down and patted
Valadan's flank.

Minstrel had stayed respectfully mute until they'd ridden
some way beyond the tower's sound. Then he took to the
air and, after a few moments of silent acrobatic flight, returned to perch between Valadan's ears. He spent the rest
of the day lifting their flagging spirits with his trills, and
sometimes begging seeds from Tristan's pack.

In the afternoon the rains began again, softly now, but
insistently. The way turned muddy. It did not greatly delay
them, though the horses were weary. True to Polassar's es-
timate, they had Kôvelir in sight as the sunset light was
coloring her sevenfold walls a deep rose.

They passed into the city along with the last groups of
returning merchants, just before the great outer gates were
shut. Powerful runes sealed them so for the night.

The space between the first and second walls was mostly
taken up with storehouses and lumberyards and a few
homes of the merchants themselves. Animals of all sorts
were much in evidence, both those used by men and those
eaten by men. They passed through a second set of gates.

Farther in, Tristan knew, were the private homes and
the greater inns, each growing finer until one reached the
middle of Kôvelir's concentric circles—the Mages' School
and the Great Library. A bit too grand for them at the
moment, though he must go farther into the city to study.
This second between-walls section, crosshatched with innumerable alleys and squares, and with tumbledown buildings
infringing on both, looked more suitable. It was crowded,
but they might safely hide in a mass so diverse. Tristan
looked interestedly about, considering. Already his ears and
eyes picked out a street hawker peddling fresh eels, stroll-

ing players rehearsing a tragical verse about the mage Duriron, and a trained horse beating out the hour on a tabor, using one hind foot most delicately.

Above the street hung the signs of noted herbalists and alchemists, and richly dressed lords rubbed shoulders distastefully with beggars beneath them. Pigs and cats wandered the rutted street, both equally at home there.

A trio of hoop-jumpers passed close by, nimbly vaulting through each others' hoops as they came, for the practice of it. The sight was too much for Allaire's white mare, who backed away, shying. Polassar quickly clamped a hand over her bridle.

Valadan led them some way through the crowds, then turned into a narrow alley that looked as if it would remain deserted.

"I think I'd best find us lodging," Tristan said as he dismounted. His cramped legs protested. "It might be best not to let Allaire be seen too closely by anyone." Even travel-stained and rain-soaked, hers was not a face to be lightly forgotten, and they wanted to be inconspicuous.

Polassar agreed with him, for once. He drew Allaire back into a doorway. out of the drizzle, and settled down to wait. Fluffing himself like an owl, Minstrel huddled in a bricky niche. Elisena chose to follow Tristan, her herb bag still clutched tight in her hand, and Thomas bounded after.

The streets about them did not remain deserted long. They crossed two squares and a narrow alley, then fetched out into a bustling market. Trade was fairly brisk, considering the rain, and the din of it at ground level made Tristan's ears ring. Somehow, on Valadan, he had seemed to be a little above the confusion, mentally as well as in physical fact.

He stood staring around, slightly at a loss. At first look he had thought the market not much different from that of Dunehollow-by-the-Sea, near his home. Bigger, yes, louder—but essentially the same. Now he began to wonder.

Torches were being lit. Lamb was roasting over a pit, sending a rich smell into the wet air. There were the usual jugglers and card readers, a bit more tawdry than most, perhaps. Many brightly dressed ladies stood about, waving and calling. What Tristan took for a woman costumed in

purple feathers minced by—and cursed Tristan in an undeniably masculine voice for not giving way quickly
enough.

He was still gawking at the combination of lavender eye-
paint and stubbled chin when Elisena took hold of his elbow.

"This way, I think. I doubt m'lady will want to be lulled
to sleep by the cries of street harlots."

A bell-capped jester gamboled up to them, thrusting his
face-topped scepter under Tristan's nose whilst he planted
a kiss on Elisena's startled lips. Tristan began to laugh,
then swung about with an outraged shout, slapping at the
fingers that had been groping into his belt-pouch. The slender dwarf-girl, costumed in motley to match the jester,
smiled sheepishly at him and vanished in a puff of green
smoke. When Tristan turned back to Elisena, the jester was
gone as well.

"Thomas, where'd he go?"

The cat was gazing blankly skyward.

*I don't know. I confess I wish I did.*

From the back of a stuffed corkindrill hanging before an
apothecary's shop, the jester gaily waved to them, then
vanished again. His winking left eye stayed a moment
longer than the rest of him.

"Swords! Warranted invincible! Forged of sky-iron,
quenched in giant's blood! Balance as true as an Ambalan
gymnast's—"

"Rings, guaranteed to render the wearer invisible, even
in rain . . ."

Elisena had a valid point. This street *was* rather noisy.
They tried another.

The inn they eventually came to was hardly in a better
neighborhood—Tristan decided he'd be very glad when it
got too dark for him to see what he was being forced to
step in. But at least the painted women—and men—didn't
gather quite up to its walls. And it was a little quieter. The
shops were small and darkly curtained, and their customers
exited furtively, not anxious to be seen. Some carried small
bags, others nothing.

Tristan looked askance at the inn's stained and dilapi-
dated façade.

"I suppose it's all we can afford. I don't know how long

we'll be here, or how much I can earn doing Blais' charms. If we can just work something out with the innkeeper—"

That worthy was small and swart, resembling a badger more than anything human. He came to the halfdoor at their hesitant knocking, and his little eyes took in Tristan's ragged cloak and patched breeches, directing his hand to shoot out swiftly for the money. Tristan made haste to explain.

"I thought we might—strike a bargain. I have some little knowledge of charms and incantations—there are probably a great many things I can do for you, in return for a night's lodging for myself and my friends. There are only four of us. I can stop your roof leaking, or charm a wart, or—"

"A wizard?" The little man began to laugh, almost cackle. Tristan took a startled half step backward.

"A wizard? You want to sell me magic in a town that's fuller of wizards, mages and apprentice witches than a cat is of fleas? Get out of here!"

Thomas hissed at him, and stalked away, more because of the insult than the order.

"Something else, then," Tristan persisted, nothing daunted. "I'll groom your guests' horses. I'll scrub your floors or your pots. Or both. We need a place to stay the night." He pulled at his cloak, trying to keep the cold rain from dripping down his neck. A waterspout shaped as a cockatrice vomited rainwater onto the cobbles, spattering his breeches and soaking his boots. It was very dark now and the streets were lit only sporadically by smoking torches.

"Cash on the nail. Or nothing."

Tristan stared at him, hopelessly. He finally started to turn away, shoulders hunched a little.

"That sword, now." The innkeeper's voice brought him back around. The sword was swinging against his leg, its hilt winking a little in the torchlight. "It wouldn't be enchanted?"

"No—" Tristan said, puzzled.

"Pity. There's always a ready market for enchanted swords here. All the heroes come to Kôvelir to buy themselves swords of power. Sell faster than the mages can turn them out. I try to keep a supply for 'em."

The innkeeper fingered his none too clean chin.

"Of course, how is a hero to know if a sword is truly enchanted? It belonged to a wizard, that's truth. Something might have rubbed off, eh? A sword like that should be worth a night's lodging for you—and your friends too—even though it's not much to look at. Saying it's been long-used and well-proved might lend it a certain air of mystery—and I'll throw in a meal too. There's beef roasting on the spit, done to a turn. What say you, master wizard?"

He was speaking very rapidly, in the harsh tones of the southern merchant. Tristan recalled the saying that the best bards come from Calandra's cold, the shrewdest business-men from the warmer lands. He was sure he'd not be getting the best end of this bargain. His sword—it was all he had of his own. The thought of parting with it made him feel ill.

But what else had he to sell? Nothing but his worthless magic and the clothes on his back, which weren't worth a lead slug. He couldn't think of any other way to get a roof over their heads that night, and it was raining harder every second. Allaire *must* be gotten out of it. He'd never forgive himself if she took sick because of his failure.

He touched the sword with trembling fingers and looked back at the innkeeper. The man had his hand out for the weapon already, anticipating.

Tristan began to unfasten the scabbard from his belt, slowly and with great pain. It's only a bit of metal, he told himself sternly. It's not alive. Who'd have thought parting with it could hurt this much?

Elisena caught at his elbow.

"No. Don't be ridiculous."

He stared open-mouthed at her. She led him away quickly, to the accompaniment of the innkeeper's derisive laughter. They were around the next corner before Tristan found his voice and stopped her, jerking his arm away and grabbing her wrists.

"What did you do that for?" Humiliation made his voice shake maddeningly.

"You can't sell your sword," Elisena said matter-of-factly. "It's all you've—"

"It's all I've got to sell! What are we going to do now? We can't sleep in the streets."

"Why not?" She was very calm in the face of his shouting. "We've slept in the rain before. We've done little but that lately. And he would have taken your sword and then sent thieves to rob us while we slept. It you've not seen his like before, I have." She wrenched her wrists from his loosened grasp and turned.

She walked away from him, silently now. After a moment he followed her.

After fifty or so steps, he cleared his throat hesitantly. "I'm sorry."

She continued walking, but did not increase her pace. It seemed to Tristan that she wasn't trying unreasonably hard to stay angry with him. He caught up to her again.

"I didn't mean to shout. You did me a service, I don't think I could bear to part with that sword, after all these years. I'd feel unclothed without it." He didn't pause to wonder how she could have known that.

He caught a sudden glimpse of himself in a torchlit fragment of window glass, and halted.

"No wonder he wanted his money in advance!"

His clothes—never fine—had been thoroughly soaked in muddy Est water, and two days of hard riding through the rain and sleeping on the soggy ground had hardly improved their appearance. The rest of him had fared no better. His bruised cheek was still purple, and he now sported a livid scratch on his neck from that tree branch. His hair was uncombed and long uncut, his eyes bloodshot and shadowed and a trifle wild. A wonder the innkeeper hadn't called for the Watch, or set dogs on him. He looked at his reflection again, and the look and the thought made him begin to laugh and continue until he was breathless. The laughter felt good. Elisena began to smile too, as she stood beside him peering into the glass.

Her gown and cloak had fared a little better, since they had been less worn to begin with, and she was more skilled at caring for them, but her hair was tangled and full of grass stems and leaves. With her skin rain- and dust-streaked, she looked like a wild witch-woman from out of the hills.

"I wonder what he thought we were?" she asked, pointing delightedly at a mud smear on the tip of her dimly mirrored nose.

They giggled together until they could barely stand and then tried to go on their way, through the twisting streets.

"We'll think of something else. Maybe Polassar has some silver." Tristan paused to watch a juggler doing truly remarkable things with wickedly flashing axes.

"If he does, he might have given it to you." Elisena's tone was tart.

"He probably didn't think. Was it this turning, or the next? He won't be used to it, I doubt he's ever been refused lodging."

"This one. Then round that corner."

Valadan snorted, as they came near. Polassar squinted warily out from the doorway, hand on sword until he recognized them. Allaire was sitting behind him against the doorstep, and it wrung Tristan's heart to see how weary she looked and how eager to see them she was.

"I couldn't find us lodging—" he began, with a sinking feeling as he saw her look change to despair. He tried to speak more gently. "They wanted money in advance, and it wasn't a very good place anyway. I don't know what to try next—"

He looked askance at Polassar. "We wouldn't need much. Not for a night's lodging."

"Wizard, I've not got a copper on me. Never expected we'd need 'em."

Allaire made a gallant attempt at hiding her disappointment, but they could all see how she longed for warmth, and quiet, and a dry bed, as they were each longing for the same things themselves. She drew her sodden fur cloak around her, cherishing the slight comfort it promised.

"We can at least try to find someplace out of the rain," Tristan said, more hopeful-voiced than he felt. They weren't likely to find any unoccupied space much larger than the doorway they now huddled in. He spared a thought for the horses' misery. They were too large to take advantage of even a doorway's scant shelter.

Minstrel winged silently to Tristan's shoulder, settling his feathers with rough jerks. Tristan touched him gently with one finger.

"You're no better off than the rest of us, little one. I wish I could think of something—"

Thomas mewed at his feet, insistently. After a minute, Tristan looked down. It was raining hard again.

"What?" He really was a complete failure, if even Thomas was reproaching him.

*Pay attention. A blind cat could have seen your dithering with the innkeeper wouldn't come to anything. I've found us a place.*

He trotted away from them rapidly, and Tristan made haste to follow him. He caught up Valadan's reins, and Polassar swore, and lifted Allaire back onto the white mare. She moaned a little as she felt the saddle under her again. Tristan hoped they hadn't far to go.

While he had thought this bit of the city evil-looking before, idly, he'd never believed it could get worse. This was the city of the mages, after all. But after a hundred paces, there were no more torches, and he heard Polassar drawing his sword free, for fear of thieves and worse. Minstrel nestled close to Tristan's neck, as if seeking comfort. Tristan looked nervously up at Valadan. The stallion's eyes flashed and flickered over him in the dark.

He seemed to have lost Thomas, and their way. They moved ahead a little longer, until the street became choked with refuse. A fitful wind was tearing the rainclouds, letting a little moonlight through. What the light revealed was not reassuring.

The buildings about them were in an advanced state of decay. Even by day, they'd doubtless be black. Heaps of rubbish and brick clogged the doorways, spilled into the street. In places, the walls were closer to being rubble than masonry. The only sign of life was a thin alley cat that ran squalling as Valadan kicked at it.

"Wizard—" Polassar's voice held a storm warning. "Are you sure we should have followed that cat?"

Tristan was not sure. Far from it. He was frantically trying to recall all the twistings and turnings they'd made, in hopes of retracing their way to relative safety again. He could light his crystal, but who knew what the light might draw to them? If the dark confused them, at least it hid them—or so he hoped. If the blackness hid other things as well— He peered about with deepening anxiety.

Something slithered against his ankle. Tristan thought at once of rats and was hard put not to shriek. He took a step back, until he was pressed against Valadan's side. The thing found his boot again, with instant and uncanny precision. It rubbed again, harder. Forcing himself to look down, he saw two great green disks shining as if with their own light.

"Thomas," he realized, with enormous relief.

*Who else did you think? You've got no sense of direction, I must say.*

He bent down to the cat's level, hoping Polassar wouldn't hear his uncertain whisper.

"Did you mean to bring us here?"

*Where better? You wanted someplace safe. No one else would come here.* Thomas fell to licking a raised forepaw. *That one on your left has part of a roof, and it costs nothing.*

Tristan straightened and looked dubiously in the direction Thomas had indicated. Fickle moonlight now washed the alley, and much of the building's interior as well. He walked closer to it, Valadan clopping after. Polassar held his peace, probably more out of disgust than respect.

A loose board lay in the doorway. Tristan scuffed it aside, disliking to poke his head into the dark room. Blais had always warned him of messing about with holes and dark places. As easy to discover a death-adder as a rabbit's nest.

*Oh, where's your spirit of adventure? You walked right into Darkenkeep without a quiver.*

Valadan snorted at the mention of the place. He wasn't any more willing than Tristan to cross this threshold.

"Are you sure this place is empty?" Tristan whispered, daring to put a hand on the doorframe, steadying himself to peer inside without getting too close.

Thomas yawned.

*As empty as makes no difference. And what do you care about rats and spiders?*

Did the sound of water dripping and splashing within mask other sounds, shufflings and squeaks?

"Rats?" Tristan said, too aghast to remember to keep his voice low.

"Rats?" Allaire echoed, and there was a rustle of fabric as she pulled her skirts well out of rodent reach. As she still sat her horse, the action was hardly necessary.

"No, it's all right," Tristan said hastily, just as Polassar seemed about to explode, by the growling that had begun in his throat. "Thomas will take care of those. And it *has* got a roof."

"Aye, but will it hold? I've not come so far to be buried alive."

Tristan decided to risk lighting his crystal. The stone responded quickly, with a flash that hurt his eyes, and it was some seconds before he could see clearly, though he hastily damped the light. He was relieved to see that most of the roof beams were still in place at the end nearest the door, and were solid looking. Thomas strolled casually inside. Except for him, the place was empty.

*Well, what did you expect? Cave bears? I said it was safe.*

"You also said rats," Tristan admonished, very low and somewhat angered.

*There are rats all over Kôvelir. We won't be bothered here more than elsewhere.*

Tristan eyed him doubtfully. Valadan was sniffing at the mossy walls. A bit of blackened candle still sat in a niche by the door.

*No one has been here for a long while. And the roof will hold.*

Well, he could trust Valadan, surely. Tristan nodded to the others.

They followed him in, after Polassar had made a few token protests. He was loath to sell any of his armor to buy better quarters, though, and so he agreed at last, and Allaire was too weary to do aught but agree. As Thomas had said, at least the place had a roof.

It also had fresh water. Part of the floor had long since fallen in on a sort of sub-basement, which rainwater had filled to a depth of several inches. They could hear yet more water trickling in.

Tristan managed to keep the crystal alight, though it flickered badly—he was as tired as any of them. By its pale light they saw that perhaps a third part of the small room was still roofed, and free of fallen rafters. It was very dusty.

That did not seem to bother Allaire, who slipped off her

horse and sat down at once in the corner, leaning against the wall.

Polassar made a rough couch for her from his cloak and some dusty straw, while Tristan dragged the drier fallen rafters together to make a fire, close to the roof opening so the smoke could get out. Its light might show from the street, but at least it would keep the rats away while they slept.

He tethered the horses near the door and began to unharness them, trying to make them comfortable. Small sounds behind him told his ears that Elisena was heating water in his pot, about to brew them something warming. A pity they couldn't have a meal as well, but their food was certainly all gone by now.

They'd need money to get more. He was going to have to think of something, some way of supporting them. This place might be made comfortable with a few hours of work, but they still had to eat. How they would manage that had him at a loss for the moment.

Thomas lay on Valadan's now shining back, watching him. Tristan reached up to stroke his fur, and the cat closed his eyes in deep contentment, saying nothing as Tristan scratched his chin.

"Thank you," he whispered. "I don't know what I'd do without you."

Thomas purred at him, then jerked his head up, eyes wide. The wailing cry of a street cat came again, from somewhere outside. Thomas leaped through the door and vanished into the night, off either to battle or love without a word or backward glance.

Tristan sighed and turned to the other horses. Grooming made his arms ache, but they could not be allowed to stand dirty all night. He was shocked to see how the white mare's ribs stood out, and how rough her once satiny coat had become. She was not used to such travel as they'd given her, and it was a wonder she'd not gone lame. For all her elegance, Polassar had not made a very good choice in her, Tristan reflected.

Tristan did his diligent best, but his head was buzzing with weariness, and his sight became blurry long before he'd finished. His one consolation was that the horses were almost as tired as he was, and he was in little danger of either bites or kicks. Polassar's roan made a half-hearted attempt, but Valadan fixed her with a furious eye as she lifted a hoof. Tristan thanked him, and resisted the temptation to skimp on the roan's grooming or ask Polassar to tend her himself.

A soothing herb smell was filling the room, which helped a little. Tristan put down the rag he'd been using on the horses' legs and straightened painfully.

Elisena offered him the cup, and he drank it down greedily as he realized his thirst, never noticing its taste. The bit of liquid reminded his stomach that it was otherwise empty, but that could be managed. He was too tired to be hungry, he told himself sternly.

Polassar was already snoring. He'd flung himself down just as he was, face down between Allaire and the door, as if to guard her even while he slept. Tristan hoped there was no pressing need to set a watch, then recollected that Valadan would warn him if anyone approached. Allaire slept also.

With her hair undone and her face still dirty where she'd had no strength to wash it, she looked very young. One fresh cheek was pillowed on her hand as well as Polassar's cloak, and the glitter of the rings showed through her moonlit hair. Tristan stood gazing at her until he began to feel guilty, as if he did her some wrong by feeling as he did, watching her thus while she lay unaware.

She looked less majestic than she had on her shining couch in Darkenkeep, but not a whit less lovely. The rough straw she snuggled in only offset the fineness of her skin, and her rags only showed her sweet body more fully. Her sable cloak rose gently and more gently fell with her breathing. Now Tristan did feel uncomfortable, knowing that he never would have dared look at her so if she'd known he was watching. He sighed and stretched himself and looked covertly around.

He could not have been standing there long, not half so long as it felt. Elisena was still busy at the fire, banking it for the night. Tristan rolled up tight in his cloak, sneezed once at the dust, and finally allowed himself to fall asleep.

# Magickery

ELISENA NUDGED him, whispering his name. Tristan half sat up, blinking at her. The room was barely light enough for him to make out her face.

"What's the matter?" Even his voice was blurry. He rubbed the back of one hand over both eyes. "It's not morning?"

"It's early. Give me your clothes."

"Why?" he asked, startled, still sleep-stupid.

"If I wash them now, they'll be dry when you wake up again," she said, as if he ought to have known. Then she helped him with the sweater—he seemed to keep getting tangled in its sleeves. His breeches she let him handle himself. "No, keep the cloak. I'll do that later." He'd have thought she was suppressing a laugh, if he'd been more awake. "You might need it—these may fall to tatters when they're cleaned."

She tucked the cloak around him, and he snuggled down into it, gradually getting warm again. He drifted off to sleep, lulled by the sound of water splashing, and soon forgot he'd wakened at all.

The sun slanted in through the roof and fell warm across his eyes. Tristan resisted it a moment, squeezing his eyes tighter shut. Even so, the brightness made a pattern of reds and oranges behind his eyelids. He turned his head, a straw pricked his face, and Tristan finally opened his eyes.

Elisena was kneeling beside the fire, poking at something in the embers. She heard him move and looked up.

"Are you hungry?"

His stomach answered for him with embarrassing promptness and loudness. Tristan looked down at it ruefully.

"Is there anything to eat?" He spoke wistfully, knowing full well there could be nothing left.

"Some bread." She held up a crust, toasted on one edge. "I tried to keep it dry, what the river didn't ruin." From the bag she'd brought out of Radak, of course, along with her herbs and who knew what other useful things?

"And somebody had a garden once, two houses from here. A long time ago, but I found potatoes, and a few very tough carrots." She prodded a blackened potato out of the ashes. "I think it's done."

He burned every one of his fingers on it and a second like it, before he forced himself to stop.

"Save some for them," he said, gesturing at Allaire and Polassar, through the last delicious mouthful. It was difficult—after all, Polassar had simply gone to sleep the night before, while he and Elisena had been working so hard doing the necessary chores. But in fairness, they couldn't claim all the remaining food as their reward. He gave the rest of the potatoes a longing look, and told his stomach that it was full.

He looked harder at the two in the corner. Allaire had not stirred all night, it seemed, and Polassar's moustache was still gently waving to the accompaniment of his snores. Even Minstrel's loud singing did not rouse them.

"Are they all right?" He felt belatedly alarmed. Allaire had looked so exhausted—

"There are herbs to help sleep come, and to prolong it. You should have slept longer yourself."

Tristan stretched till his joints cracked, and yawned. That drink last night, then. Stupid of him not to have noticed what was in it. He wasn't sure he liked the idea of being drugged, but he had to admit he was feeling no ill effects from it.

"What time is it?"

"The four hour past sun-high. I heard the chimes."

So late? It surprised him greatly. How long had she expected him to sleep?

Seeing he meant to stay wakeful, Elisena brought his clothes. With the dirt off, they looked more worn than ever.

"They're patched on the patches. How is it you don't freeze?"

He shrugged and tried to smile it off, since he'd long passed the point of being embarrassed by his shabby clothes. The smile developed into another yawn.

"I have water hot, if you want to wash."

The water felt—he had no words to describe it. This was far the happiest thing that had happened to him since he'd left Blais' cottage, Tristan thought. He got out his belt-knife, too, and shaved himself by his reflection in the pool, although he was barely beginning to need to do so. His growth of beard was neither as thick nor as coarse as Polassar's, so he went bare-chinned, unlike most wizards and persons of importance.

Finished, he poured a handful of hot water over his head with a sigh of contentment. He'd have liked a long soak in a whole tub of steaming water, and lavender scented towels, and fresh new clothes to put on after, but for now this was fine indeed. The High Mage of Kôvelir himself couldn't have asked for better under these circumstances.

"Feels good, doesn't it?"

Tristan nodded, drying off on the bottom of his cloak as usual. Elisena must have had her own wash earlier, and he saw as he dressed that her hair was combed as well as it might be, thick curls falling cleanly about her scrubbed face. Her cape even looked as if it had been brushed, and was hanging neatly on a peg.

She was grinning at him. "So that's what you really look like. I was wondering what was under all those bruises, and the dirt."

By that, he supposed his face must be healing, finally. By what little he could make out, it seemed to be about as good as new, save for the spot where Polassar had marked him. And his eyes, of course. It was becoming distressingly obvious that he hadn't been eating or sleeping properly.

"You're looking better yourself," he observed dryly. "Compared to last night."

"Any change would have been to the good." Her eyes were dancing.

He heard splashing, and looked around to see Minstrel taking his own turn at a bath, in a little puddle Tristan had dripped out. He put his head into the water, shaking it, fluttering his wings and tail rapidly in the spray. His head came up, he looked to see if anyone might be watching, then went back to work, sending drops flying and sparkling in the sunlight.

"We'll be needing more food," Tristan commented, when he'd had enough of the diversion. He stood up, and stretched till his leg muscles protested. Tristan winced, but persisted.

"Thomas caught two rats. Want those?"

"No. I was thinking of doing some hunting myself." He whistled the now clean Minstrel over to him. "I'll try to be back by dark, but if I'm not, don't worry. And don't let anyone else leave. Better we don't all start wandering around. Not that they look much like doing it." Polassar's snores might yet bring the rest of the roof in.

She didn't ask what he was going to do, which was just as well. He had no clear idea of it yet himself.

Thomas met him at the door with a cry of delight, and fell into step with him. Minstrel chirped scoldingly down at him from the safety of Tristan's shoulder.

*What are you up to?*

"I'm going to get us supper."

*If you get caught stealing, they cut your right hand off,* Thomas told him cheerfully. *Even for a first offense. A one-handed wizard should be most amusing.*

"I'm not going to steal anything," Tristan protested.

*I suppose that makes more sense than saying you don't expect to be caught. What am I going to steal for you?*

"Nothing. We aren't going to steal, either one of us. Now be quiet. I'm planning."

*If you're doing the planning, it's a good thing I came with you.*

The alleys did not look so frightening by daylight, or so unnervingly narrow. Just dirty. Tristan struggled to commit all the twists and turnings to memory, as he dodged heaps of refuse and rotting masonry.

This bit of the city looked the sort of place whose inhabitants might spend their days sleeping and their nights doing things best not thought of. They were beginning to wake now, as evening drew near, and Tristan passed through little knots of people. Ladies, bright as birds and of dubious virtue were shadowed by tough-looking men with very long knives, while a yawning man tugged his sluggish dancing bear along by a rope looped through its jeweled

collar. Thomas bristled his fur at the sight of the creature—no great bravery, since it was safely muzzled. Tristan thought it might be best to observe from beneath lowered eyelids—staring might well be taken as an offense.

He was busily examining a runestone set among the cobbles—like a jewel set in clay—when a troupe of street players danced out of a courtyard nearly on top of him, star-
tling Minstrel so that he flew up to clutch at Tristan's hair.
The players gamboled about them, saluting either him or
the stone with mock magic, then passed on.

Something about the players gave Tristan the spark his
imagination had been waiting on. They reminded him a
little of the wandering mages of Calandra, those skilled in
the lesser magics. They entertained at weddings and festi-
vals and markets, with cheap tricks, and no true wizard
deigned to pay them the slightest attention. They lowered
everyone's standards of magic with their chicanery. But
they always seemed to get people's coins thrown at them—

And, Tristan thought, what was it that Blais used to do
with fireworks and purple smoke? It wasn't very difficult,
if he remembered aright.

He found a likely looking corner of a now crowded
square and began to let green-colored cold flame run
through his fingers. Thomas kept a respectful distance, until sure just how well this was going to work. With a grand
gesture, Tristan made a ball of the flame and juggled it
about.

No one seemed to be noticing, much to Tristan's dismay
when he covertly glanced about. The ball dropped to the
ground, and sent a pale pink smoke column coiling about
his legs.

Startled, he tried ineffectually to do a shadowplay, shap-
ing substance from nothing. He finally achieved a flimsy
sort of a tree, and Minstrel obligingly hopped onto it for
him. The bird even began a song.

Something was wrong. No one was paying them the
slightest attention. Tristan almost let the shadow slip away,
and Minstrel ceased singing and fluttered his wings for balance. No one seemed to know he was even there. The bus-
tle in the square passed them by as utterly as if they'd been
walled off from it.

Thomas decided to take matters into his own paws.

Without a second's warning or a hint of his intentions, he leaped into the tree after Minstrel. The canary vacated the shadow branches in a flurry of feathers and landed on Tristan's nose. Thomas followed just as Tristan lost hold of the tree altogether.

He grabbed at the cat, who must surely have gone mad. *Play this for all it's worth! They're noticing now. Do some smoke rings.* Thomas writhed out of his grasp effortlessly.

Tristan did as he was bid, trying to gather his wits at the same time. The first few rings were not very round. Minstrel managed to perch inside one, swinging to and fro. Thomas stalked him, stepping lightly from ring to ring as they floated through the air, with no more concern than had he walked the merest earthly fence.

Something hit Tristan's boot. It gleamed in the late sunlight—a copper coin of medium value. He nearly let the smoke rings fade in his surprise. Thomas hissed wildly at him as he sailed by, and Tristan hastily steadied the spell.

More coins followed the first. They worked the crowd for several minutes, improvising their act so, their ideas dovetailing nicely. Minstrel had entered into the spirit of the game now and put more showmanship into his last-minute escapes from Thomas, even hiding briefly behind Tristan's ear, peeping out in mock surprise to find Thomas poised on Tristan's shoulder. By now a few harlots were throwing Tristan silver bead-coins, for which he made white doves seem to appear from their hands—a charming incongruity. Thomas walked among the crowd, daintily collecting the coins in his mouth, to lay them on the growing heap at Tristan's feet.

There was quite a pile by the time Thomas sensed their watchers' attention wandering and suggested a halt. The torches were lit by this time, and the evening's business pressed their onlookers.

*Come on. That's enough, don't be greedy.*

Tristan gathered up the heap of copper and gently winking silver and stuffed it carefully into a leather pouch.

"Enough for food, and maybe some grain for the horses. But Allaire's gown is nothing but rags now. I'm sure she's cold. We really should keep on while we can."

*This crowd's tired of us. And it's past Minstrel's bedtime.*

"We'll try another square, then. Just for a little. Wouldn't you like some milk?"

*Not really. But it's your show.*

Thomas convinced him to buy the food first, though, and stash it carefully along their homeward route. Someone might think they'd collected enough by now to be worth robbing. From the look of it, nearly everyone they met fell into the robber category.

They bought bread, meat, oats, and milk, haggling for a good price, then passed over a few streets to the next crowded spot.

Thomas judged the climate of this one to be subtly different from the last, composed as it was less of women and more of men—most missing teeth and eyes or even arms and legs. Not apt to appreciate the gentler sort of entertainment. He went into his act as before, perhaps a shade more frantically, overplaying shamelessly.

It went well, after the first few uncertain moments, somehow. They even got a goldpiece, albeit a small one. Well enough, until Tristan decided to add a new trick to their repertoire. The idea of doing it had long captivated him—a miniature raincloud, no bigger perhaps than a cat, floating inches above the heads of the crowd and scattering minuscule raindrops. He made the passes, remembering the grimoire's instructions about it.

Nothing happened, so he repeated them. Thomas mewed anxiously, but Tristan ignored him and shut his eyes, trying to concentrate.

He did the passes a third time. Still no cloud. He ran through the spell again in his mind.

Some of the crowd was looking up, though, gesturing skyward. Maybe something was beginning to take shape after all—

They were pointing at a balcony which overhung the square. Perched on its narrow edge was a large chamberpot, which was rocking back and forth furiously to the time of Tristan's movements. A few prudent fellows tried to step back, but they were not in time—Tristan finished his last pass, the pot wobbled to the edge, and emptied itself into the crowd.

There was a moment's silence. Then a blur of motion, and the wall behind Tristan was dripping smashed tomato. Other missiles followed, as outraged shouts rang through the night air, but most were truer to their mark. Tristan ran.

After a few harrowing minutes of dashing through alleys and shadows, he hoped he'd lost them. He looked back to see, tripped and fell headlong. He prayed he'd lost them all then, as he lay panting. He couldn't run any longer. He was thoroughly lost, and had no idea of where either Thomas or Minstrel might be.

He didn't even have the money, he realized with a sickening jolt. His pouch was still back at the square. He'd left it on the ground at his feet, while Thomas dropped coins into it, and never thought about it when he bolted. He felt tears beginning as he wiped rotten melon bits out of his hair.

*It's hard to earn any kind of a living by magic in a town where it's over-familiar. They're most unappreciative.*

Tristan's stomach did a quick flop of relief.

"I spoiled your act, Thomas."

*You don't have the instincts for this sort of life. No sense of theater. Always grab the money when you run, for instance.*

He dropped the clinking bag by Tristan's face. With a bright chirp, Minstrel landed beside it, a tiny coin dropping from his beak.

"I got the running right anyway." He sat up, feeling at a new rip in the knee of his breeches and a scrape on the knee beneath. "Almost."

*Do you remember where you left the food?*

"No." Tristan continued to try to dust himself off, without much success. Most of the stuff on him was malodorous and clung stickily.

*It was this way. They're not looking for you anymore, so it ought to be safe. Crowds are so fickle.*

Allaire's joy at the sight of the food should have made all Tristan's troubles worthwhile. Instead he was just intensely conscious of how foully the rotten vegetables plastered on him stank, as he watched a now rested and immaculate Polassar dig through the food. A joint of cold meat disappeared in seconds.

Tristan sat down and leaned his head against the wall. At this rate he'd never keep them fed.

He tried vainly to analyze what had gone wrong. For those few moments he'd been in command; the magic had been doing exactly what he wanted it to. He'd felt like a real wizard at last, even though it was only a small magic. At least it had worked. And now—

"Tristan? Don't you want anything to eat?"

"Let him be, if he's determined to sulk. Come and finish your own food, my lady. Just let him be." Polassar's tone was as chill as the Winterwaste's breezes.

Allaire stayed beside Tristan another moment, in spite of that, holding out a bit of bread that he didn't even see. She had spoken his name three times, and he'd never even looked away from the wall or shown the least sign that he'd heard her. He just kept staring—

"It's not easy, is it—selling magic in the streets?"

It was Elisena by him now, he saw. Allaire was dutifully back at Polassar's side, roasting bits of meat in the fire.

"How did you know?" He wasn't very interested.

"What else? You come back with half the night gone, and you bring food and small coins. You're covered with melon juice and tomato pulp. What else could you have been doing, that they threw coins at you, then garbage? And stones too?" A little horror crept into her voice, as she touched a fresh cut on his cheek.

Tristan's fingers followed hers. He sighed. More work for the butterfly box's ointment.

"I don't remember how that happened. I was busy running. Probably when I fell—Thomas says I have stupid feet, always tripping on things."

"I will go with you to the Library tomorrow, if you like." Her eyes were troubled. "I can read some of the old tongues. I may be able to help."

"Thank you." It would be useful to have a second pair of eyes seeking clues.

She held out a chunk of bread, filled with bits of meat and potato.

"Please. I didn't let them gobble everything, I saved this for you. I thought you might be hungry later."

"I almost had it for a while," he said, looking at the food in his hand, thinking only of magic. "I was in control. That almost never happened before. And maybe it never will again."

"It will." She spoke with certainty, even after he'd told her exactly what had happened in the square. "Be sure it will."

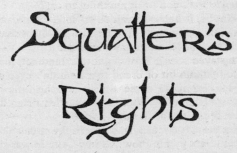

# Squatter's Rights

TRISTAN WOKE EARLY, his depression of the past night lifting only a very little with the day's first sunlight. He might have taken some comfort at Elisena's words, but what did she really know about magic? His pride—what was left of it—was stung. Had he looked so in need of pity that she'd been moved to lie to him? Glumly, he washed the sleep out of his face and went to water the horses.

They'd been moved outside, where there was some hope of their finding grass—also, Polassar had been overheard making a nasty crack about sleeping in a stable. It made a long trip for a person carrying water, particularly when that one had only a small cook-pot to do the carrying with, but at this moment Tristan didn't mind. The longer the chore took, the longer it would be before he must face the problem of the Library.

He wished he knew what the procedure was. Could any mage just walk up to the Library's great gates and demand entry privileges? He would like to think so but doubted it would prove that simple. Would Blais' name be enough to gain him entrance, or might he be put to some sort of test? Until it happened, there was no knowing, but that didn't rule out his worrying. Balancing the sloshing pot, he stepped out into the pale sunshine.

Half a minute! Something was wrong here. This alley hadn't been that cluttered the night before. He would never have got through it. The narrowest stretch was blocked completely. Come to think, that pile of rubble yonder was unfamiliar too. And he remembered starlight shining on windows in those buildings across from him; only now there weren't any windows, just gaping holes.

"Stop right there!"

Tristan's right hand dropped instinctively to his belt knife, in lieu of his sword, which was hopelessly far off with the rest of his gear. The pot dropped with a clunk and a splash at his feet.

"Don't think about it," the voice advised. "You'd be dead before it cleared the sheath."

A fist-sized lump of brick splattered against the wall, inches from his head. Tristan dodged, nearly losing his footing on the wet cobbles, and somehow wound up facing the direction he thought the brick had come from.

A figure rose from behind a broken wall.

A woman. She shoved back tangled waist-length red hair with one hand, hitching her skirts up with the other as she picked her way around the wall and into plain view.

"Now that I have your attention, I'd like a few words with you, master wizard."

"Certainly," Tristan replied, very courteously, he thought, in view of the circumstances.

The woman stalked closer, eyes appraising his face and clothing with swift darting glances.

"You're not from Kôvelir," she observed flatly. "It figures."

"Excuse me?" Tristan asked blankly. He wished he could see her left hand. She was keeping it too well hidden in the folds of her skirt; he suspected another brick.

"Where are you from?" she spat. "And *who* are you?"

Tristan's jaw muscles tightened. He resented her tone—who was she, to take him to task so? What had he done, anyway? He drew himself up to take advantage of his full height and said proudly, "Tristan of Calandra. And whom have I the honor of addressing?"

For once it wasn't difficult to assume the bearing of a

commanding mage. He'd decided he had little to fear from her now, so long as he kept a wary eye on her. A brick was useless unless she caught him totally by surprise, unlikely out in the open like this.

The woman's eyes slitted, and he glared back at her, taking in her ragged clothes, the filthy red skirt, the indigo blouse—between the stains and ropes of beads, that was—and her bare, dusty feet. If not for the force of her personality, he'd have been totally unimpressed. But brick or no, she didn't mean to be taken lightly.

"Crewzel," she said, as proud as he'd sounded, or prouder. "And this is *my* street!"

"Your street?" Tristan dropped his hauteur and tilted his head to one side. "I'm afraid I don't follow you."

"My street! All my work, keeping the alley blocked, all my money spent on expensive illusions to keep the nosy out, all my labors to make a home for my poor fatherless boy, someplace safe out of the weather for us both—not that it's much, but we make do, we get by! And you waltz in, free and easy, and just move yourself in!"

"What?" Tristan asked, still not comprehending and amazed at the amount of speech she'd gotten from one breath.

"Let me spell it out for you! This is my home! Mine! Get out!" She advanced a pace toward him, fists balled at her sides.

"Now just a minute." He thought he finally saw what Crewzel must be driving at, but he needed time to make full sense of it. "This street was deserted when we came here."

"Ha!"

"It was. And with the shape it's in, I can well understand that. It was dark, I'll admit that, but there was no one here."

"We work nights, earning our pitiful crusts."

"Are you trying to tell me that you and ah—your son—live here?" He waved a hand at the squalid alley.

"Aye. For the past two years, since my man died untimely."

Tristan found he was standing beside one of the strange piles of rubble. He peered at it with new interest.

"And part of this decay is just illusion?"

*"Don't touch that!"*

She stormed toward him with such obvious purpose that Tristan jumped back from his examination of the spell, spreading his hands placatingly in front of him.

"All right. *All right!*" He wondered what harm his touch could have done. Was the illusion so fragile? Interesting.

Crewzel gave her head a toss.

"Are you going now?"

"What?" Tristan stared at her. "Of course not. I can't— we can't—I—why should we?"

"You scurvy dolt! You've had the gall to move in not only on my home, but my livelihood as well!" Crewzel thundered, apparently remembering another grievance by the irrelevance of her latest accusation. "Even my very best street-corner!"

"I'm sorry," Tristan said hastily, anxious to soothe her quickly and hardly attending to her words.

"Yes. You are sorry, and so's your magic. I caught your act last night."

"My act," Tristan repeated stupidly, beginning belatedly to understand. If Crewzel were one of the itinerant street magicians, living a squatter's existence here, then this might make sense at last. No wonder she resented him, and was trying so stridently to drive him away.

"Are you going?" Crewzel demanded, her eyes slitted again.

"No." Tristan opened his mouth to explain why he and the others needed to stay here and how that needn't necessarily inconvenience her, now that they knew she was here, but Crewzel got her breath first, and put it to use.

She spoke a word of witchery—unfamiliar, but Tristan recognized the purpose of it by its sound—and her waiting hands filled with what looked like millions of bright sparks. Smiling nastily, she patted at them and said more words. Chanted them, really, and odd rhythms formed.

Tristan was so intrigued by her methods that he hardly noticed what she was actually wreaking. When the lump of sparks was sufficiently ball-shaped, she hefted it, and with another cry flung it at his face!

In a proper duel of magic, he would have immediately spoken the correct counterspell. Only he didn't know it. In a proper duel of magic he would have at least been prepared for this, but she'd surprised him as if he were the greenest of children. All he could hope to do was dodge, and he managed it twice. Gouts of hot white sparks sizzled by his ears harmlessly.

The third time, the sparks were suddenly inside his head.

"Wait a minute," Tristan said, lying on his back in the alley mud and waiting for the lights inside his head to dim so that he could see. Several Minstrels gyrated worriedly in the air over his face. "Can't we discuss this sensibly? For the sake of variety?"

"Wizard? What's amiss?"

Tristan was greatly relieved to see Polassar's bulk darkening the doorway of their shelter.

"Our neighbors," he answered casually, getting to his feet but carefully stepping to one side so Crewzel might have an uninterrupted view of Polassar's size.

"Oh. Very polite of 'em to welcome us."

"Well," Tristan said, "it *would* have been." He'd never have suspected Polassar of having such a refined sense of humor.

Something else was moving, beyond the tumbled wall. Tristan glanced that way sharply, and Crewzel saw his head turn.

"*Delmon!*" she shrilled. "Ruuun!"

She meant, of course, for her boy to run away, saving himself, but Delmon ran straight at Tristan, as ready for a fight as his mother.

The boy couldn't have had more than six summers under his braided leather belt; he looked undersized even for that age. At least Tristan thought so. He'd no chance to form much of an opinion, beset as he was. In seconds he was kicked, punched, trodden on, and bitten. He staggered back, trying to get a grip on the child that would keep him harmlessly at arm's length, and crashed into Polassar with a thud that rattled his brains.

Polassar disentangled himself with a timely step to his left and pinioned Delmon neatly, forestalling both kicks and bites. The three adults panted and glared at each other. Delmon writhed like a hooked trout, with about the same hope of escape.

Crewzel whirled, driving her sharp right elbow into Tristan's midsection. His breath left his lungs in a rush and he doubled over, falling to his knees. Crewzel went down with him, and not by accident or loss of balance. She flung an arm around his neck, pressing a shard of window glass to his throat.

"Hostage for hostage," she said coolly, to Polassar. "Let him go."

Tristan stifled his burning need for air, afraid that too deep a breath might thrust his neck against the glass splinter.

With a snort of disgust, Polassar took his hands away from Delmon, who leaped well out of his reach.

Crewzel smiled and stepped back, dragging Tristan to his feet. Or so she would have done, had Thomas not tangled himself around Tristan's feet, causing him to stumble and fall again and Crewzel to lose her hold on him.

This time, Tristan didn't even bother to get up. He wiped a hand over his throat, half expecting to find it bloody, and said, "This is absurd. If we've done you any injury, it was purely accidental."

"You can't just barge in here and throw me out of my home—poor as it is, wizard!" she howled.

"No one's throwing you out of anything! I'm sure we can work all this out if we sit down and talk like civilized folk. And do stop shouting," Tristan added. "You're making my head ache."

Elisena appeared in the doorway, spoon in one hand, seemingly unconcerned about the brawl.

"Would anyone care for breakfast?" She gestured indoors with the spoon.

Crewzel froze in alarm, and lifted her skirts preparatory to flight.

"Wait," Tristan said, trying to sound reassuring. "No one's going to hurt you." He saw Allaire peeping out curiously over Elisena's shoulder and realized that Crewzel had no idea of their numbers. She'd thought he was here alone, and now suddenly there were four of the invaders. Four to one was hardly good odds; small wonder she was ready to run.

He introduced them all with great care.

"This is Elisena, that is the lady Allaire, and this is m'lord Polassar. I'm not at liberty to speak more of our names and lineages or our business in Kôvelir, but if you'll

join us in a meal, I'll tell you what I can. You've nothing to
fear from us, and we only intend to be here for a short
while. Please." He swept a hand toward their shelter.

Wary as any wildcat, Crewzel stepped through the doorway, Delmon pressed safely to her side. Allaire greeted her
gently, and Crewzel dropped an unpracticed-looking curt-
sey.

"I thought you were just a street beggar," she whispered
in a cracked voice to Tristan. "I didn't know—"

The reason for her sudden politeness was obvious. Tristan supposed it was only the reflection of the sunbeams
striking the water in the pool, and the fact that Allaire
stood with her back to the light, but she did seem to be
glowing. Her rings were unmistakably bright. He looked at
them too long and found he needed to blink back tears. For
the first time since Darkenkeep, even in her rags, Allaire
looked a queen.

Elisena knelt by the fire. She'd pounded some of the oats
Tristan had intended for the horses into meal and mixed
them with the milk Thomas had not wanted. With anise
seeds crushed and stirred in, it made a fragrant batter. She
dropped spoonfuls of the mixture onto a fallen roof slate,
which was serving her for a griddle. The room filled with
pleasant smells and a sizzling sound.

Crewzel lost all her outrage and most of her arrogance
with the meal. She swallowed the last mouthful, having
thoroughly chewed its smallest crumb, sighed, and shoved
her hair back with both hands. Tristan suddenly noticed
that she looked not very much older than he did himself,
once the anger had gone from her face, and doubtless she
wasn't. Under the curling red hair, her features were as
sharp and pointy as any ferret's, but it wasn't an unpleasant face when she was calm.

"We've had a lot of trouble, since Giffyd died," she said
quietly to no one in particular. "Maybe I'm over-suspicious,
but I protect what's mine." Her eyes went to Delmon, who
sat watching Thomas. Thomas likewise watched him. A
dark, silent boy, mostly eyes, much as Tristan supposed
he'd once been himself.

Minstrel settled on Tristan's shoulder and made scolding
noises. Wasn't he ever going to be fed? Must he forage for
grass seeds on his own, like a common sparrow?

Tristan fetched the birdseed, pouring some into his cupped hand. Later, he would spread more seed on the windowledge, so the canary could eat whenever he needed to, but he knew Minstrel liked the companionship of perching on his thumb and taking the seed from his palm. After a while the bird began to sing, as a counterpoint to their conversation.

"What sort of trouble?" Tristan asked.

"Free lodgings are scarce everywhere." Crewzel's slanting eyes glittered at him.

"Even these?" He cocked an eyebrow at the gap in their roof.

"Even these. And I'm a woman alone—that doesn't make it any easier. Every man's hand against me."

*Ha!* Thomas sniffed. *I wager that one always lands on her feet. She's more a cat than I am.*

Tristan smiled at him. Delmon was just screwing up his courage and reaching timid fingers into stroking position. Thomas knew it and, ever the sensualist, was looking pleased already.

Bored, Polassar excused himself from the conversation as soon as the food was gone and set about straightening up their gear.

"How do you come to be travelling with that one?" Crewzel whispered, leaning close. "He doesn't seem overfond of you."

Tristan shot a quick look at Polassar—Lassair's lord was safely out of earshot.

"We've had a long trip. He's just tired." He didn't dare say more—they had no guarantee that Galan's men wouldn't cross the Est, and come searching here. Kôvelir was the only likely place they could have made for, and they hadn't troubled to hide their trail, as much from exhaustion as stupidity.

"These past two years have been frightful," said Crewzel, returning to her earlier complaint.

Two years? "Oh. You mean since your husband died—"

He hesitated, not knowing if she wanted to talk about whatever had happened to Giffyd. He didn't want to seem to pry—in case it set her off again.

"In a duel of magic," Crewzel informed him bitterly.

"And let that lesson you, master sorcerer. Don't mess with magics that are beyond you."

Tristan solemnly agreed that it was best not to.

*You're a fine one to talk.* Thomas was luxuriating under Delmon's increasingly daring caresses.

Crewzel went on to describe her view of the past two years, expanding at incredible length on the slights and setbacks and troubles she'd suffered, all through trying to keep life in herself and her son. Tristan decided that she'd been deprived of a sympathetic ear—or at least an open one—for a very long time. Still, this was better than having lumps of hurtful sparks thrown at him. He listened quietly, offering comments only when she really seemed to require them. Most of her strident and insistent questions turned out to be rhetorical, or else she answered them herself before he ever had a chance to.

After half an hour, Allaire also excused herself, and went to find Polassar, who'd gone outside to examine what was left of the roof. Tristan had seen him fingering his ears as he went out the door and he smiled ruefully to himself, noticing that Elisena also kept herself quite busy at the fire, some distance away from Crewzel's tale of woe. Delmon had doubtless heard it all before; he never looked up even when he was the subject under discussion.

". . . so I hawk my magic in the streets, to keep meat on our bones." She looked at Tristan, face unexpectedly pert, younger even than her narrow span of years.

"Tell your fortune?" she mimicked in what must have been her most winning street voice. "But dip your finger in this cup of common water, and all's revealed." She mimed a cup, holding it out to Tristan. He smiled, and touched a finger to the empty air between her palms.

"I see marvels, lordly sir, both done and yet undone. And mysteries—"

Her eyes had gone smoky black, until she gave her head a little shake, and dropped all pretense of the cup.

"I can read you even without the water—and that's passing strange. I can read you, but not quite make your meaning out. Like a book fairly printed, but in the wrong tongue."

Her attitude was strange, as if curiosity had stripped

away all her posturings, leaving an altogether different
person gripping Tristan's hand. From her words he'd long
since pegged her as a card reader, skilled in the small
showy meaningless magics, but now—Crewzel was as startled as he was by the change. Confusion in her face, she
snatched her hand away.

"Well, I've told your fortune, as well as any might. Cross
my palm with silver now, if you'd not offend a mighty
witch, sirrah!" A little wild, her voice. He wasn't sure if
she meant what she said or not.

"Gladly, lady, if I but could," he replied, playing the
game. "But I've no silver. And none of your skill at earning it, either."

"That's no little truth! Despite what your hand says."
The spell was broken. She was her noisy self again, brash
and immodest.

"You're an honest man, Tristan, and as such, will you
not keep your word now, and tell me why you're here?"

Tristan swallowed hard. Had he really promised that?
With her free tongue, it certainly wasn't the wisest course
he might steer. He cast back for his exact words.

"I said I'd tell you what I could. We're on a quest—and
I can't tell you what its object is. It's likely better if you
don't know. Then no one will bother you."

Crewzel looked disgusted, as if all her lamenting had
backfired on her.

"All you can tell me is that you can't tell me?" she inquired sarcastically.

"No, of course not. I don't play that kind of game. We're
seeking something, and hoping to find leads on it in the
mages' Library. Only we have to live quietly while we're
searching because we don't want it known that we're here."

"And you're broke." Crewzel amended pointedly. Tristan nodded gravely.

"That too. That's why I went out magicking last night.
I'm sorry I appropriated your corner. You should have said
something, I'd have moved elsewhere."

"Just see it doesn't happen again." There was an unmis-
takable flash of steel in her tone. "Who're you on the run
from?"

"Let's just say that we are," he stalled, wondering how
she'd guessed that, and just what she'd really seen in his

hand. There were witches who could read men so, but he'd have sworn she wasn't one of them.

"So if you stay here, you're putting me in danger, aren't you? There'll likely be packs of assassins after you, murdering me in my bed by mistake."

He winced at her hyperbole.

"No! We lost them—I mean there weren't any assassins, it was soldiers— Toadstools! You're not in any danger. We wouldn't be stopping here if I thought they were still after us."

"All right. I believe you. Now to business."

"Business?"

"Yes. You said you'd be staying here. Well, as I told you, free lodgings are scarce. Scarcer than snake's feathers. And this is my street."

"So you keep telling me." Were they going to go into this again?

"If you four are going to stay here—there *are* only the four of you?—coming and going at all hours, maybe someone snooping around looking for you, or following you back here and finding out that my costly illusions of the street being blocked are just words and air—for all that inconvenience to me and mine, you've got to make payment." She eyed him calculatingly. He could almost see silver gleaming in her eyes.

"I told you, I haven't got any money. We're going to have a very hard time keeping ourselves fed. If I could pay rent, we'd be at an inn."

"And not having half the privacy you'll get here!"

"Or the fresh air!" Tristan exclaimed, gesturing at the roof. He sensed that the haggling was going to proceed unstoppably from here on.

"It's very healthy. The rains are nearly done for this year. And as for money, when you're magicking for your dinner, put back a few coppers. It won't be difficult for you."

"I don't intend to spend all my time in the streets charming pennies out of tight purses. I told you we're here to learn something, and I need to be at the Library for that. It's apt to take long enough as it is. And as you're not actually living in this deplorable excuse for a hovel, I seriously question your right to charge any rent at all!"

"This is my street!" Crewzel insisted dangerously.

Tristan glowered at her, then brightened. "I don't think Polassar will like being thrown out," he said sweetly. "Especially as he's been working all morning on this roof. I certainly would hate to be the one to break the news to him."

A roof slate slithered to the pavement with a crash, and an amazingly inventive stream of curses floated through the hole in the roof. Tristan rolled his eyes meaningfully.

"There's magic, you know," Crewzel muttered, then changed tacks. "All right. You've no money and no real prospects. We can settle on something else."

"What?" Tristan asked apprehensively, wondering if it mightn't have been safer just to pay her.

Crewzel's eye lit on Delmon, sitting now with Thomas in his lap. Her glance took on a little glow of motherly pleasure.

"Fond of it, isn't he?"

Tristan's heart slammed to a stop.

But Crewzel went on.

"I worry about him. Without more schooling than I can give him, he'll end like his father did—too much talent and no sense of how to use it without killing himself. I'd like to see him safely settled."

Tristan managed to resume breathing. For an awful moment he'd thought she was going to ask for Thomas.

"Don't the mages have a school here?"

"If you can pay—and have an established mage as a sponsor. Or if he had a great blazing power that they'd have to notice—but he's only got enough to get himself into trouble."

Thomas opened one eye briefly.

*He is a lot like you.*

"Crewzel, I don't think they'll take my word, as a sponsor. I'll do what I can, but—"

"Of course they won't! Who are you, anyway? But if he can't go to their school, he can at least be tutored. That your grimoire?" She pointed at the bound volume lying by Tristan's saddle.

Tristan nodded. "My master's. But it's mine now."

"Good. Then if you can't remember the spells, you can read them to him. That will do very well, master wizard."

Useless to protest that he was too unsure of his own magic to dare instruct someone else. She'd either disbelieve him or cook up some worse means of payment. Tristan took Crewzel's outstretched hand, and together they spoke a word of binding to seal the bargain.

# Instructions Magical

"GOOD," Crewzel said. "That's done. Now just to show you that I'm not a heartless creature—altogether—I'll do you a favor, Tristan. I'm going to show you how to earn a decent living here, with your magic. It's the little niceties that ensure only coins are thrown your way. Clean yourself up—when a crowd sees those tomato stains, it'll only give 'em ideas they don't need—and wait for me here. I'll be back at sunfall."

She was off, crooking a finger for Delmon to follow. He put Thomas down with a sigh and gave his new tutor a look of inspection as he passed him.

*That boy'll go far. Knows how to treat a cat.*

Tristan tickled Thomas' chin.

"So do I. And look where I've got."

*You haven't spent a whole morning petting me since the day we first met. Growing up spoils boys.*

"The same might be said of kittens," Tristan said, standing up. He'd plenty of time before he needed to think about cleaning his clothes. The talk with Crewzel had taken a long time, but it was still only a couple of hours past sunhigh. He'd better make himself useful. Polassar would never think that the mere securing of their lodgings was sufficient employment for him—he'd better set about cleaning the place as well.

He spent the afternoon sweeping and scraping at the dirt floor, getting the loose debris out and removing the bumps from their sleeping corner. Then he scoured the neighborhood until he found a well-grown patch of bracken and made them a more comfortable bed of it. They could burn the straw in place of wood.

Allaire's afternoon was equally full. She sat atop a wall near the roof and listened to Polassar's stories of his heroics, which proved to be as endless as Crewzel's list of grievances at the world.

Apparently Crewzel's word was as good as her vocabulary. The sun had barely dipped below the edge of the city's walls when she reappeared, clad in motley and carrying a tambourine. She slapped it smartly against her leg as she inspected Tristan.

"I don't suppose you've got any other clothes?" she asked critically. "Well, never mind. Just keep your cloak about you."

Tristan meekly did so as he followed her out the door, pausing to drop a quick word in Elisena's ear. He didn't know if he would be late, and Polassar and Allaire should be occupied with supper for a good while, but he didn't want them deciding to have a look at the town afterwards and strolling off without his guidance.

*I feel exactly the same way about you,* Thomas said, trotting busily after him.

With the rain holding off for the evening, Kôvelir's nightlife was more varied than ever. They passed acrobats and tumblers, sword throwers, and sword swallowers. When they came upon a rope walker, Tristan had eyes for nothing else, until Crewzel annoyedly dragged him away. Tristan simply couldn't understand how anyone could juggle oranges, balance a ball on the crown of his head, and dance a jig, all while teetering on a rope strung fifteen feet above the pavement and a jostling crowd.

*He's probably got a glue-spell on the rope,* Thomas said deprecatingly.

"All the same, I know what'd happen if I tried that kind of trick."

A conjuror was pulling incredible lengths of silk from his clothing—miles of the stuff, by the varicolored heaps that already lay at his feet. When the pile lapped his knees, he spoke words to it, gathering up as much of the cloth as was possible in his encircling arms. The silk shimmered, writhed, and somehow there was a lovesome wench in his embrace. She smiled, kissed her master, and ran off into the crowd, her silks trailing after her like the feathers of the Timbrid bird.

Tristan watched that and other marvels as they passed through the crowds, silently resolving that he'd try nothing of a magical nature again so long as he was within Kôve-lir's walls. He felt a fool, utterly incapable of the smallest magics, far less a brilliant, moneymaking creation.

That ill-considered resolve was swiftly tested, as Crewzel finally selected a spot for her night's work and jabbed a finger in the direction of the paving stones at her feet.

"Make me a table," she directed.

"A table?" What in the world—

"To lay the cards on," she explained patiently. "Any sort will do, though 'twould be nice if you'd cover it with bright silk. This act could do with a higher tone."

"But I can't—I thought I was just going to watch—" His past inadequacies and outright failures danced before Tristan's dazed eyes.

"Wolfbane! Are you a wizard or not? Make a table, I say! You should be glad to oblige a lady. A nice solid table, mind. Nothing rickety."

Tristan swallowed hard and gave in. No failure of his spell was as potentially humiliating as the tongue-lashing he was going to get momentarily if he didn't make Crewzel the table she required.

He shut his eyes, tried to set a spell from the grimoire glowing in the dark inside his head. It wasn't strictly applicable, but if he rearranged it thus, and so—

His fingers weaving, Tristan knelt and described the outlines of a table with his hands, eyes still closed. Something was happening as he spoke the spell—already he felt the knotty wood under his fingers. It would be a rough sort of table, but Crewzel had said nothing fancy. Yes, it was definitely taking form. It might not be visible yet, though, so he kept his eyes tight shut, for fear of losing his precious concentration.

There. It was surely solid now. He spoke the words that locked it in.

Someone giggled. Tristan opened his eyes, lost his balance and fell over backwards as a table-sized turtle lumbered toward him. It regarded him mildly, nibbling at his sweater before wandering off through the crowd in search of food. A silver coin spun through the air, rebounding painfully from the tip of Tristan's nose. His audience departed, still laughing side-splittingly.

"I suppose you think that's funny—" Crewzel said furiously, dragging him to his feet with a tug that wrenched his whole arm. Tristan rubbed at his wrist, and said nothing.

*Actually, I thought it was pretty good. Very lifelike, no one would ever guess it was only a magical turtle.*

Tristan just glared at the cat, then made haste after Crewzel, who seemed to be doing her best to lose him in the crowd.

He finally caught up just as she seated herself on the tiled ledge that rimmed a splashy fountain.

"As good a table as any," she sighed resignedly, signing him to sit beside her. Tristan watched the jets of water playing about the unicorn in the fountain's center and tried to tell himself that none of this mattered. He wouldn't be here that long, or need to see any of these folk again—

"Never mind," Crewzel said, unexpectedly soothing, as she patted his arm.

"Are you sure you still want me to instruct your son?" he asked bitterly.

"You probably just weren't trained for this kind of magic," she said. "I assume you haven't had to live by it, since you've obviously lived to grow up?"

"No. My master and I did mostly weather-witching, rain and all that, and some love charms. We weren't on the road. Nothing like this was ever called for. But I should still be able to—"

"You're just not a creative showman," Crewzel interrupted. "As evidenced by your performance last night. You don't know yet what people want. They don't like pretty magics, not enough to pay for them. Folk like a touch of the unknown, or a bit of spice, and to think that they might see blood spilled—specifically, yours."

Tristan surpressed a shiver.

"And remember, not everyone in Kôvelir's a mage, able to appreciate the fine points of a sorcery. A lot of 'em are just here for the magic-market—swords, rings, advice, cloaks of invisibility. They're impressed by different things. It may be that your mistakes will amuse them, if they don't know they're mistakes."

*It's a thought.*

"If you could just do those screw-ups to order—"

"I can't do anything to order," he said angrily.

"Never mind. Just be quiet and watch, then."

She began to deal the cards, laying them out one by one on the damp stone. The figures on the cards seemed to shimmer. Tristan blinked, thinking the shimmer to be caused by barely held-back tears in his eyes.

Within the shallow framework of the cards, the figures came to life at Crewzel's touch.

Two tiny swordsmen stood up, challenged each other and began to fence, their blows ringing lightly, as sewing needles might if hit together. On another card, a woman lovely as a miniature Allaire lifted a golden cup, pledging a man seated by her at a banquet table. The man turned his head to thank her for the cup, and Tristan saw his own face there, unmistakably. Shaken, he looked to Crewzel, but she was as intent on the cards as he.

"You must still be charged up from that magic," she muttered. "I can't pick up anything except your influences, and you're not even touching them! Would you mind damping it down a bit so I can get a bearing on someone who's apt to pay for my reading his future?"

Useless to say he'd have already done so, if he'd known how. Tristan watched the cards, fascinated. Now the figures of the man and the woman were rising to their gemlike feet, embracing. Their pinpoint lips met—

Thomas' paw fetched him a needle-pointed wallop on his left ear. Tristan yelped, and the cards went dark, lighting again eventually, but with an aimless glowing that was very different from their former light.

"Never seen anything like that. The cards taken over totally, and no hand but mine on them. Whatever that was, you must want it a lot—"

Tristan rubbed at his ear.

"Can you do it again?" She shoved the cards at him. Tristan took them reluctantly, but there was no reaction from the cards this time. He'd somehow known there wouldn't be.

"You're full of surprises, aren't you, wizard?" Crewzel asked, her voice soft and puzzled, both of which suited her, unfamiliar as they were to her lips.

"Where'd you get these cards?" Tristan asked, afraid she'd see or guess her way too close to the truth of his quest. He fingered the back of one card, wondering at magic signs embossed there, unlike any he'd ever seen.

"Giffyd made them. I told you he knew more than was good for him."

One of the cards lit, but Tristan could make out only a dark shape on it before both Crewzel and cards were turned away from him as she said, "Your fortune, sir? Shall it be by card or water?" She dabbled a hand in the fountain, looking up at a raven-cloaked man who'd paused by them.

He was peering intently at Tristan, though, not at Crewzel or her spread deck of cards. Alarmed, Tristan did his best to look nondescript, and felt Thomas go stiff against his leg. The man was more than common tall; that and his clothing gave him the semblance of a cypress tree's shadow.

"Who's this? I've not seen him about the city before. Pick him up on your travels?" His voice was fully half as chill as the worst wind off the Winterwaste.

"A friend of my late husband's, sir," Crewzel lied, easily as cold as the caverns of Darkenkeep.

"Ah? You'll do well to remember, wench, why your late husband *is* your late husband."

He stalked off, and Crewzel spat on the pavement behind him, narrowly missing the trailing edge of his long shadow, while Tristan gazed in perplexity at the scene.

"That swine! I took him for a customer at first, he's disguised his face—ware of him, should you meet again."

No fear, Tristan thought, but only nodded, wondering how to avoid a man who could change his face at will.

"Who is he?"

"An old acquaintance. I doubt he'll seriously bother you, though perhaps you'd do well not to be seen with me—it's me he wants." She sounded annoyed now, not panicked, though he'd have sworn at first that she was closer to terror.

"What he said about your husband—he didn't—"

"No. But he could have helped, at the time, and that he didn't do."

Just then the black shape faded from the card, and Tristan felt easier. Crewzel apparently did too; her face altered, and she brightened as she laid the cards out once more. Tristan wondered how he'd thought her merely bothered by the man.

"Telling futures isn't so tricky," she explained briskly. "My only gift's in being able to see exactly what the marks want to hear. And that wanting's oft far from the truth, I assure you. In fact, that's your first lesson."

By the end of the evening he'd had others, many more than he could absorb at once. Crewzel was almost continually busy with her future-telling. It seemed she was well known and sought after despite her poor-mouthing of herself. Persons of all classes came to consult her, the better dressed somewhat furtively, as if they'd no wish to be seen in either the place or the company, here amongst the lowly. They paid well, though, either in coin or in small cloth bags that might have held anything but smelled of spices. Tristan poked into one, disappointed to find only peppercorns inside. He'd been half expecting gems, camouflaged by the smell of spices and herbs. Crewzel slapped his prying fingers without looking up from her cards, but seemed willing to let him continue holding her night's take. Better she remain unencumbered, he supposed, wondering if he were taking Delmon's usual job.

She played her customers skillfully. There was never any doubt. Each person got exactly the sort of news he or she expected, but so deftly worded that none of them suspected the simplicity of her readings. Crewzel's speech could be terse or flowery, but always it was carefully keyed or counterpointed to her listener's character.

And when he grew tired of her readings, there was always the rest of Kôvelir's unending show to amuse Tristan. He noticed now a bell-capped jester, who kept disappearing into a brass mirror carried by a tall lady whose head was wreathed in purple pasque-flowers. And there was a trained pig, for whom second-sight was claimed, and the blind juggler who worked with poison-tipped knives . . .

Everywhere were men garbed in flowing robes in somber colors—gray, brown, murrey, black. Tristan knew those robes marked their respective grades in the Mage's School, from apprentices to acolytes to the mages themselves, though he couldn't quite recall just which color signified what. There weren't many of the black robes about, so those must mark a high grade indeed, or a dangerous one. Despite the hubbub in the square, his eyelids were drooping. This had been a long day for him though he couldn't remember when the bells had last chimed or guess the hour. Thomas had long since expressed boredom and departed.

Crewzel elbowed him awake.

"You're worse than Delmon, and you've not his excuse of youth! Come on now, time we bought some supper."

Tristan was agreeable to that. He had a few coppers to call his own—some of Crewzel's better-dressed customers had been generous after a good reading, especially since he'd held their fine cloaks safe out of the mud while they conferred with her. Even a cloak-rack was worthy of some sort of hire. And he could do with a meal, the sooner the better.

Crewzel seemed pleased with her night's income. She tallied the coins rapidly, hid a few in the hem of her skirt, and proceeded to a wine shop. There she bought a medium-sized dark jug, which Tristan was constrained to carry for her.

"We'll have a fine evening," she promised with an expansive wave of her hand. "Your big friend too. In payment for whatever he did to the roof—I might keep a few chickens in there, when you've gone. And wine may make him a trifle friendlier to you."

They bought hot pastries next, envelopes of rich dough filled with meat and potatoes and gravy. The price was fair, and Crewzel said they tasted fine cold too, and kept well. From the savory odors they exuded, Tristan doubted that many of them got a chance to cool.

He bought more oats, with Elisena's griddle-cakes in mind, and, because Crewzel's mere presence seemed to get him better prices than he might have haggled for on his own, a little pot of honey, a jug of cream, and a fish.

"I hope that's for your cat," Crewzel sniffed. "Because if you're intending to eat it yourself, there'll be nothing left of it once you've boned it. And what are those for? Going to start a flower patch?"

She pointed at a little sack of sunflower seeds Tristan was carefully tucking under his belt.

"A surprise," he said, smiling. He gathered their various bundles into his arms and indicated that he was ready to follow her.

"Well, at least you can carry more than Delmon—"

They were just passing into the darkness beyond an archway when Tristan felt part of his load slip and heard something hit the ground with a soft thud. He knelt, groping for it with one hand; as he did so, he felt the air stirred by something beside his left ear.

It might have been Crewzel's skirt, but it wasn't. Metal rattled on the cobbles, and he stared transfixed at a dagger hilted with a silver panther's paw.

Luckily, his fencer's reflexes were still sharp. Tristan's sword was clear of its scabbard and in a low guard position before he was back on his feet.

For a moment he couldn't make out his assailant, or even Crewzel. Curse these deep shadows—

One of the shadows shifted a little, and he saw a white blur behind it. It took him an instant to realize that what he saw were Crewzel's fists, as she flailed at her attacker. With a shout, Tristan came to his feet and lunged simultaneously.

His point hit the shadow dead in the center of its back— and passed right through.

There was no sensation of his having struck anything. Tristan overbalanced and landed on his knees and outflung left hand, skidding. There was no sound except for the clang of his sword on the pavement and Crewzel's gasping. Then there was a little *pop*, and the dagger vanished.

"A seeming," Crewzel finally managed. "Cheris—the man we met tonight. It's his style and his dagger."

Tristan didn't venture an opinion. He was too busy keeping his heart in his chest and out of his throat, where it threatened to choke him.

"But why didn't you run?" Crewzel blurted out, in a bewildered way. "He was after *me*—"

Tristan fingered a deep scrape on his hand. Lucky he hadn't broken his wrist, landing like that. Serve him right, he'd ignored everything Blais had ever tried to drill into him concerning the importance of balance in swordplay. When he had his breath again, he began gathering up the parcels, pleased that nothing seemed to have broken or gotten stepped on, not even the wine.

"Why didn't you run?" Crewzel repeated insistently.

It simply hadn't occurred to him, but Tristan hated to admit such unself-preserving stupidity to her, somehow. She wouldn't understand it.

"Let's just go," he growled.

"You certainly do have your uses," Crewzel said, sounding as if his snap had brought her back to herself, and led off lightly. From her manner, no one would ever have guessed that death had brushed them so close.

They were late rejoining the others, but the sight of the wine jug improved Polassar's temper remarkably. Once he'd opened it and sampled the contents, he seemed willing to forget all anger over their "dawdling" while the rest of the party "had waited hungry." He didn't even bother examining the food they'd brought until much later.

Elisena had brewed a tea of mint leaves, which was wonderfully freshening, and more to Tristan's taste than the wine. He took a few long swallows before spreading out their supper. Allaire smiled at him, and even helped set the things out. The touch of her fingers as their hands accidentally brushed was so sweet as to cancel out the pain of his scratched hand.

The fire's glow encouraged feelings of comradeship. Crewzel left briefly, returning with a sleepy Delmon who would have been better left abed, and they settled down close to the flames, swapping stories and pleasantries as they ate their meal. Tristan said little, being content to listen and overly aware that Allaire's silk-clad thigh was only a palm's width away from his own leg.

The unexplained bag of sunflower seeds was opened now, and Tristan fed them one by one to Minstrel, who loved them inordinately. He chirped impatiently when Tristan was slow shelling them for him. After critical examination, Thomas was pleased with the fish, too, and had eaten it neatly to the last shred before indulging himself in a thorough washing. He climbed to Tristan's lap then, fixing the yellow flames with his uncompromising gaze.

"You'd think he saw all the secrets of the universe there," Elisena said.

"No," Tristan answered blithely—he'd just had a swallow of the wine, which was singing in his tired head. "Those are in the Mages' Library. And tomorrow we go to seek them." The wine had lulled his anxieties about that, too.

"I'd almost forgot why you were here," Crewzel said. Delmon was asleep again, leaning against her side.

"Now, wizard, surely you don't expect us to spend another day penned up here, while you go wandering?" Polassar only sounded half drunk, so he might well mean that at least half seriously.

Tristan waved his hand dismissingly.

"Of course not. You could check the bazaars—never know what you might overhear that might be useful to us. But you will be discreet, won't you?"

He was belatedly alarmed, not sure he ought to turn Polassar loose in the city. Asking Polassar to show caution was like asking a thunderstorm to be careful of flowers.

"Aye, no fear, wizard. We'll speak not a word of our purpose, no matter how trusty the folk may seem. We'll be ears only—"

That seemed unlikely. But Tristan was too sleepy for debate. Better to sit here and watch the soothing flames.

Things magical aside, no one seemed to be feeling too badly about him now, Tristan thought happily, just before sleep claimed him and stopped that nonsense.

# Master Cabal

TRISTAN HAD NOT SUSPECTED that the main part of the city would be quite so big, or half so noisy, or so grand. Nothing in the squalid, half-glimpsed alleys had prepared him for it. The morning was new, the air around him and Elisena bright and chill.

"Is it really autumn?" he asked her.

"By the rains, it is. Need you ask?" Elisena pointed at a glistening puddle.

"It was summer, when we went into Darkenkeep. Just begun, really. We were only there a few hours: I'd swear to that. Not even a full day. Yet now it's nearly winter. And I can't account for any more than two weeks, out of all that time."

"Nímir's time is not as ours."

Once she'd mentioned reading the old languages, he'd stopped being surprised at the things she knew. With access to books anything was possible, and who knew what had been mouldering unremembered in Radak all these years? She was perfectly correct about Nímir's time, too. It was a fact remarked upon in many histories.

The streets they passed along now were wider, straighter, and the buildings fronting them were covered in marble of many colors, in place of the former thatch, wattle and obscenities. Now and then a well-dressed servant hastened by, intent upon some morning errand.

Their way coincided with one such, and thus brought them out into a square that was serving as a food market. Piles of vegetables and fruit brightened the gray pavement, more lovely than flowers to the eyes of hunger. They each had a tart apple by way of breakfast. The fruit vendor levitated their coin into the till with a gracefully negligent gesture that much fascinated Tristan. He watched closely, trying to pick up the fingerplay. Truly, this city was built on magic. Small wonder his own impressed no one.

They strolled by a noble building with elegantly fluted doorposts, its walkway edged in pale green marble inlaid with garnets and sapphires in delicate tracery. Gryffons and winged deer sported among hellebore flowers within the design. The paving tiles themselves were set in an elegant fan pattern.

"It's nice to see Kôvelir isn't all thieves and cut-throats," Tristan said. "This is more like the city the bards sing of."

"It all depends on where you enter. That's the great Water Gate, over to sunward, by the Est. I believe the way we came in is called Thieves Gate."

"That explains a great deal. Still and all, it's likely the last place Galan will think to look for us."

"I doubt he's really looking at all." She bent to examine a hedge of rosemary.

"Is he really—" Tristan began, breaking off in confusion.

"Really what?" She looked up brightly, tilting her head to one side.

"No, forget it." His face felt hot. "It was very impertinent of me. I'm sorry I—"

"You were going to ask me if he's really my father," she said simply. "Well, you heard what Polassar said he called me."

"Changeling?" She couldn't really mean—

"Exactly. He's old enough to have fathered me—barely. And my mother was his woman, of course, or so others have told me. She died in childbirth, so I cannot ask her of it. I'm not sure what to believe. He wouldn't own to me, except when it suited him. Otherwise he says I could be anyone's. For all purposes, I can't say I ever knew parents."

Her tone, far from being depressed by the sense of her sad story, was nearly gay.

"He kept me because I was useful. I'm quite good with herbs, so it was handy. I suppose he never thought how easy it would have been to poison him." She smiled at Tristan, sidelong.

"My own story's more romantic than that," he countered, trying to match her playful boastings of misfortunes, or top them. "I was left in an orchard. On Midwinter's Night. My parents can't have thought much of me, because it was surely bitter cold."

"It prepared you for the Winterwaste." That odd wisdom again.

"Yes. I suppose it did." He sobered, as he fell unwillingly to thinking of it, and all lightness of mood left him.

He had never felt any burning desire to learn about his real parents, nothing like the zeal which might have been expected. Blais had always seemed sure they must be dead, though he'd never mentioned why he thought so. As if living folk never abandoned a child! But Blais had doubted that Tristan was some Dunehollow fisherman's by-blow— or that those phantom parents had been local folk at all. That corner of Calandra was simply too small; the secret would never have remained so. And no one from those parts would have possessed that great battered sword, or left it beside a squalling baby if they had.

In any case, Tristan didn't wonder about it now, any more than a cast-off kitten might have done. Blais' books had early taught him that wizards were often nameless, until their deeds made their own names.

"And the wizard took you in, then?"

"Mmmmmm?" He was too far away for casual recall. "Nothing. I think we want to go left here."

The gates of the great Library were hewn of hard green stone, almost as dark as spring grass. Their surface was inlaid with shining brass, in whorls and spirals and arcs— not an angle in the lot, as if straight lines had no place in its magic. They drew closer, and Tristan discovered that each curving line was in fact a string of letters or words. Some were in tongues he knew, and some in languages long forgotten, their last speakers ages dead. He saw musical notes and magic runes among them, some picked out in silver, as if they had special virtue. The sheer labor involved was staggering.

The bell was of brass, delicately silvered, shaped in the likeness of a singing bird on a quince branch. Its feathers seemed to tremble in the wind, so exquisitely were they wrought.

"Minstrel would fall quite in love with this." Tristan put

out a cautious finger to it, and it answered with a sweet chiming before he'd even touched the metal. "He'd try to outsing it all day." The chimes gently faded into the cool air, and he regretted that he'd asked the canary to stay with Thomas. He might as well have come. But were animals permitted in the Library? Even familiars, one of which Thomas for all purposes was, despite his disclaimers?

A panel, invisible when closed, opened suddenly in the left-hand gate, making Tristan start and step back. A slight young man stood within, proudly wearing the scarlet robe of an adept.

He inquired as to their business, eyeing Tristan skeptically the while. Tristan half winced, knowing the poor impression he must make. The adept's robe was surely silk, and the thread that stitched the runes at his throat could be nothing less than gold. He wasn't only well-schooled but apparently he was wealthy, advantaged, at the least, and very self-sure. Tristan stammered maddeningly as he told the youth why they'd come and that he begged admittance. He felt sick—he might have known those stains would never come out of his clothes. The spell he'd tried had only set them. Why hadn't he thought of riding up on Valadan? Curse his stupidity—

"You say your master sent you?" the adept asked disinterestedly. "Pray, what is his name? I'm sorry, but I don't see how I can let you in. I—"

Tristan didn't hear the rest. He had already turned away, to hide the flush of shame spreading across his cheeks. To have come all this way and then not be let in— after all, as Crewzel had said, who was he?

This defeat was crushing, for all he'd expected it from the moment he set eyes on the adept. What were they going to do now? Everyone had been trusting him, expecting he'd make everything right. He was a wizard, wasn't he? And now simply because he was a stranger here, didn't have proper clothes, or know the ways of the place— The adept's voice rippled smoothly on, conciliatory, explaining.

"This library is really only for the mages, you understand that? I'm responsible for admissions today, and—"

"What's the trouble, Howun?"

The speaker was an old man in a black robe, bearded so

lushly and so whitely that Tristan was reminded painfully of Blais—save that he'd never seen his master gowned so fine. The mage had been passing by the door, intent on a page from his grimoire, but he'd heard enough to invoke his curiosity. Under his glance, Tristan wished himself very small and invisible. At least the adept hadn't slammed the portal in his face, but one of the mages of Kôvelir certainly would.

Elisena stood just behind him, neither helping nor hindering.

The adept stepped back from the gate diffidently.

"They wish admission, m'lord Cabal. He says his master sent him. I've never heard the name, and I don't know who she is. I apologize if I did wrong, Master, but as I say, I don't know them, and—" he glanced meaningfully at Tristan, curling his lips in distaste. "Well *anyway*—" *How provincial*, his tone seemed to say.

"Yes, I see. It's all right, Howun; you may go. I'll handle this. Have you travelled a long way?" The last remark was directed at Tristan.

Tristan nodded, surprised at having a second chance to plead.

"Yes. We only arrived in your city a day ago."

"And your master sent you? What is his name?"

"Blais." Not that it mattered. If only the name of a mage could gain him entrance, what use was the name of an old wizard no one here had ever heard of?

"*Blais?* Blais of Calandra?"

"Yes, m'lord," Tristan said slowly, curious as to the interest in the old voice. It took him a moment to realize that he had never mentioned Calandra.

The portal swung open, so swiftly that Tristan had to step back smartly out of its way. The mage's wrinkle-hatched face was now broken by a broad smile. He waved them in.

Half stunned by the suddenness of the move, Tristan stepped through, Elisena after him. The mage quickly led them to a bench beside a splashing fountain. He sat Tristan down there, while Elisena bent discreetly over some herbs that grew by the water. Many of the herbs were planted in tubs, so that they might easily be moved to shelter during cold spells, Tristan distractedly noticed.

"Blais of Calandra! I have not heard that name or thought of him in years!" The mage sat, sprang up, then paced rapidly about, as if in the grip of some great excitement. "We studied together, in the Mages' School, many years ago. We were both young then." He saw Tristan's blank look. "You did not know that he studied in Kôvelir? I should have thought he would have spoken of it. That was longer ago than I care to think, but we both pledged we'd return one day. I never left, as it chanced. I instruct the young boys now, in the school here. Has he sent you for further training? Come, how does my old friend?"

"My lord, I'm sorry. He's dead." The words came so matter-of-factly, betraying none of the searing pain inside him. He'd been so close to Blais for so long—was that why he could hardly recall what the mage looked like? The tighter he tried to clutch the memory, the more elusive it became.

"Dead?" The pacing stopped. Their eyes locked. Tristan saw that his pain was shared, perhaps surpassed.

"That's why I'm here. He didn't really send me," Tristan admitted reluctantly. "That was my own idea. It was the only thing I could think of—this was the only place left to turn. Blais entrusted me with the quest, you see. And I don't know what to do about it."

"Quest?" Cabal had sat down beside him once more, and spoke from behind a hand which covered his face.

Could he truly not understand? Not know? Or was he only distracted by grief? Tristan opened his mouth to elaborate, but Cabal spoke first.

"Wait, I—yes, I recall it now. For sure, he was always speaking of it! Whatever we did, or studied, it was never far from his thoughts, not for long. His quest. Something about a ring, wasn't it?"

"*His* quest? Surely all the world's, m'lord."

"Oh. I'm sorry—what did you say your name was?"

"Tristan." Was the man wandering in his mind? For certain he was old, but the mind didn't always age as the body did.

"I'm sorry, Tristan, I didn't think. Of course it was all the world to Blais, and would seem doubly so to you, with only him to teach you."

All the world to Blais? Something this important must be

known to everyone—this was the one place in all the wide
world where he'd have expected to be instantly understood.
Tristan felt suddenly alien, lost, as if all the colors of the
world had gone wrong and he were falling helpless from a
great height while hideous flying things screamed and
snatched at him.

His own voice, so calm it came perilously close to hys-
teria, was saying, "Are you trying to tell me that no one
here knows the story of Allaire of the Nine Rings? But
surely all the mages must know, it affects the whole—"

"Well, there's a song, I think, or there used to be. Some
of the bards sing it, but it's never been what you might call
popular. And of course I recall a bit of what Blais used to
say about it, but—" Cabal seemed suddenly to become
aware of Tristan's shocked face, and read his feelings from
it.

"Tristan, you must forgive us. Try to see what it's been
like here. Blais raised you alone, did he not?"

Tristan nodded dazedly.

"Yes, I thought as much. And I'll wager you've not been
so far from home before?"

If he could only know, Tristan thought; but he couldn't
find his tongue, or trust it if he did. He felt ill.

"This may have seemed recent history to Blais," Cabal
went on. "But it really happened long ages ago. Mages
from all the world may once have followed the quest, but
so few ever returned. You'll know that from your studies, I
expect. Yes? None have left here in the last several life-
times. And with Calandra at war within herself for so long,
no one goes there at all, unless into exile. Even Esdragon
we barely trade with, except for farm goods, and as for
contact with the mages there—" He spread his hands helplessly. "Blais was the only man I ever met who'd lived
there. It has become impossible to learn what goes on
across the Est. So it has all been ignored and ultimately
forgotten."

Tristan looked more horrified than before, if possible.

"Forgotten?" He stared around the courtyard, wild-eyed.
It was their business to remember it here, along with all
other deeds of magic and sorcery. A whole land, and all its
wizards, simply cast out of the collective mind of Kôvelir's
mages? Forgotten?

Tristan stifled a groan. And he'd been so careful to mention nothing of their quest to Crewzel, and had taken such pains to find them secret lodgings and keep Allaire hidden! He needn't have bothered, no one here would have guessed the slightest truth about her. He'd been running from shadows. All that pointless secrecy!

"I'm sorry, but it's true. I'm possibly the only man in the city who would guess what you were talking about. You've been fortunate to find the one man still in Kôvelir who knew Blais really well. My name is Cabal, by the way."

Tristan sat up straighter, forcing his mind to order. He wasn't a child, was he, to fall apart at a minor setback? However much it forced him to revise years of thinking. He shoved a thousand questions and sidelines to the farthest cobwebby corners of the back of his mind—let them torture him later, when he'd time—and thrust straight to the heart of the current problem. Blais had trusted him with his quest, and if he could expect no help from the mages who'd forgotten their great enemy, then he'd do without that help.

"My lord Cabal, the city *will* take this seriously when Nímir spreads his power into Kôvelir. I know his might. I've felt it."

Cabal smiled uncertainly.

"I suppose we've trusted to the Est, all these years. It's a mighty barrier to magic." His tone suggested that he merely humored Tristan's inexperienced worries.

"I crossed it."

"Of course you did. How else does one get from Calandra to Kôvelir? We control the ferry, and it's protected by the most powerful runes years of research have devised. Nímir will not—"

"Not by the ferry. Upstream, by horse."

Cabal looked startled. Tristan could see his thoughts working: a wizard crossing running water on the scale of the Est? Tristan began to suspect he'd be taken more seriously now.

"And it's only a barrier as long as it's flowing," he went on. "Nímir will probably freeze it solid from source to seaflow. He must be stopped before he reaches the Est."

Cabal nodded, as if the notion was no stranger to him. Glacial cold seemed to lap the room.

"Is that why you've come, to be trained for the fight?"

"Trained?" Tristan came back to himself. "No, m'lord. I need to see some of your books. I think there are things here that are nowhere else to be found now."

"Of course. At your disposal. And the girl?"

Elisena had such a quiet way about her, Tristan had forgotten her entirely. She stood near now, waiting—not expectantly, or even patiently, but effortlessly, like a tree or a grassy plain with the wind stirring over it. His face flushing with an embarrassment which Cabal waved away, Tristan explained why she'd come with him, without bothering to go into details. If she didn't want to trade on her iffy relationship with Galan, he certainly wouldn't.

"A second pair of eyes will be useful to you, certainly. Pay no mind to stares, girl; women don't often venture into the Library . . ."

He rose, and led them along a cloistered walk between the gateway and a row of windowless buildings. The mages had taken no chances—their home would survive sieges other than the magical sort. The blank-faced buildings would serve as a second wall for defense purposes, and doubtless there were other features whose uses were likewise double and unobtrusive.

"A shortsighted policy, to exclude women from our schools—well, nay, discourage only, but 'tis the same in the end. Many useful things they contributed in the past, especially in the herbal arts. Though of course we manage to keep those up—"

This was obvious enough. Even the spaces between the paving-bricks were thickly grown with cresses and mosses whose seeds had medicinal value. Not a speck of ground within the encircling walls was without its valued crop, not a crumb of the magic-laced soil was wasted.

"No one will trouble either of you. I'll set my mark on you. It will be your password." Cabal touched their palms with the tip of his oaken staff, leaving a single rune glowing painlessly there. The rune was not one Tristan had encountered before.

"That will grant you free passage here for at least a week, before it begins to fade. No more difficulties with Howun, eh?"

Cabal clapped an arm about Tristan, much as Blais might have done.

"Howun means well enough. It's not his fault that he's never gone hungry. I confess if it hadn't been for Blais' name, I might have turned you away myself. We're used to receiving disguised royalty here, and others who'd prefer their true identities not be known, but we get our share of mendicants too, and must discourage them—so long as we're ruled by a Council which insists we do so! But pay my grumblings no mind, we must live by rules, however some rules may chafe."

They'd halted before a flight of cedar-wood steps, wide and shallow, which led to a crystal-roofed building. It was far from the tallest building in Kôvelir, but it might well be the largest in terms of interior space. Tristan knew the whole of it couldn't be seen from any one spot. Only birds perceived the Library entire.

Cabal was silent a moment, and his next words were soft.

"I'm sorry to hear about Blais. You can't know. Are you sure you wouldn't like to stay, if only for a little while?" His glance brushed the stains, travel and otherwise, on Tristan's clothes.

"I heard rumors this morning about a street magician, some sort of misfortune with a chamberpot? Blais didn't quite finish your training, did he?"

"No. He didn't live long enough. There's still so much I don't know, don't understand—" No harm in admitting it, certainly. And no shame. He'd long since passed that stage.

"Then stay with us a while," Cabal suggested. "We can help you finish up that training. And afterwards, who knows?"

"Thank you, Master Cabal, but Blais had close to twenty years to teach me what a wizard should know. If he couldn't teach me, I doubt you can help me."

The mage seemed troubled.

"We can discuss this at greater length later, perhaps. I'll show you to the book rooms now. I'm late for an appointment; you've excited me so that I quite forgot it. I should like to talk to you again, soon. Tomorrow, perhaps."

"Perhaps. I can't promise."

"Make a point of it." His sternness sounded almost fatherly. Cabal took them to the top of the steps, then stopped.

"I don't suppose you could tell me what success Blais had with his quest?" he asked wistfully. "You've brought back such memories of him. I'd forgotten how his talk of it intrigued me."

Tristan looked long at his face—the first kind one he'd seen turned to him since they arrived in Kôvelir, if he discounted Crewzel's enigmatic behavior.

I really could stay here, he thought. He truly wants me to, he treats me as if I were Blais' son. I'd have a place here, a future, and maybe I could learn. To be a real wizard, at last—

"No," he said, feeling the renouncing of his dreams keenly. "It wouldn't be safe—for you. Blais died for what he knew."

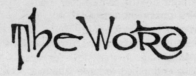

THE SCROLL was a ram skin, well seasoned and tanned whole. The letters sketched on it were so minute and closely spaced as to make the skin appear solid black, even from a few inches away. Tristan finished the line he was reading and unrolled the next section carefully.

He sat back, rubbing his eyes with the heel of one hand, while the other held his place in the writing. The daylight that filtered through the crystal roof was fading—it must be near sunset.

Elisena looked up from the herbal that had tempted her away from their search.

"Did you find something?"

"I'm not sure." Tristan took his other hand away from the scroll and began massaging his temples. "I've read so much these last three days, I can't call back any of it. I hope it will come later, when I'm not so tired." He shut his eyes for a long-promised minute.

She came to stand behind him.

"No wonder you're weary. What language is that?" She fingered the black letters hesitantly.

"It's so old it has no name. Blais had a book in it, too, and he didn't know what it was either. I wonder how long it's been since there was anyone here who could read it?"

"I've never seen its like before." She frowned, leaning closer.

"This looks like the same hand Blais' book is in, too. It may be a cipher only used by one mage." He sighed. "I wish I thought these spells would work for me. Or that they applied to our problem." Or that anything he'd read did.

"They have a look of power, even unread." Her hair brushed his, and he felt a crystal touch his cheek.

"I wouldn't dare read some of them out loud, Elisena. This might even be the grimoire of the Master Mage of Calandra, the one who made the rings! It was never found, supposedly, after he disappeared. Neither was he, for that matter. I wonder how it came here? Think of it lying here all these years, unknown, unread!"

He let his eyes rest on it again.

"They can't have known what it was—look at the dust stains here. It's hung on that wall for ages, before I happened to see it and asked to have it down. And how lightly they gave it to me! As if it weren't valuable at all. Surely they haven't so many great books here that such a treasure is nothing to them?"

"Does it mention the ring?"

He sighed again.

"No. Not so far. Or not directly. Sometimes there are spells hidden between lines of writing that you can't see unless you know the key-rune. Like something you only see out the corner of your eye—that goes away if you look straight at it." Tristan rubbed at his nose. "It really might come to me later, while I'm thinking about something else. It's like that sometimes. I've only a little more to go on this section. If the light holds I can finish it today." He bent back to the task, hating the inconsiderate haste he must use. Such a thing was meant to be savored, absorbed little by little, and there were shades of meaning—the words claimed him again, he thought of nothing else, not even recent past events and discouragements.

* * *

Tristan had seen Cabal twice more, briefly, both times in the Library, and once asked his help with an obscure concept. Cabal had been both patient and helpful, explaining far more than he needed to. He tugged at his beard, arranged his robes around him on the marble bench, and paged through several books in search of the most cogent explanation.

"Let me see. How far did Blais take you with this? Do you know of Jehirmick's precept? Farinon expresses it most clearly, I think, though Ingenlin's works have value also—"

Cabal broached the subject of his entering the school again, of course. There would be no need for Tristan to begin as an apprentice, he said, as if that might have been the problem. His training with Blais would certainly give him some sort of higher status, however unofficial. It would be worth his consideration.

With perhaps a shade more regret, now that he'd had a taste of how fine life here might be, Tristan declined again. He had no business even to consider such a thing, with the quest still unfulfilled. He would have liked to explain that more fully to Cabal, but was reluctant for the same reasons as before. He liked the elderly mage, didn't want to endanger him. Let all Kôvelir forget Allaire, then; it was safer so.

The excuses he gave to Cabal sounded exactly like excuses, though, and he was guiltily sure that Cabal recognized them for what they were. He hated to think he was hurting the man, however good-intentioned his motives.

He finally had a sudden happier idea.

"Master, there is something you could do, that would be a great favor to me personally."

"Yes?" The sadness had not left Cabal's eyes, though he tried to mask it.

"Consider another student. I can't vouch for the extent of his talents, but he has a spark of sorts, and he hasn't been able to get a hearing here at all. His mother asked me to instruct him, but I've such poor control over my own magic, how could I teach someone else?"

Cabal shook his head at that, but Tristan pressed on.

"If you'd just see him. It would mean a lot to him, I know."

Cabal's stubby fingers styled his beard.

"What's his name?"

"Delmon."

"And how old?"

Tristan thought briefly. "I'm not sure. He might be small for his age, or bright for it. Between five and six, I'd guess. Do you take them that young?"

"Oh yes. They've no time to form bad habits, that way."

"Then it's just as well I haven't had time to give him many lessons."

Cabal smiled. "Send him, then. You understand, I can promise nothing?"

"Of course. He'll be glad just for the chance. And if it should develop that he has no talent, he's better off out of the business early. I'm well qualified to speak on that subject."

Certainly, Tristan knew, he wasn't qualified to teach magic.

His progress with Delmon left much to be desired. If he could have taught the boy alone he might have made a better beginning, but Crewzel of course sat in on the lesson, and kept intruding with her own comments and questions, until she'd gotten Tristan far off whatever track he'd been trying to follow. He was left wondering who was teaching what to whom.

Delmon caught on to fire-lighting quickly—most boys did—so Tristan sent him off to locate a fire-stone of his very own as a graduation exercise. He remembered how proud he'd been when Blais had sent him on a similar mission—his first, as it happened—and how he'd scoured the countryside in search of just the perfect stone for days.

Delmon was back, stone in fist, inside of half an hour.

"You were supposed to find a stone, not buy one," Tristan reprimanded gently. "It makes the stone more answerable to you, more your own—"

"I didn't buy it. I stole it." Delmon smiled up brightly at Tristan. "That took more doing than just picking it up off the ground." And when put to the test, the stone worked perfectly for him.

*Cheer up,* Thomas advised. *It may come in handy some day to know such an accomplished pickpocket. Besides, he showed initiative. If he'd gone out foraging for a stone that*

*way you did, he'd have been gone a month on the errand.
Or were you looking forward to postponing lessons?*

He might have been, Tristan admitted to himself. Since
they'd gotten to Kôvelir, it had been nothing but magic for
him, day and night. Reading it, pondering it, instructing,
being instructed—he'd gone out briefly with Crewzel each
night—practicing a little, when he was alone and not too
weary. He could have used a break.

Allaire and Polassar had been having a fine time, roam-
ing the city at will. Heroes of Polassar's type were always
in good supply in the city, and if any noticed the more than
common beauty of his companion, or her be-ringed hands.
Polassar's size and high temper ensured that neither was
ever mentioned to him. Tristan had finally decided that
Allaire was safe enough with Polassar and had stopped
fretting about her every moment he couldn't personally be
by her side.

She'd noted his concern at first, though. When he and
Elisena had returned from the Library that first time, Allaire and Polassar had just gotten in also, and she came
shyly up to Tristan, fingering her silver hair.

She'd gathered all the shining mass into one thick braid
down the middle of her back.

"See," she said. "So no one would notice me." Her face
lit. "Oh, this city is so wonderful!"

There was no doubt she'd needed the outing and enjoyed
it. Her old sparkle had returned. But hiding her in Kôvelir,
Tristan despairingly thought, was rather like trying to conceal a candle's flame in a dark room. Even if no one knew
who she was, the situation was not a comfortable one.

And it had soon become less comfortable.

Yes, there were other heroes in Kôvelir, conceivably
there might even be one who resembled Polassar. And the
dice game was shadowed as much as lighted by the flickering wereflames. But it was as impossible to mistake anyone
else for Allaire, as it was impossible to mistake a glowworm
for the gibbous moon, even with her hands hidden carefully
in her gown and her hair nondescriptly plaited.

Tristan, on his way homeward from another eye-
straining day at the Library, almost paused and spoke to
them. Only the heat of the game stopped him—that and
the sight of Polassar casting a bejeweled armband at a be-

velveted gambler, in return for getting another cast of the dice. The armlet's mate was already gone, and either one of them would have purchased a week's lodging at any hostel in the city for their entire party. Tristan had noted sickly, as he slipped away unnoticed into the crowd. He was hardly surprised that Polassar had hit upon this means of passing the time, but that he should make Allaire a partner to it beggared the imagination. Was this his idea of lying low, of careful and discrete searching?

Still, Tristan said nothing about it at first, not wanting to provoke Polassar. He was irritated that Polassar should gamble his jewels away, when he'd been unwilling to sell them to buy lodging, and that he would take Allaire into such questionable company, but another fight would solve nothing. He would only be badgered about how his own search was going, and it was going none too well at the moment. And he didn't care much for the thought of having his recently healed face smashed in again.

Coins clinking in his pocket as he moved reminded Tristan that he might as well add them to the rest of their small cache before he lost them. He'd pried up one of the hearthstones, under which he'd dug a cavity, and pulled out a small leathern bag. It felt light. They must stand in worse need of money than he'd thought. Maybe Elisena had done more marketing that day.

He'd have assumed so, anyway, if he hadn't caught Polassar's quick glance in his direction and an even quicker one away, as he opened the bag. So. Maybe the armbands hadn't been all that had been gambled away.

Tristan was first suspicious and then certain, but some deep streak of caution directed his tongue that evening, and bid him frame his questions carefully, even innocently as he spoke to Allaire.

What delights of the city had she and Polassar sampled that day? he asked lightly, as he fiddled with the fire. Truly, Kôvelir never ceased to amaze him with its variety and complexity, so different from anything he'd ever known—why, just today Tristan had heard of the Circle of Chance, wherein all manner of games of luck and craft might be found, the streets were oftimes literally paved with wagered gold.

Allaire looked him straight in the eye, so guilelessly that

he might have believed her if she'd held the magicked dice in her white and silver hand even as she spoke. She said sweetly, "Aye. Just this very day I heard its name. As we walked along the Street of Jewelers we met a poor wretch who'd lost even most of the clothes on his back there, in some game or other. Polassar felt such pity for him, he gave him his armrings, so that his family might not starve."

She then favored Polassar with quite the fondest smile Tristan had ever seen, exactly the sort of smile a man gallantly generous might expect to receive from his lady—a lady not over-familiar with simple economics or concerned with the whereabouts of her next meal.

She was lying to him, straight-faced. If he hadn't seen them with his own eyes—and Thomas' too . . . It was enough to make Tristan seriously question the state of his wits. He felt sick to his stomach. *She'd lied to him*—how could she lie to him? She who was above all deceits.

"Wasn't that a marvel?" Allaire asked him.

"Oh yes," Tristan replied numbly. "Oh yes, it certainly is marvelous."

He would certainly have been ill. Maybe right there on her little white feet, if he hadn't gotten himself away quickly, stammering something about looking after the horses. He fled, somehow only tripping once or twice as he went.

It was better outside in the dark, even if the cold air made him acutely aware of the hot tears on his cheeks. At least no one could see them there. He almost fell over Thomas and wound up at last sitting on the ground behind a heap of rubble, his head resting on his knees.

If she'd even lied about something that mattered!

That still hurt, and he didn't know what bothered him most about the lie—the senselessness of it, or that she'd told it to protect Polassar from his own folly, or that she'd thought him stupid enough to believe it.

The fact that she'd lied at all was staggering. Tristan felt as if a bit of the ground had been yanked out from under his feet.

Thomas was full of advice.

*You've got to stop being shocked when people lie to you. Just because Blais never did, your world needn't fall apart the first time it happens. Grow up.*

Tristan made no attempt at an answer, but sat in the darkness, miserable and colder than the night air warranted.

A jingle of crystal finally made him lift his head, but he didn't rouse swiftly enough. Elisena went as silently and quickly as she had come, but there was a bundle resting beside him, and inside it Tristan found a roll of pastry stuffed with nuts and honey, a favorite of his, which made him smile despite all.

None the less, he lost much innocence and a lot of trust over the incident, and a dark gloom fell over him at times, as if someone had shoved a pane of smoked glass between his eyes and the city and his friends. Everything about him seemed subtly changed, altered and artfully transformed.

Tristan and Elisena left the Library of the mages at dusk, when even the red sunset light had failed them. He had finally finished with the ram skin, but still had found no mention of the ring. The writing was obscure, as if the writer had not dared say more, fearing the hands his work might fall into. There were only shadowy hints, too insubstantial to do more than prick at the senses.

They separated—she with their few remaining coins to buy food, he to try his luck at getting more money so they could eat the next day.

"I don't expect to be long," he said. "I ran across some interesting bits of business today, before I started on the ram skin, and I'd like to try them out. This search is taking longer than I'd planned. We need real provisions, and a few coppers here and there won't do. I need to start really earning. No rain spells, though," he added quickly, in response to her concerned look.

Alone, he worked the crowds for an hour or so, never staying long at any one spot. He missed Thomas' company, and was sorry he hadn't let the little cat follow him that morning.

Nor was the crowd so ready to toss coins to him alone. Despite all the tricks and glittery showmanship he'd absorbed from Crewzel, Tristan knew that he himself was nothing out of the ordinary. The cat had been the novelty worth rewarding.

Rain had begun again, adding to the evening's lack of

cheer. Cold drops got down Tristan's neck, setting him
shivering and ruining a fine rainbow illusion which he'd
been some minutes setting up. His audience, not large due
to the rain, hurried on before he could begin again. Tristan
wished he could do the same.

He was anxious to pass his news on to Crewzel, whom
he'd not seen since the last time he talked with Cabal.
Doubtless Cabal's offer was more than she'd ever dared to
hope for—Cabal was pretty high up in the mages' hier-
archy, Tristan had discerned from the deference he had
been paid by apprentices who'd seen him with the old man.
It was only a chance, of course, and Delmon's acceptance
was provisional, but if the boy applied himself, there would
be few upward limits to his career. Tristan could safely say
that he'd done well by Crewzel in return for her hospitality.

He crossed the square and insinuated himself into a half
dry spot at the edge of an awning beneath which a cook-
stove and some few persons were gathered. Smiling nervously, he started up his soggy magic again.

Someone touched his elbow, just as he'd finished giving
a moth the semblance of a bejeweled butterfly. He turned
his head sharply, one hand tight to his purse and the other
falling to his sword hilt.

The man who'd accosted him was not armed, at least not
visibly. He was, in fact, a wizard-in-training, wearing the
neophyte's gray robe, though he seemed somewhat old to
be still at that low grade. He spoke clearly but softly, so
that none might overhear.

"That was very nice. Now if I were you I should get
clear away from here at once—the Council has had its eye
on you. They know that you have no license for street
magic. They're not lenient in such matters, and Master Cabal won't be able to help you once you're in their hands.
This is near as bad an offense as stealing, to the Council's
mind. If you go now, you'll be but one step ahead of the
Watch."

Tristan opened his mouth to question this business of a
license, new to his ears, but the man in gray did not let him
speak.

"Unauthorized magic for profit in the streets is strictly
forbidden. You've been amazingly lucky, but no luck holds
forever. And the crowds have gone, with the rain." It was

true. Tristan had not noticed how the square had emptied, or when, but it was nearly deserted. "I'd not linger. Cabal won't be able to help you—"

Tristan glanced instantly at his palm, where the mage's sign still faintly glowed. When he looked up, the man was gone, perhaps melted away behind a passing train of pack oxen. He might as well have turned to smoke, the color of his robe—

A businesslike tramping reached Tristan's ears. Nail-soled boots, such as guards might wear? The Watch? He heard a shout, and lost no time darting into the darkest near alleyway.

Tristan ran a few hundred paces, twisting at every opportunity to confuse the trail. He was as good as lost anyway, in this part of the city, until he happened upon a square he might be able to recognize. Just now his best course was to hug the shadows. His worst fear was of entering a cul-de-sac which would trap him unwittingly.

He was going in the right direction, in a general sort of way, so he wasn't too concerned otherwise. Yet the sounds of pursuit and the feeling of it persisted for a disconcertingly long time. He felt the pursuers should long since have given up. Was the Watch that hot to catch him, then? Would those faint bootsteps never die away?

It occurred to him that his pursuers would know these streets far better than he could hope to. He couldn't get far enough ahead of them now to double back safely, and they might cut him off at any instant. It was illogical to think that he could outrun them; if they were magic-trained, they might well ensorcel him on sight.

He came to an intersection, too tiny to be called a square, too broad to be incautiously crossed. Tristan stopped short and peered about.

There was no sign of any living thing—just rain and puddles and shuttered windows, closed doors and heaps of rubbish. Alleys opened in profusion. From here he could run in any of half a dozen directions but he had no idea where any of the streets led. Tristan glanced around again, then up.

The building nearest him had a fairly shallow roof, before it gathered itself into a second storey. The tiles were wet, but he should be able to keep his footing. He could hear bootsteps again.

Tristan scrambled atop a wobbly rain-barrel and dug his fingers into the crumbling brickwork. A heave, a couple of wriggles and a slip which slammed his chin painfully against the roof's edge, and he was up. By the time the small sounds of his climbing had died away and the rain-barrel had stopped rocking, he was up on the next-highest roof, safe enough behind a carven stone wyvern which served as a rainspout.

Besides being well out of sight and in the last place anyone would look for him, Tristan found he now had a fine view of the alley below. He watched tremblingly as dark-cloaked figures cast about like a pack of hunting dogs in the square below. There seemed to be some discussion among them over which way he might have gone.

They left nothing to chance. Some few split off at once, checked the shorter alleys, and returned swiftly. There was more discussion, then the whole bunch set off at a fast pace, in a tight group. Tristan counted them very carefully, to be sure that none were left behind as a trap. Then he waited a good while longer, for safety's sake—and another bit longer, figuring out how to get down from his lofty refuge and building up the necessary nerve for the descent.

On the ground at last, Tristan paused in a doorway, panting, and felt about in his pouch for the night's takings. He might as well tally them while prudently letting the Watch move farther off.

By feel, all were coppers, with one small bit that might be silver. Not worth being chased over. He hadn't done so well tonight without Thomas' help. Still, there should be enough, if it were spent carefully and it didn't have to last too long—and if he hid it better. By this time, there should be a good store of food, Elisena no doubt being a more thrifty marketer than he.

Rested, Tristan got his bearings and headed back to their shelter. From his rooftop perch, he'd been able to make out some few landmarks, at least. His goal was at no great distance now, easy enough to reach if there were still daylight; but it was dark, and he daren't make any sort of light now, in case he was being followed. Rain drizzled down from a dark-clouded sky. After a time, he fancied that he could almost see in the dark, like Thomas. He scrambled over heaps of wet rubbish and walked through others which were illusion, only occasionally confusing the one with the other.

This might be it. He heard horses stamping, and recognized Valadan's greeting neigh. The stallion seemed restless, but Tristan didn't pause. Later, or in the morning—right now he wanted only to get back to the light and his friends, out of the cold wet dark. He still had a few doorways to go. He searched the wall with outstretched fingers, eerily reminded of the night they'd first come here. He'd have been glad to have Thomas at his feet now. Almost—there!

The room was dark, they must have let the fire go out, and Elisena wasn't back yet, though she should have been. Could they be sleeping? Really, he'd have thought Polassar might have stayed on guard, if he'd nothing better to do—at least kept the fire going to warm the place. It made Tristan angry to know he'd been working so hard, getting soaked and chilled and chased, to earn the price of their living, while Polassar slept. And where was Elisena? She should most definitely have been back by now.

He stepped quickly through the doorway, tripped, and was flat down on the floor before he could think to catch himself. Coins went everywhere, rolling and jingling.

Was a roof beam across the open doorway Polassar's idea of a defense or a joke? Tristan picked himself up as best he was able, rubbing a bruised knee, and fumbled out his crystal to make a light. He would have been muttering a curse, too, but he wouldn't give Polassar that small satisfaction.

There was no beam in the doorway. Polassar lay there, his head in a small puddle of blood.

The crystal slipped through Tristan's fingers and went out. He scrabbled for it wildly, all the while trying to feel whether Polassar was still breathing. Polassar was, quite strongly as it happened, and he moaned when Tristan held the relit crystal near his face. The blood came from a gash on the back of his head, and there seemed to be no other injury. His sword was not even half drawn.

Tristan looked around in the wavering light, shouting for Allaire, but he somehow knew that she would not answer. The room was deserted.

Not quite. There were flutterings and frightened cheepings, but Minstrel could tell him nothing beyond his own relief at seeing Tristan again. It was night; he'd been sleeping, of course. And Tristan already knew that Valadan had been too far away to help. That left Thomas; perhaps he'd followed—but followed what? Who could have done this? Galan's men?

Thomas should have contrived to leave him some sort of trail. If they had stealthily attacked Polassar from behind, then there couldn't have been many of them—

A dead rat landed almost on his head, making Tristan jump so that he nearly fell again. Looking up, he saw Thomas perched on the windowledge, an unfamiliar bewildered look on his face. The cat regained his composure in an instant.

*I wasn't gone long. And no one was here then.*

"Then they can't have got far!" Tristan sprang for the door, the cat leaping behind him.

"Minstrel, search from the air as best you can. But beware of owls," Tristan shouted as an afterthought, while he ran down the alley, his sword at the ready.

He ran hard, knowing he must be behind them by only precious minutes. If he could overtake them before they expected pursuit—! Cold rain began again, destroying every hope he had of picking up their trail. The city seemed to dissolve into a nightmare of walls and passageways. Allaire could have disappeared down any one of the dark alleys.

His boots lost contact with the slippery mud, and he plunged smack into the middle of a malodorous puddle. Tristan picked himself up and ran on, but a shade less purposefully than before. His sword was dripping mud.

Why hadn't he thought to saddle Valadan? Then he'd at least have had a chance to overtake Galan's men. What if they'd had horses hidden? They'd be out of the city by this time, if the attackers really were Galan's men.

Or perhaps they wouldn't escape. The gates were shut and sealed for the night. He and Allaire and whoever had abducted her were sealed in, too. He had a few more hours, then—and only the whole city to search! The idea of Allaire in peril drove him relentlessly.

He stopped running sometime after his third fall. He'd

hit his head once, hard enough to make him see stars, but he staggered on somehow, even when he'd half forgotten why. His chest and throat burned horribly.

Minutes later, Tristan slowly realized that he was no longer moving at all, but was sagging against slimy brick-work. His cheek was pressed tight against it, and all he could see was his own hand a few inches away, fingers gripping the rough bricks desperately. His sword lay at his feet.

He bent dizzily to pick it up, then leaned against the wall again, his heart hammering. He was unsure just how long he'd been running almost aimlessly, with still no sign of Allaire. This was surely hopeless; the attackers would be miles away, could be anywhere in the city or even watching him now from any of these buildings. But he couldn't just stop looking.

Water ran down his face—rain, sweat or merely tears. Once he got his second wind he'd begin again. Tristan took a deep breath, felt fire stab his side. His legs were rubbery, not to be trusted just yet.

This is senseless, an inner voice protested. Sit down, get your bearings, then use magic to find her. It's what you should have done in the first place. Or go back for Vala-dan. This useless dashing about in the dark only wastes time.

A rat paused in passing him by, shook rain from its pelt before scuttling on.

But going back for Valadan would waste more time. And in the crowded alleys he'd move faster afoot, if he only knew which direction to move. His breathing was still ragged, painful.

This was hopeless. If he were going to find them, he should have done so by now. Suppose he went to Cabal? Could some sort of alert be raised without lengthy explana-tions? He spared a thought for Minstrel, who probably couldn't find him and might well be frightened.

Thomas crouched beside him. His ears pricked suddenly at a distant cry. Tristan took no notice.

*Come on. That was close.*

He set off at a rapid cat-trot. Tristan wobbled after him, rather than be left alone.

Two turns, one dung heap, and a long alley later, they

burst upon a crosspath. Tristan saw a dim flicker of white, and heard another cry that mingled rage with despair. He blinked, and the scene cleared slightly.

One ragged man held Allaire fast, while a second was doing his best to remove her rings. She writhed and kicked at him, until he struck her in the face and shook her. Still she would not quiet, and the man drew his knife roughly.

"Cut them off, then!"

Tristan answered that with a yell, and lunged for them. The surprise of the attack and his momentum gave him a small advantage. The first man he encountered fell back before him, until stopped by a wall. There, knife in hand, he stood to defend himself.

Tristan hadn't troubled to count the abductors. One or twenty, it didn't matter; he was committed to his attack. Fortunately there seemed to be just the two of them, armed only with knives, long and wickedly pointed. Tristan held his man easily, until the other hit him a shoulder-numbing blow with a barrel stave. Thomas leaped at the man's head, spitting, and the odds were equal again. Tristan had expected his opponents to run, for they plainly weren't soldiers, and a sword outmatched their weaponry.

They must have considered two knives against one tired swordsman fair enough odds, though. The pair closed in warily, eyes fixed on his sword, but they smiled ferally. Tristan couldn't quite see the joke. Maybe he didn't present the heroic picture he hoped to.

He was nearly spent from fear and running. And his boots kept slipping in the wet filth on the ground, so that he couldn't move as nimbly as he should. If he once went down, it was all over. Tristan backed and dodged, engaging one knife, helpless to keep the second man from slipping behind him. His first thrust had missed narrowly, and there was no time for another. Even if he hit this time, he'd likely be dead before he could pull his sword free to try at the second man. He slashed briskly, trying to back one or the other of them off, feeling something catch and rip at his cloak.

Allaire tried to come to his aid, having been let free in the confusion. She belabored his second attacker's back with her fists, though with little success. She had only a moment to act before she was caught and held again, then slapped and flung aside. Thomas sprang for his man again, yowling fit to wake the dead.

Tristan's first opponent was getting in a good share of kicks every time they closed. And Tristan had to finish that one off fast; Thomas couldn't be expected to hold the other off forever. Tristan's blade whistled and leaped in his hand like living metal, but a heavy belt turned the blade once, and he nearly lost his hold on it when he tangled with the knife's guard.

Minstrel swooped out of the black sky like a falcon, but without a falcon's talons or weight which would have made his attack something more than diversionary.

A squeaking puff of thistledown, he vanished into the night, but he gained Tristan a moment in which to parry a slash with a heave of his arm that sent the man crashing into a wall.

A cut from the second knife glanced off his unicorn buckle's horn. Wouldn't that be a fine trick to play on a swordsman, he thought wildly, if there were a spell to activate that buckle, let it really fight? Silver responded well to magic, if only he had time to perfect the incantation.

*If you don't think of something that's useful now, there won't be a later.*

His boot hit something yielding, and Tristan trod on it ruthlessly, only to have his ankle wrenched savagely out from under him. He only missed getting a knife in the throat because he landed so awkwardly that his throat was nowhere near the spot his attacker had expected it to be. Gasping desperately for the air just jarred out of him, Tristan swung his blade windmill fashion. He hit nothing, but the gesture must have looked impressive to his attackers, since one took a step back and the other held his ground instead of moving in, long enough to let Tristan regain his feet.

It occurred to him that Blais had never mentioned fencing against knives. His advantage was reach, theirs numbers; and maybe they had more practice at this sort of thing. Both of them were heavier and taller than he'd ever be.

Something dragged at his cloak again, trying to pull him off balance. He saw Thomas tensing to spring again, fighting by his instincts, and Tristan knew he'd have to do the same. If he couldn't reason out a defense, he'd just have to scrap reason.

Then he gasped, as cold steel scored his ribs and a sudden weight hit him from his left side. He rolled, trying to get his sword up again in time to account for at least one of them. Then they were too close, inside his reach. He was off balance, falling again, and his swordarm felt so heavy . . .

The word came up out of his mind, fresh as when he'd first read and then forgotten it, scribed on the ram skin. His lips shaped it, wondered at it as it burst free, and then he fell back to the cobbles, waiting for the knife's inevitable touch.

Nothing happened to him. His heart kept on beating rapidly.

Tristan opened his eyes and looked about—at two heaps of white bone that lay movelessly gleaming.

# A Hero's Reward

HE WANTED to gather Allaire up in his arms and carry her back, closely cherished so. She needed it, for she was weeping and could barely stand on her own. But beyond getting her to her feet and keeping her there, Tristan could do nothing. He'd enough work keeping himself upright.

She clung to him, her disordered hair falling over his chest like melted silver, her hands clutching at his ragged sweater as to life itself. He bent his head close to hers, to catch her words as they passed haltingly along the alley.

"They wanted to cut my hands off, because I wouldn't give them the rings—" A fit of weeping shook her again. "We'd only been out for a little while, seeing the shops, looking at the rings there. Polassar said it would be safe, it was still light even though it was evening. I never saw them. They must have followed us, and then——"

She could not go on, for the tears choked her. Tristan held her, smoothed her hair as best he was able, marvelling as he did so. Somehow through his tiredness he was intensely aware of the softness of her body, pressed to his. His hand grazed her cheek, strayed to her neck. She was softer than the petals of roses. Her lashes were tear-spangled, like grass after a heavy dew. Somehow, her lies to him no longer mattered.

He whispered encouragement to her, reassurances. And all the while he tried to erase from his own mind those piles of bones in the alley, the sudden disappearance of the would-be thieves, which she'd not questioned. He felt a little ill——more than a little——thinking about it. Tristan glanced around nervously, then urged Allaire on again. Nowhere seemed to feel safe now; it was as if something *watched* them——and particularly watched him.

Allaire's hands were bloody, cut deep when the thieves had tried to rip the rings from them. She looked at them now and moaned softly, as if she had only just noticed the pain.

"My lady, we must try to hurry. They might come back," he said, knowing full well they wouldn't——couldn't.

She was near to fainting, though, and leaned on him like a weary child, her head on his chest. Her whole exhausted body drooped against his, drawing comfort from him. Tristan stumbled, but managed to right himself. They moved slowly on.

Light spilled out of their doorway now. The sight of it relieved Tristan tremendously——Elisena must be back, and safe. She ran out with glad cries at the first sound of their halting footsteps. Minstrel was with her, fluttering. Elisena had a yard-long stick of firewood in her hand and a determined look briefly on her face——Minstrel must have been fetching her to help.

Tristan supported Allaire with gentle hands, half carrying her into the warmth and light of the fire. He could see now how her face was stained with tears and dirt, yet was lovely all the same.

Her wet eyes flew wide open.

She straightened in his arms, twitched free, and ran to Polassar, who sat by the fire holding a rag to his head. Tristan hadn't realized that she must have thought Polassar slain, hadn't thought to tell her that he'd only been stunned. She wept aloud now, touching him in wonderment with her bleeding hands, exclaiming, as overcome by joy as she'd been by grief, and then he pulled her to him, and she grew quiet at last.

Tristan allowed himself to collapse against the wall, sliding slowly down it till he was sitting on the floor. He was so lightheaded that he thought he'd have fainted otherwise.

"Is he all right?" He gestured limply at Polassar. Allaire's behavior did not bother him as much as he might have supposed it would. Afterwards, yes, but not at the time, and that fact bothered him more than Allaire's reactions. He ought to have felt worse about it than he actually did.

"Oh yes." Elisena bent over her bag of herbs. "Just a headache that will put him in a bad temper for a few days." She knelt down by Tristan. "Let me see."

"What?" He stared at her, bemused, wondering if he'd heard properly.

"You're bleeding." When he still stared as if not understanding her, she drew his sweater up firmly, leaving his chest bare.

Tristan was mildly surprised to see the long red slash across his ribs. He barely remembered the prick of the knife, and it had hardly seemed to matter. It was bleeding, but not a great deal.

"It's only a scratch," he protested, as she laid out an alarming array of powders and salves and rags.

"Oh? And I suppose the knife was clean, too? This will probably sting," she warned him, just a second too late.

His ointment in the butterfly box might have done the job as well and less painfully, but he was too tired to argue the point. And aside from that first smarting, which probably wasn't her fault, Elisena's hands were gentle enough and coolly capable. Tristan found he wasn't flinching from her touch, even the very next one. She smelled of lavender, like clean fresh air, and all at once Tristan felt as if he were at home again, lying hidden from his lessons in the midst of the herb garden, with wild strawberries at his fin-

gers' reach and the sweet lavender for his pillow and cover-
let as he napped. In a little while he would venture sleepy-
eyed into the cottage, sit down to a meal of savory stew
and then sit longer beneath the bright summer stars and
listen the night away as Blais spoke of his youth and other
long-ago marvels in colors rich as the last of the summer's
twilight.

Elisena served up supper after she'd finished tending his
wound and had bathed Allaire's hands. The meal was a
sort of soup or stew, with Allaire and Polassar sharing the
pot and Tristan being awarded their single mug. He paid
scant attention to it, and Elisena spoke his name twice before he showed any sign of hearing.

"Are you all right?" She reached for her herb bag again,
frowning.

Tristan blinked at her, then sighed, looking down at his
very muddy self. Memories of Blais, of happy uncompli-
cated childhood drained away. Thomas nestled in his lap,
rubbing his head tenderly against Tristan's wrist. Tristan
could see a bruise there, felt others all over himself.

"I could use another bath. My head aches, and I'm so
tired I can't stand up. Save for all of that, I'm fine. The
cut doesn't hurt at all now—only part of me that doesn't."

She sat down close beside him, all attention—true attention and not mere politeness. He tried to find words to
explain to her what was mostly wrong with him—about the
two thieves, the spell, the dark, nauseating horror of what
he'd done to them. He'd never meant to kill them, not in
that terrible way. He'd only wanted to get Allaire back. If
this was what magic really was, he wanted no part of it,
none at all. The things Blais had taught him—were they
really kin to this dark power, this sudden death and destruction? Was not magic light and growth, healing and
beauty? So he'd always thought, at his very core, though
his mind, of course, knew that couldn't be wholly true and
was probably a childish concept.

He didn't even know how he'd learned the spell; he
had no recollection of having studied it specially. He
couldn't remember it now—just as well, maybe, but it
scared him to think of that kind of power lurking inside
him, ready to explode out of his control as all his other
magic did.

He wanted to tell her, but the words just seemed to mill about in his head without sense. He couldn't order them. Nothing at all came out except a few whispers about failure.

"A failure as a wizard?" Elisena's dark brows arched. Her fingers brushed a few straying hairs out of his eyes. "I would hardly say that about someone who made a fog to blanket a hundred miles out of nothing more than a stone and a feather."

"A hundred miles?" It nearly made him laugh, once he remembered what she was talking about, but mirthlessly. "That's a child's trick, it doesn't extend more than a few hundred feet." She surely wasn't that naive. It was a nice trick, to be sure, but not that nice.

"Are you so certain? Drink your soup now." She pressed the cup more tightly into his hand, tipped it against his lips.

The cup warmed his fingers, the soup his insides a little later. He felt like trying to explain to her again, more clearly. It would be nice to have someone understand, for a change. But that would take too long, need too much effort, when he was so bone-weary.

Elisena caught the cup as his fingers slid away from it, smiling as she saw his head nodding. She eased him into a less uncomfortable position, put his cloak over him, and let him sleep.

Back to
Calanora

TRISTAN LAY on his back in the bracken, wishing he knew why they were really here and what he hoped to find and yearning to relax for just a little while. He was stiff all over, either from nerves or from the fight. He held a sunflower kernel between his lips, and Minstrel stretched to take it, returning to Tristan's shoulder with his prize.

He wondered briefly why Crewzel hadn't put in an appearance the night before. She usually did but, aside from Delmon, she'd seemed pretty independent; perhaps she'd simply grown bored with them and moved on.

The watched feeling had persisted when he woke at dawn, indeed seemed to have been with him all night, ever since he'd used the spell. He shrugged it off, got up, and washed himself. The others still slept, save for Thomas, who'd curled himself in the warm spot Tristan had left in his bed.

He was restless, filled with a strange resolve. He could hardly sit quiet after the others awoke. While they ate breakfast, Tristan sat deep in thought, barely mouthing a few bites.

He'd learned about all he was likely to in the Library. If he stayed longer, he'd just retrace the same ground and be caught up in a pointless search after a place for himself, a way to fit in here, which he knew he'd never find. The quest couldn't be ignored; he knew that plainly. They were all doomed to seek after the ring, or else to abandon it entirely. They couldn't search with half a mind to it. This gray middle ground strained nerves and tempers alike and rotted their souls like a cold psychic rain. Or else, with many freezings and thawings, it stressed and aged them till they'd eventually shatter, their bright objective forever lost.

*My, aren't we poetic today?*

He ignored Thomas and watched Polassar squatting by the fire, endlessly cleaning his sword, and Allaire staring sightlessly at the door and starting at every least noise. They weren't safe here any longer. Only a fool would ever have thought they were, and now that had been made very plain.

"The ring is not a wedding ring." Allaire jumped at the sound of his voice; she looked startled, as if she'd forgotten what he spoke of, what they'd come to Kôvelir to learn.

"Eh?" Polassar grunted. He ran possessive fingers over his sword, admiring the blade's sheen.

"It was merely intended to be used as such." Tristan's voice sounded strange to his ears, caustic, biting. Elisena offered him a cup of fittingly bitter tea, which he drank before continuing.

"A wedding ring might be any ring," he said. "The tenth ring was made when the other nine were, and by the same hand. I suspected this before, and my readings here have lately confirmed it." Just how, though? he wondered to himself. He'd thought he'd learned so little here, except for one awful word of power and many small disappointments.

He looked into the fire, thinking hard, trying to organize what he knew, put order to his new insights, shape an explanation. Or grab at any lead, however slender, if one looked at the matter that way.

"Allaire and her rings came from Esdragon. But the final ring was in the King of Calandra's possession, as a surety until she came to him with the rest, and we must assume he had it with him when he died. Nímir may have taken it then. If it is not lost, then it will be hidden."

"Or destroyed," Allaire suggested fearfully.

"If Nímir could destroy it. But if it were destroyed, there would have been no need to imprison you. So perhaps he couldn't destroy it. No, not while all the other nine exist. If it were destroyed, so would they be. And if he could not destroy it, he might have no power to use it, either, without you, without your consent. So, he might have hidden it. It must be in the last place we'd think to look, a place we wouldn't search well because we were so anxious to get away from it."

Something was still wrong with his logic here, but his certainty increased as he spoke.

"Start packing up. We've got enough coppers put by now to buy a good store of travel food, so I'll go see to that. Also, the horses' shoes may need looking at, and there's the ferry to arrange. We'll cross the Est in a bit more comfort, this time." As if anything could ease that journey for him!

"But where are we going?" Allaire asked petulantly.

They were all three watching him intently, as he realized with surprise that no one else had recognized their inevitable destination.

"We must go back to Darkenkeep."

No one, to Tristan's constant amazement, said what a stupid plan it was. Perhaps he'd happened on the right idea after all. Surely they couldn't have become so blindly dependent on him in such a short while. He certainly hadn't the leadership record to support that kind of faith.

Such black thoughts held him only a while before he set off for the markets. This time he was determined they'd be better prepared for travel; he was weary of going hungry. He strode swiftly through Kôvelir's alleys, with Thomas casting curious glances in his direction—glances which Tristan didn't note.

At the markets, Tristan flattered himself that he did as well as Elisena might have. He ignored those stalls selling hot food, despite the tempting sights and odors abounding in their vicinity. He bought instead a good supply of salted beef, dried to the consistency and keeping quality of leather, and went on to collect oats, beans, bread, and a small cheese. He held back enough money to pay the ferry fee, and a little beyond it for emergencies, but otherwise spent everything on food. They'd at least start this trip with full saddlebags.

By unspoken agreement, Allaire was not left alone, or even alone with Elisena. So when Tristan returned heavily laden, Polassar went out at once, on an errand he'd trust to no one else. After a bit, seeing that Elisena was packing their scanty belongings, Tristan fetched the horses and groomed them, paying special attention to their feet.

He was more than a little annoyed to see that Allaire sat listlessly staring into the fire, while Elisena bustled about trying to gather up their things and cook a meal at the same time. Whatever misgivings Allaire might have about moving on toward such a destination, could she not lend at least a hand at turning the oat-cakes? Tristan did the job himself, grumbling, as soon as he'd done with the horses, then looked guiltily at Allaire. What did he expect, anyway? She was too well used to being served, and that wasn't entirely her fault. What could he possibly know of the torments that might be passing through her mind? He hadn't been prisoned in Darkenkeep for hundreds of years. He had no right to judge her behavior.

Polassar returned quickly enough, minus his cloak-brooch but greatly pleased with himself. Green velvet and scarlet satin flashed in his arms, and a heady perfume filled the air as he shook his bundle out before them. He was grinning broadly, well satisfied with his selection.

Allaire had badly needed a new gown; her rags were closer to tatters after her struggles during her abduction. Yet she looked less than happy, even disconcerted, and Elisena's face plainly said that the dress Polassar produced was in the worst possible taste for adventuring through rough country. Allaire was blushing as she slipped it on, while the men carefully kept their backs to her. The furred neckline was so very low, and those slits in the skirt would of course prove handy for riding astride——but need they be cut quite so high? She seemed glad to wrap her cloak about her, and very tightly she wrapped it too. Polassar looked crestfallen, unsure of how he'd failed to please.

Another whiff of the scent found its way to Tristan, and he roused a little, even to hastily smothered laughter, as he finally placed the smell he'd thought familiar from the first. He remembered it well now. That cheap scent had filled the whole square on his first night of street-magicking. A painted face, hennaed hair——he'd made a butterfly for the harlot, pulled a flower from behind her ear——it was to be hoped she had gotten as good a price as she'd wanted for her cast-off gown. Probably she'd gotten better.

They retired early, for they'd be starting as soon as the city's gates opened. Kôvelir did a brisk trade with Esdragon's farmers, if it ignored all coming from Calandra, and the ferry ran from first light till last.

For all his determination to rest, Tristan got little sleep. The darkness was too filled with memories and speculations, each more dear or fascinating than the last, and all desperately worthy of his close attention. He lay quietly, to rest his body at least, and watched the night away.

He was first up before dawn, too empty emotionally and physically to care about a meal. He'd saddle the horses while he waited for the others to wake and prepare themselves. Fog swirled lazily among the rubbish heaps in the alley, and he saw it wasn't properly morning yet.

"Tell your huge friend that he forgot the undergown to the surcoat he bought yesterday. Geneve may like to go without it, but I doubt your fine lady shares her tastes."

Crewzel held a length of gray cloth out to Tristan. Except for her voice, she was insubstantial in the mist, as if he'd conjured her up out of his imaginings.

"You're going," she said flatly, not questioning.

"Yes," he answered, his words fog-puffs in the cold air. "Well, you kept asking us to go," he continued, trying for a joke.

Crewzel stepped forward and flung both arms about him, hugging him so fiercely that she took his breath away. Doubly so, for she squeezed the knife slash too, which had barely begun to heal. After a moment, she held him back at arm's length.

"Not with *that* look on your face, I didn't! What's happened? You're not on the run again?"

"Not quite. The time's come for a move, that's all."

"Well, you'd know best about that. Foul of you to slip off without a word to me, though." She dropped his hands.

"I'm sorry. You didn't come yesterday, or I'd have told you. We only decided then." He told her what Cabal had said about Delmon and when the boy was to present himself at the Library.

She nodded, and they stood facing each other for a long while, not speaking, not seeming to need to. Crewzel fingered a pouch that that dangled from her belt. By its shape, it must hold her cards.

"You have a destiny," she said. "That's odd, most people don't. They just muddle along, and nothing much matters. I hope when yours meets you, it uses you gently."

She said nothing more, and when Tristan had blinked away a bit of warm fog which had blurred his sight, she was gone. He called after her, something inane about Delmon, and how things would be better for her now that he was under Cabal's tutelage, but Crewzel never answered— or even heard, for all he ever knew.

Finding a boat to ferry them across the Est was no difficult matter, for there were many waiting to serve. Much of the river side of Kôvelir was interlaced with canals and shallow lagoons—boats were popular forms of transport for all manner of commodities, shooting like water beetles between the numerous islands in the estuary. Even the horses might ride. Allaire cast longing looks back at the bright city.

The passage was not too uncomfortable. Tristan's mind seemed to flee his body, though part of him knew he still

stood beside Valadan in apparent normality. He remembered nothing of the crossing, or of what he thought while
they made it. It was as if it had never been. Not till he
reached the Esdragon shore did he find that he'd picked up
a sea-green and sea-rounded pebble from the far beach,
and clenched it so that his palm was white and marked by
it. Its color recalled Crewzel's eyes suddenly, and he
blessed whatever thoughtful woman's magic she'd wrought.

## Decision-Making

"You're not thinking of dragging her with us any
longer? Not when we're so close to her home? We've no
need for another—"

"Woman?" Tristan finished, incredulous. "She's earned
her place. We'd not have gotten this far without her. And
what else would you do with her? She has no friends, no
family. Maybe you think Galan would welcome her back
now?" He shook his head disbelievingly. "Valadan makes
nothing of carrying two."

The object of the debate crouched a scant six feet away,
peeling potatoes into the stew pot with a fine disregard for
Polassar's outrageous speech, though she was plainly within
easy hearing of it.

"I was going to say *witch*. I saw enough in yonder city—"
Polassar jerked a thumb in Kôvelir's rough direction.
"Enough of trickery and shadow-shows to last any sane
man a lifetime. We've troubles enough with magic now.
Are you certain we really need to do this?"

Tristan considered the point.

"If Nímir has the ring, where else would he have hidden
it? Darkenkeep is his securest fortress. Lost in that warren,

the ring's safe where none would dream of looking for it. But *we* must."

"Could we not simply go back to Lassair and live as normal folk?"

Tristan glanced at Allaire, who was watching a hawk's circling flight above them. A trick of the light was responsible, mayhap, but the glow was about her again.

"Do you really think we could?" he asked.

"There's no moon tonight," Polassar protested, changing tacks. He wanted to postpone this trip to Darkenkeep as long as might be possible. Tristan didn't blame him for the attempt.

"That doesn't matter. Valadan knows the way now. And I think you'll find the trip less difficult this time," Tristan said slowly. "Nímir will be anxious to have us back. He'll have his best welcome out. A short journey and an easy one." He felt a greater strength of purpose than at any time since he'd first set out from Blais' cottage.

Still, Tristan was mildly surprised to be proved so right so quickly. They must have embarrassed Nímir very much, and he was most eager to have them back, before too many learned of what audacious things they'd done. The Gates were in sight before they'd travelled an hour in the Waste, and the air was hardly even cold. They'd crossed the Winterwaste more easily than the wind might have.

The Gates rose, darkly glittering. They dismounted into the snow, Allaire last of all.

"Must we?" she whispered.

"It's the only way, my lady." Tristan lifted her gently down, ahead of Polassar for once. She felt lighter than a child. "We will search every inch of it, if we must." She seemed to take little comfort from the thought.

She'd been complaining bitterly every step of the way— of the number of miles they covered daily, the food, the weather, her mare's stumbling and her saddle's discomfort, until Tristan was irritated with her to the extreme. Her trepidation seemed now of a different sort, but Tristan saw at last that the complaints and the timidity were but different faces of the same fear, and could hardly blame her for it, though she'd made their return journey as difficult and

unpleasant as it was possible for her to do. He himself
would have done almost any deed to avoid Darkenkeep,
but he knew that might not be.

They entered in, four small figures scaled even smaller
by the great teeth of ice. Thomas kept close by Tristan's
feet, and Minstrel refused to stir from inside his sweater.
Allaire shrank beside Polassar, her hands wrapped furtively in her skirts, while Elisena stood looking about her,
as curiously calm as Tristan himself was. Her only response to Darkenkeep was to lift her skirts safely above the
steaming puddles on the floor.

The path still glowed, and led deep into the hill. The
same path they'd followed before? Or another?

"Don't follow that, Polassar. It probably leads straight to
whatever the Cold One has prepared for us." Since Polassar apparently could see the path, that seemed sure, and
exactly Nímir's style. Allaire quivered as Tristan went on.
"And I think we'd best skip his welcoming party. You can
be sure he'll not lead us to his treasure, save to trap us."
He caught Polassar giving him a somewhat uneasy look.

Tristan lit one of the torches they'd remembered to bring
and chose a tunnel that was dark. He wondered momentarily how he knew which direction to take. What sorcery
guided his steps? The way shelved roughly down, twisting,
slippery. Thomas followed him readily enough, so Tristan
supposed that there was no danger down here greater than
that in the chambers above. But the cat was silent, refusing
to answer when Tristan spoke to him.

They scrambled perhaps half a mile, before arriving at a
small round chamber from which a dozen other doors led
out. The frozen floor was mostly covered with bright heaps
of gold and jewels. Tristan's boots slithered among them,
making his footing unreliable. Yet where better to hide a
small object than among many other small objects?

"We might as well start here. Thomas, Minstrel, you
must help too. Let nothing be overlooked."

The search grew quickly tedious, as any of them might
have predicted. After a few moments the vision blurred,
and Tristan was not wholly sure that the fault lay with
their smoking torches. Nothing was as it should be in this
place. The gold seemed to be crawling, moving under their
hands. A thing would be put down in one place, and reap-

pear at the bottom of quite another pile a few minutes later. Tristan caught himself going over one heap for a third time and was certain the trouble lay not with his eyes alone. He rubbed wearily at them all the same.

Of course, Nímir would know exactly where they were. How much time do we have? Tristan wondered. And how will he strike, when he does? Yet on the surface, his mind remained calm, as if nothing could happen, but he was at a loss to explain his assurance. Something more would come; this little inconvenience would never be enough to stop them, ultimately. It just set tempers flaring a little—

"Wizard, we shall all die of doddering old age ere we find the ring this way! Is there no other? What of spellcraft?"

What of it? It would do no good, unless Nímir wished it to, for his own purposes. Tristan shook his head, and the movement dizzied him.

"This is the best way I know. If there's another, I would be glad to hear it." He straightened a little, trying unsuccessfully to unkink his back.

Allaire let a pile of jewels slide through nerveless hands, to lie glimmering about her knees. She bent her head to the task again at once, but not before Tristan had seen her eyes.

He should have thought of that. She would soon be under Nímir's influence again, if they stayed here long. Fear was taking her, part of him insisted. Her mind was going dark. She would stop fighting, and it would all be over.

What ever possessed me to bring her back here? It's the most senseless thing I've ever done. What can we possibly do, if we don't find the ring soon? And it could be anywhere in vast Darkenkeep! A careful search made sense, but action would have felt better. He felt his lips moving.

"My lady, have courage. We'll soon be out of here. Just keep trying these rings." He offered the handful of silver he'd gleaned.

"What's the use?" Tears gleamed like silver on her face. She looked exhausted and frightened past all reason. Ignoring Polassar, who was diligently ransacking a far corner, upending chests with imprudent crashings, Tristan dared slip an arm about her shoulders. Her face buried itself against his chest.

"You're only tired," Tristan said, the scent of her hair filling his mind, her silver rings shining fit to blind him. "We're all tired, but this will be over shortly, I promise you—"

His prophetic encouragement was interrupted by a great slithering, loud enough to drown out Polassar's racket, coming from a side tunnel. At first he hoped it might only be an icefall, but he listened and knew it came closer with each heartbeat. There was no mistaking its cause—the Guardian!

They froze. Stay small, instinct screamed, it might not notice them, might pass on. Only Thomas grew large. He bristled like a wildcat, ears laid back and fur erect, and his torch-thrown shadow loomed big as a dragon itself. But his eyes were wide with terror, and he made no sound.

It hissed closer. A sudden chill blast swirled ice crystals around them. The air glittered briefly.

"I don't think it can get in," Tristan whispered. "The doorway is too small."

Then the walls started to shiver, and he remembered that they were only ice.

"Wizard, what treachery is this? Why have you penned us thus?" Polassar's sword rasped. "I was fey indeed to follow you here a second time!"

Tristan shook his head at him, wonderingly. Treachery? What if it really was? Why had he brought them here?

All at once, for the first time in weeks, Tristan's eyes and mind came into clear focus. Of course the ring wasn't here. It was nowhere in Darkenkeep and never had been, except in a suggestion skillfully planted in his desperately searching mind. A groan escaped him, unheard even by himself. They were trapped, and for nothing, for less than a dream and a longing.

Allaire let out all her pent fears in one shriek and fell back, silent, as if she would nevermore have voice again. Tristan shook her and got no response. The room seemed to be growing darker. He forced it firmly back, and spoke a word to bolster the torches.

"Wizard, what's happened to her?" Polassar knelt beside Allaire, roughly shoving Tristan away from her side.

"The dragon's spell—it can still reach her, even if its body can't get through." He seemed to need to shout, as if the air were crowded with sounds. Bits of the doorway were beginning to fall into the room.

Polassar sprang to his feet, blade in hand.

"Foul beast! Let my arm make an end to this!" Grabbing up a gold-bossed shield from the treasure heap, he lept for the tunnel.

"Polassar, no!" Tristan felt his shout die in his throat.

He looked at Allaire, gowned in green and scarlet suddenly magnificent, glowing with her own light. From very far away, he seemed to hear the singing of a sword. Her hair and rings outshone the torch, the nine rays leaping up from the rings once more, rebounding from the ice walls and the gold until he felt they knelt at the center of the sun.

No ordinary sword could slay that monster. Polassar would die, instead. Even if he were too angry for the spell to affect him, the dragon would still kill him. It had many weapons.

It would be so easy, Tristan thought, black spreading to cover the green of his eyes. I can have her. If we leave here without the ring, she's of no use to Nímir. Polassar will die, and she'll have no one to turn to but me. She'll forget him, in time. Surely she could love me, then. I can wait. And I want her so, Tristan insisted, as if he needed to convince himself. I've had nothing but winter all my life. Don't I deserve a little spring? Just a very little sunlight? He flung a glance about the golden room, as a vagrant thought crept hesitantly into his mind, so odd that he couldn't recognize it as his own—was he perhaps longing for her from force of habit? He thrust it from him in dismay.

They could escape now, while the Guardian was occupied—which he fully was. Sword-steel still rang loudly. The dragon bellowed, breathing frostfire. A little of it touched Tristan where he crouched beside Allaire.

Why should they both die, fighting it? Who would save Allaire? She must be gotten away to safety, whatever happened to Polassar. That was right and proper.

He put his arms about her, tried to lift her up from her knees. She was rigid, eyes straining, her flawless face turned away from him and toward the sounds of Polassar fighting.

Tristan shook her again, trying for some reaction. She moved all in one piece, like a wooden doll, and never blinked. Yet she did not sleep, and her open eyes dripped agony.

He seemed to be the only living thing in the room still able to move. Elisena sat motionless, her head bowed, and Thomas and Minstrel were hidden. He looked into Allaire's eyes again, pleading with her.

"Move! Wake! Wake for me, as you did before." He tried to conjure the flowers again, but his mind was barren of songs. All the magic in the world seemed useless to him.

But what about Allaire herself, her needs?

Her eyes held no feeling at all for him, only the screams that could not pass her lips. She did not even see him.

His life had gone totally out of his control with Blais' death. He'd been led, driven, tricked, beaten and starved, nearly drowned, and was now intently pursued by Galan's soldiers and Reynaud's magic. He no longer had a home, or the smallest of families, or anything in the world beyond the clothes he stood up in. Death was imminent if Galan's men found him, and worse was probably in store if Reynaud got to him first. Neither thing mattered much here, in Nímir's clutches.

Was it all to be for nothing?

Since I set out on this quest, I've made no single decision of my own, Tristan thought wildly. Blais sent me off, told me where to go and what to do when I got there. He took me to Valadan, released him—how did I dare think I could have done that on my own? It's as if I were in a dream then. I don't feel I did anything at all. It was his life's work. And it was Minstrel who saved me from the dragon, taught me how to wake Allaire. Valadan has saved me with his speed, fought for me. I owe my life ten times over to Thomas' wits; and it was Elisena, not me, who got us out of Radak. I've done nothing.

He was unskilled at deciding things. And there was no one left who could choose for him now.

# The Forging

THIS IS MADNESS, Tristan told himself. It will take an enchanted sword of great power to slay the dragon. A mighty magic. No mage has ever battled this creature and lived. I could never handle a spell like that—and this poor old blade would never hold the charge if I did. It will shatter into a million little bits and destroy me with it.

He looked at Allaire, at Elisena, and at the drawn sword in his hand. He stepped through the doorway.

Polassar's great blade was rimed inches deep with frost. Near the hilt it reddened, as his blood ran down onto it. One edge was yet clear, sharply gleaming, and he was still standing fast between the dragon and Allaire.

His armor was cut half away, his helm dented, and few spots could be seen on him that were not either red or white. He was as frosted as his sword, on which he leaned now.

Man and dragon both took a moment's respite. Polassar breathed hard a few times, then sprang back to the battle, hoping for the advantage of surprise. His strokes were still thunderclap quick, but now the blows were a shade less powerful. Tristan watched the encounter, feeling his mouth drying out.

Polassar had jammed his torch into a heap of fallen ice, and by that fitful flicker Tristan got his only clear look at the Guardian.

If it hadn't been moving, he might have taken it for another heap of ice, frozen from a fouled pond, maybe. It seemed to flow as it crawled, in a way that looked somehow wrong for a living thing. The awkward body was inadequately supported by four short legs, all nastily clawed. From the sides of the front legs another claw sprouted, like a spiked thumb.

The neck twined and coiled, raising the head mostly above the torchlight, except when the thing closed in to strike. The head was shaped mostly as a narrow wedge; the great, dead-white eyes were deeply socketed, but Tristan didn't think it was blind. The Guardian's mouth gaped wide, like a toad's. Its throat seemed lined with icicled teeth, as well as its jaws.

The dragon's vast wings flapped, beating at the walls, and snow swirled to Polassar's knees, so that he stumbled. The blade struck again as he fell. Screaming sleet lashed the room as the dragon retreated. Tristan shivered and cringed back.

They battled back and forth across the narrow space, while Tristan watched for his best moment. Several times he nearly moved, only to lose his nerve at the last second. The dragon's lashing tail missed him narrowly as he hesitated. The very air was loud. Then the red blade rose a fraction too slowly. As claws slashed out past his shield, Polassar fell back, and the claws were red, like the sword. Still, his blade came back to guard.

Tristan formed the spell in his mind, holding it tight with his whole being. He must control it, letting it out slowly, and still more slowly yet, using a restraint beyond anything he'd ever attained.

He had to be careful. The sword-blade was cold iron; he dare not touch it as he cast the spell. Its nearness would add a wild unpredictability to the spell, which he must adjust to, if he could.

He found himself climbing, scrambling up the giant tail as if it were some immense stairway. A wing's edge hit him hard on one hip. He nearly fell, but he caught his balance somehow and reached the slippery icy-white back. Here, now, just between the wings—

No fine swordsmanship was required here. Just a simple hacking blow, fit for chopping firewood. He had only to match spell and steel, making sure that his timing was perfect.

The words exploded out of him, with a tongue of their own, and he plunged the sword in. It flamed in his hands, hit the scales and slid through irresistibly. He felt the power coursing through him, through his arms and legs, like life, like death. His head was ringing with it, his body jerking.

The dragon writhed, its head and neck lashing about like

a snapped cable. It screamed and strove to fly, but he held firm to the sword and was somehow not thrown. The spell's power waxed, until it seemed to Tristan that the sword melted and he was melting with it.

Well, he'd known he couldn't hold it.

*Let the end come quickly now, please.*

## The pledge

THE CRASH SOUNDED as if the roof had split open, though that remained whole. The sound shocked Allaire and then had the beneficent effect of rousing her from the dragon's trance. Thomas crept from the treasure room, followed by Elisena. Minstrel chirped loudly at Allaire and fluttered his wings in her face, until she rose and went along after him.

Polassar half sat, half lay against the far wall, the dead dragon's head inches from his legs. He wiped his sword mechanically on his leggings and stared in amazement at the blood on his hands. Already the dragon's eyes were changing, running into pools the color of glacier-melt. Elisena lifted her skirts and stepped around them.

She looked where Polassar had been looking, her face filled with an uncanny calm. Then she knelt down.

Beside the dragon's bulk, Tristan lay on his face, unmoving. There was a burned-flesh smell. When she lifted his right hand, she saw that his sword was gone. All that remained was the silver from the hilt. Melting, it had flowed into a ring of metal round his finger, burning him badly. The metal glowed dully and was still warm to her touch. Otherwise, he was completely cold.

"Is he dead?" Polassar's voice was bleak. "He slew the dragon to save me." The bleakness was slowly replaced by wonder.

Elisena bent closer to Tristan's face, listening.

"He's not dead yet. He breathes. We must go from here

in all haste, Allaire. Come help, Polassar. He is sore wounded."

Thomas mewed at her feet. He had fetched Valadan, somehow, and they laid both men across his back.

"Shall we go without the ring after all?" Allaire whispered once, and then all was silent.

The world was vast, and Nímir's projects in it likewise varied and innumerable. Or else the dead dragon had been his eyes in Darkenkeep, and his Hounds hunted too far away to be recalled. There was quiet, and no retribution fell.

The wind howled about them like the dragon's unlaid ghost. Allaire followed Elisena unquestioningly, little knowing if the girl had any idea of which way to lead, less caring. She climbed up behind Polassar's sagging body, holding him in the saddle, and wept snowflakes. Valadan plodded steadfastly into the Winterwaste. The roan mare staggered after him courageously, but the white, unridden, could not follow, and no one marked when she ceased to do so. She simply was no longer there.

They feared to load the horses heavily, in the deep drifts, yet walking they should all have been lost. Each horse must carry a double load. Polassar held on somehow to his rat-tailed roan, while Allaire clung sobbing behind him. Elisena bent low over Valadan's neck, trying somehow to support Tristan and shield him from the worst cold. Thomas huddled as close to him as possible, and Minstrel fluffed his warm feathers against his throat, but Tristan's face was white and still, and the falling flakes struck his face without melting.

The sky was the color of metal, then eggshells, then ceased to be. They no longer walked the seam between earth and sky, but stumbled ahead in a frozen fog. Elisena was loath to move—each step might drop them into unseen and unguessed at peril.

Valadan staggered forward as if uncaring. His head was sealed in ice—it broke and reformed as his nostrils flared to draw breath. The roan followed as if spellbound to his side.

To cease to move was to die, to feel ice taking hold in every vein. The intense cold was curiously warming; they drowsed upon the horses, lulled by the always shrieking wind. Somehow Valadan continued to move, gaining them inches in the swirling whiteness.

They came out of the Waste at some point, for there were trees about them again, but all the land looked gray and nearly as lifeless as the Winterwaste. They stopped, after a long while, and Elisena led them into a blackberry thicket.

They laid the men down—for Polassar had long since fainted—and they anointed and bound up his wounds. There was nothing to be done for Tristan. The sun, what faint glow there was of it, was setting.

Elisena lay down beside Tristan, wrapping both her cloak and her arms about him. He was as cold as an ice block, and as stiff.

She opened his fingers with difficulty, and looked again at his hand. Most strangely, it did not seem at all burned about the silver ring now, but only on the palm, in the shape of the sword hilt. She held the hand close to her bosom and pulled his head onto her shoulder.

They passed the night so, and she felt him grow gradually warm. Once he sighed. Minstrel, roosting on a branch close above, heard and pulled his head from under his wing. Thomas crept a little closer to them, eyes like lanterns in the dark. But there was no further sound.

It was morning, and a bird was singing. The song mimicked the sound of running water, a sweet-singing brook. A man might easily listen to it forever and be forever refreshed. Tristan lay lapped in warmth, through which no pain penetrated. He could hear the wind-chime now, the one that hung in the apple tree beside Blais' cottage. Its ringing was the sound of high summer, of lightly breezed mornings, sleepy afternoons. Even now the breeze brushed his face, smelling of clover and butterflies.

He opened his eyes, expecting to see leaves and green apples arching overhead, and beheld Elisena's silver eyes in their place. The still-echoing crystals hung down from her hair. He reached a hand up to touch them and looked past her at Minstrel, warbling on a blackberry cane just over her head.

He tried to speak, to tell her that those were sights he'd

never hoped to see again in this life, but she laid a cool finger on his lips and drew him back down beside her, and he slept instead.

He heard singing again, in sleep it seemed. Minor in quality, it was like the keening of the wind through Kô-velir's windtowers. After a while, he dimly recognized words —it was the ballad some call the Lament of Kings. He wondered who was singing it, and why she did so. Crystals chimed like harp notes among the words.

His eyes slitted open, and he saw a face haloed with soft dark curls. Some far-removed part of his numb brain discovered that Elisena was doing the singing, and for a space he wondered fuzzily if Galan had had her trained as a harper. She held the pure, formal notes until they melted back into the clear air, yet they lingered with him as he slept. Strange, he thought. She never sang before.

She woke him later, feeding him bits of bread dipped in broth. He heard crunchings and, turning his head, saw Thomas gnawing a rabbit bone.

*Don't fret. I'm looking after things*, the cat said and went back to his meal.

Thus reassured, Tristan sank back into warm and silent peace and slept all that night again, with Elisena beside him.

She was not beside him the next morning, and so he sat up cautiously, as far as the low thorny bushes would allow, and began looking himself over. His right hand prickled when he moved it, and he stared astonished at the ring on his middle finger. He examined his palm, from which the burns were fast fading, and was at a loss to explain where either burns or ring had come from. He noticed then that his scabbard was empty at his side.

It would be a pity if he'd lost the sword or stupidly left it behind. They had been friends a long time. And so senseless, to lose it carelessly, when he'd resisted parting with it at such cost in Kôvelir. He absently rubbed Thomas' ears, feeling out of place, out of touch even with himself.

By the lack of any human sound, they might have been alone on the hillside. A little wind sighed in the grass, and somewhere a stream flowed.

Thirsty suddenly, he stood up and followed the sound, letting his ears lead him to the water. His legs seemed to work well enough, and the lightheadedness he felt at first soon passed.

Someone was filling a pot at the stream. By the brown cloak it would be Elisena. He joined her, but she refused to let him help with carrying the pot. Indeed, she seemed amazed to see him there at all, though he didn't understand why. They walked back up the hill, Tristan insisting that he did indeed feel quite well and half wondering why she thought he should not. She had made a little fire, among the purplish blackberry brambles, and Polassar lay beside it, his head in Allaire's lap. He smiled as they came near and drank the water as quickly as Elisena would allow. Allaire never looked up from her tending of him, not even to greet Tristan. Some icy shadow seemed on her still. For his own part, Tristan was somewhat astonished to realize that he'd not once wondered where she was, or even seen her face in his dreams.

The pot was set on the fire, and Elisena made a soup of the mushrooms she'd gathered by the stream, stirring the mixture with a peeled stick. He ought to try to get another rabbit, Tristan thought, seeing how few were the scraps of meat she added to the soup. But he didn't see Thomas about, which meant the cat was probably taking care of it. Frankly, he was loath to leave the warm fire. Darkenkeep had settled in his bones, and he felt unable to stay warm.

They all huddled close about the tiny blaze, still exhausted and stunned by their defeat. It was both too late and too soon to rejoice that they were all alive and free. And there was the question still of pursuit, which might come at any moment, and which they had no means of preventing or preparing for.

Elisena sat stitching a tear in the sable cloak, offering Allaire her own while the work was being done. She worked quietly, without visible shivering, but the wind was chill, and her hands much whiter than was usual.

How alike we are, Tristan thought with tardy insight. And how easily Allaire allows us both to wait on her. But then she is a princess, and no doubt takes servants for granted.

A great anger rose up in him as he watched, and spilled over. He wanted to shout at Allaire, order her to do her own mending, cook her own meals, lift a hand to help just

once. At the same time he trembled, not knowing if the rip
had been made by a blackberry bramble or an icicle, or a
sword during their escape from Radak, so long ago. Whatever, since awakening her he'd led Allaire into only deadly
peril, it seemed to him. He felt confused by his conflicting
emotions, turned inside out.

He was surprised to find Elisena smiling at him. Everyone else seemed deeply depressed, and rightly so, for they'd
failed, even though the dragon was dead. At least he supposed it was dead—how else had they gotten away? And
what had happened to his sword?

He returned the smile tensely, stood up, and laid his own
patched cloak about Elisena's shoulders. He walked on,
right up to the top of the hill, through the blackberries and
on out of them, where he might get a view of their surroundings.

He knew this country. That lane wound over that rise,
crossed the brook, and ended at Blais' gate. This was even
the same brook, though further upstream. He'd often
come here in summer, berrying.

It tempted him mightily now, the thought of walking
back to the cottage. To have his books by him again, and a
fat yellow candle, and the big brass kettle singing on the
fire. And please, by all the nine greatest mages, let no enchanted smoke come from the lion-dog's mouth ever again!

He should be planning their next move—that was his
job, after all. He flushed to think how easily Nímir had
lured him from it. It had nearly all been over, for a while,
and he'd never even suspected how he was being used. This
aspect of Nímir's power was more terrifying than any glacier or dragon.

It wasn't just that Nímir had clouded his judgment,
duped him into reentering Darkenkeep. Nímir had even
used his deepest feelings for Allaire, twisting and distorting
them to bend Tristan to his will. Just because he now knew
how it had happened—did that mean it could never happen again? Tristan shivered.

The fields spread out at his feet, a tangle of russet and
bleached bone. Those trees would blossom pink in the
spring, and the orchard would foam with white. If there'd
been anyone in the cottage now, the smoke from its chimney would be visible from this hill.

And I would like to go home now, he mused.

Or even to Dunehollow-by-the-Sea. Dunehollow, with its dusty pink-plastered houses, its wandering cats and its yellow-sailed fishing boats returning with the dawn. He'd walked its streets often, on errands for Blais, and if not in secure confidence, then at least without feeling such a fool as he had in Kôvelir.

Hang the quest! What good had he done anyway? Let Polassar and Allaire work out the rest themselves. Maybe Polassar's wedding ring would be the right ring. Somehow the outcome did not matter to him so much as it formerly had. He was never fitted for world affairs.

I thought I loved her because I needed someone to love, Tristan thought, as Allaire's face came to mind. Anyone would have done. She's not really worth all the fuss. All shine and no substance. Has she really got enough power to use the rings? I wonder just how she was chosen for them?

For all that, he couldn't seem to think harshly of her. He'd made his own choice, as had she. He just hoped he'd chosen rightly.

Maybe they should just give up—the task was nearly hopeless anyway. What if Nímir spread the Winterwaste farther? They could always move south. Nímir's advances had always been slow. Was there any real reason to think they wouldn't continue to be? We shall have time enough, for us, he thought, and our children's children, too. It needn't be so bad.

As to the prophecies about Allaire—well, a prophecy's meaning could alter drastically, depending on how it was viewed, whether interpreted literally or subjectively.

And maybe the prophecies weren't true at all. Maybe they were just wishful thinking, a ruse perpetrated to keep the cold and dark at bay for as long as was possible.

If he gave up the quest and Allaire, then he ought to yield Valadan to Polassar as well, Tristan supposed. A no-account, failed wizard had no right to a horse who'd never carried any rider less than a Duke. He could see the stallion now, watchfully cropping grass as usual, taking mouthfuls of the brown grass in his teeth and tearing them loose with a graceful twist of his neck that set his mane dancing.

He'd miss the horse. Not just the riding, which he'd come to enjoy far more than he'd ever have guessed, but even the sight of the elegant profile as the stallion scanned the horizon and the warm grassy breath on cold mornings.

All unwilling, he began remembering little things about the fight with the Guardian, and those things made him shiver afresh. Had he really done that? He might have gotten himself killed, he really might have.

Footsteps whispered in the dry grass behind him. It was Elisena, returning his cloak with thanks both sincere and simple.

"The thanks should be mine, lady." He meant for the nights and her warming and tending him, for it came to him that she'd saved his life.

Somehow the words weren't needed. Her face seemed very close to his, until he could have counted her lashes without effort. Her skin lacked Allaire's marble purity, but it was white, and soft, and creased now with smile lines about eyes and mouth. And the touch of her fingers against his own was gentle and friendly. With that touch, the memories of Allaire's face and all the empty nights of agony over her seemed banished. And he knew he didn't want to travel home alone.

The wind blew freshly, and he slipped an arm about her back, holding her close beside him. They both gazed down the hill.

"Elisena, I have a mind to go back down there—but no, I *am* going. I know that now—it's the only home I ever had. It's not much, but the roof doesn't leak. Will you come with me?" He looked back at the berry bushes, with smoke rising thinly from the hollow on their far side. "They don't need us, not so long as they have each other. I should have learned that a long time ago."

Her eyes were very wide, brimming with tears, he thought, but her mouth still smiled. He wiped a tear away, feeling it warm on his finger. Silver-gray eyes, he observed. I swear they shine brighter than all Allaire's nine rings!

His ring was warm against his hand, and he drew it off, holding it out to her. He smiled ruefully.

"This just might be the only thing I've ever had that was truly mine to give. I think I really earned it." He slipped it on her middle finger, the finger of marriage. Was it only by coincidence that it had formed about the same finger on his own hand? It should have been large on her more slender finger, but it nested perfectly there.

Somewhere—it might have been as far away as Dunehollow—bells began to peal softly. The ring gleamed quietly on Elisena's hand.

As he kissed her he felt a loosening, a gentle surrendering, as much within himself as within the woman in his arms. A sense of safety, peace, belonging—a rightness never guessed at, though longed for all unknowingly. He tasted summer on her lips, lavender and strawberries.

# The King of Calandra

ELISENA TOSSED her head back, letting her dark hair fly free in the wind. Tristan kissed her again, and heard voices singing for his pleasure alone. The song was teasingly familiar and passing sweet. Her mouth tasted now of violets.

She pulled at his hands, laughing, and broke away, and they ran down the hill together like children. Minstrel was flying before them, doing loops in the air. Tristan felt that he could have done one himself. Elisena ran him breathless, and then they stopped, swaying, by the fire.

The soup was boiling. Tristan stooped to dish it up, but Elisena was no longer at his side. She stood before Allaire, her hands held out, palms up.

*"Sister, give to me my rings!"*

Tristan gaped at her and knew that Polassar did likewise. His jaw dropped even lower as, one by one, the rings were slipped from Allaire's fingers and onto Elisena's, where they shone like captured moonbeams.

"My thanks to you, sister. You have kept them well for

me." To their final astonishment Allaire flung herself weeping into Elisena's arms.

Tristan sat down, hard.

Her tears undried, Allaire began to smile—the first real smile Tristan felt he'd ever seen on her face. She stretched and rubbed her hands before her, as if the weight of so much magic and silver had cramped them. Her hair came loose and tumbled, heavy and smooth as that metal, about her joyful face. Had she been lovely before? That was to her now as a bud to a flower.

Tristan's face must look much like Polassar's—frozen in incredible disbelief. There were too many questions tumbling in his mind for any one to get free. Elisena began to answer them, unasked.

"A thing is better hidden if something is left in its place as a distraction," she began, looking still down at the rings. "Since Nímir stole me away, he has hidden me in many places, many guises, while she waited always in Darkenkeep, in case some hero should win so far. It made a lovely game for him, to see them struggle so, knowing that even if they found her, they would not truly have the prize they sought. She was my lady-in-waiting, but she is now in more than truth my sister, for she has shared a hard bondage with me. I hail you, Ariana of Esdragon. You are a woman of great courage."

"Forgive me, lady, that I did not know you. Yet I hail you now, Allaire of the Nine Rings!"

Elisena frowned. "I had rather be called by the name you have known me by." She looked down at her hands once more. "The name I have known best in this shape. I do not wonder that you were deceived with all the rest. I am much changed, and Nímir must have laid a confusion upon you as well." She shook her head, crystals ringing.

"As for the tenth ring, that was hidden as well, though not by Nímir." She held up the crystal that hung pendant from a silver band on her left thumb. "This will answer many of our questions, I think, if I remember aright."

Tristan thought he saw minute figures passing through the stone, like shadow puppets, or the shapes on Crewzel's cards. Elisena gazed deep into it for a long while, then sat back, her eyes closed, and began to speak again.

"When word came to the King at Crogen that Allaire

was taken, he was wroth, and swore that the Duke had broken faith with him, though once they had been as brothers. Nímir's poison worked in him, and there would be war, the war that Allaire was meant to prevent. He called his armies out at once, they coming from many lands and cities. And he cast the ring from his finger, where it had rested waiting for his bride. It might have been ensorcelled to do him harm, he said.

"But Thalia, his sister, scooped up the ring from where it fell and carried it to the king's master of magic, the High Mage of Calandra himself, for she knew it was precious beyond all else in the kingdom. The wizard knew how greatly Nímir would desire it, and so he melted it and shaped it into the hilt of a sword, smothering its power as only he who had forged it could, until the day when it might bloom again. Then he gave the sword to Thalia, and spirited her far away from the eyes of men. For she was great with child, and he foresaw that her husband and brother both might be slain in the senselessness of the coming war. And her child would be of the blood royal, the rightful blood of the Maristan kings. With Allaire lost, all hope rested on that child."

It might have been any ancient tale of war and magic, told to children and sleepy apprentice wizards on long and frightening winter nights. It seemed almost beyond belief that the story was one that could touch them so deeply.

"Thalia lodged with a poor family, and when she died of sorrow for the fate of her house, worn with birthing and grief beyond any hope of consolment, they took her child and hid it so well that no trace of it was ever found again. Nímir could learn nothing of whether it lived or died, and the ring was lost with it, in the sword, though he knew that not.

"And after long years, men began to forget what had passed, for times and life were hard, and it was the will of the Winterlord that they should forget all hope and promise. Only the mages remembered, and Nímir was well pleased. He knew how best to lure them to their dooms. By his power, a legend grew of a quest that only a mage could fulfill, and this was a thought dear to their prideful hearts. The best of them followed it and they perished. And all this was as Nímir wished."

Tristan watched her wide-eyed, like a child. This was better than any of Blais' tales.

"In all save the ring. It had never been destroyed. While it existed, it was a mighty threat. And when Nímir learned that a mage at last remembered to seek Valadan and had learned much concerning him, he slew that mage in a great duel of magic. The very heavens rocked."

She was referring to Blais, and with that realization her tale ceased to be a pretty story to Tristan.

"And when it was done, Nímir saw that there was still magic in that place, where all things of that nature should have been destroyed. A very small and nagging magic, and there was but one thing it might be. Even mighty Nímir trembled.

"He sent his Hounds after it, bidding them seek the mage's apprentice, a mighty warrior-wizard, who now held the ring and was concealing it well.

"Yet they found nothing. The magic had gone when they reached the place and it had left only a cold trail. As for the warrior-wizard, they could find no trace of such a person." She smiled knowingly at Tristan.

"Nímir cast his power far from Darkenkeep, seeking the ring. And so he noticed not at all when two entered his hold, one of them bearing an ancient sword. When at last he attended to what had happened, they had vanished. And so he set about luring them back once more, to his place of greatest power.

"He cannot have known that the ring would call me also, when it came so close to my prison—and he has forgotten what sacrifices men can make."

Tristan struggled to find his voice, but failed. Elisena went on.

"I was a silly child of sixteen, when Nímir stole me from my father's men. Ariana he put to sleep, to bait his trap, but me he left aware, to be tormented more, for daring to contest his will.

"Can you imagine the frustrations of experiencing infancy and childhood with an adult mind? To be full of knowledge that is desperately needed—knowledge that might have saved a Kingdom in those early days before men forgot and it was too late—and be able to utter it to no one because your body has not yet mastered speech? And finally to know that no one will listen to such things from a child? Can you imagine learning to walk and talk and run, to read, all without seeming to be more than you should be? Or of knowing the bright vigor of youth and finding it followed by the slow fading of age, the dark night of death—more than a dozen times? To be shuffled from one body to another at Nímir's whim? Never daring to love, because each life might be my last, or snatched from me the moment Nímir suspected I was finding my punishment a pleasure? And finally, my dearest hope becoming that each life would be the last, and release me?" She closed her eyes on the remembered pain, then looked up brightly.

"The first few times were disasters, as well you can imagine. Yet a mountain will wear away to sand in time—I learned.

"I learned. From each life, each experience, however bleak or painful, I learned. And by his vanity in leaving me alive and helpless, Nímir has created the force which will destroy him. I know how to use these rings, far better than I could ever have hoped before!"

Even as she spoke, her face shadowed, her lids closed.

"It chilled my blood, to go into Darkenkeep unarmed. But by then I could feel the ring. I knew that somehow it was connected with you, Tristan, though you didn't know it. I could not chance leaving you, no matter what danger you were being tricked into."

Her eyes had opened now, and she was looking at him.

"I think—even if you had not been tied to the ring, I could not have let you go alone. I could tell you were being led—how long it would continue I could only guess, and you were in danger for so long as it did. So I said nothing, and followed—but I did not expect we would ever see this world again."

She raised her hands, glittering and shining with more than silver. The glow lighted all their faces.

"Hail, Allaire of the Nine Rings!" The shout seemed to burst from all their throats, even Thomas and Minstrel and Valadan. Tristan caught their echoes, if no one else noticed.

"Ten, now," Tristan whispered, and then continued with sinking heart. "It was written that Allaire would marry the King of Calandra. And I'm no one, a nameless half-wizard.

Why did you agree to wed me?" Sickly, he went on before she could speak, "Was it only to get the ring? I would have given it to you freely, had you told me what it was. I see now it wasn't mine to give, in any case."

"Did you not earn it, nearly with your life?" Elisena asked. "There are many heirs to Calandra." And when he still shook his head, she said, "My rings each have a special function, which I am yet learning. But this—" She pointed to the middle finger of her left hand, which bore a sky-colored stone, marked with clouds of white. "This one I do know. It is called the Kingstone. One of its purposes is to locate that which is lost—most particularly the heirs of kings. Let us see how it responds to Polassar."

The stone, held near him, shed a soft blue glow on his face. Elisena nodded, and Polassar smiled proudly, sure that the reaction must be a favorable one.

"So he is an heir. It is said that in the presence of the true King, the stone flames like the sun. Shall we see?" She stretched her hand toward Tristan.

He could hardly get his breath, for his heart hammering. The stone came closer, impossibly large, blue like the summer sky, flecked with green and white and brown. It flashed all at once, so brightly that he had to shut his eyes against it.

"I saw one thing more," Elisena said, "in the crystal. A child, born on Midwinter's Night, and orphaned that night as well."

She held the stone near his unresisting palm, bathing it in blue radiance. There, beneath the healed burns, a small crown showed, blue to match the stone. Elisena moved the ring back, and the crown faded. With the stone brought nearer, the crown reappeared. Polassar gasped.

"Do you need more proof?" Elisena asked Tristan.

"No—" It came out more as a despairing wail than a denial.

Elisena smiled widely. "Thalia's child may have vanished into obscurity, but it lived and passed on both its royal blood and the sword. Between those spells upon the ring and those on the sword itself, it would always be close to the true heir, though we shall never know the whole story. Destiny moves strangely." She took his hand again.

Tristan looked up to find Polassar struggling to his knees.

"My liege lord—"

Tristan scrambled up and backed away from him in alarm.

"Don't kneel to me!" he stammered. "I'm not fitted to be your lord or lord of anyone else."

He walked away, almost running. Thomas fell into step beside him.

*Don't be a fool. You can't just ignore this. And Blais would be so pleased—you're a lousy magician, true, but you were starting to shape up. He always said that odd-looking sword they left with you would be good for something.*

"Leave me alone," Tristan pleaded desperately.

*Valadan knew.*

"What?" He stopped so quickly that any animal less alert than a cat would have fallen over him.

*He'd never have accepted you otherwise. He was the personal warhorse of the Dukes of Esdragon, after all. He knew you weren't a nameless bastard.*

Tristan walked faster, head down. The cat trotted just behind him through the dead grass.

*Calandra needs her King.*

He looked up to see Valadan, his eyes filled with exploding constellations once more. Tristan felt himself pulled into those eyes, saw all the glories that once had been. Battles and crownings moved across the stallion's eyes, like the images in Elisena's ring. Lives of long-dead kings flickered, a land changed, a throne waited empty.

Tristan turned his head roughly away.

"You stay out of this."

The next time he looked up, he was at the cottage, teetering across the footlog.

He had never thought how silent it would be. The door was still neatly barred, but dead leaves had come down the chimney and lay as deep upon the floor as the dust did on the table. A mouse dived through them and vanished into its hole. Thomas paid it no attention.

Well, the place would look its old self again, once he got it cleaned up. But just at the moment, it was pretty dismal. Maybe a fire on the hearth would help.

He laid the kindling, and knelt to make the passes, as he had so many times on this very spot. He'd first learned the spell here. His palm itched, and he paused to look at it. There was no mark on it, except for a few flakes of skin. Maybe it had been a trick. His middle finger looked indented, where the ring had briefly been, as if he'd worn it a long time, long enough for it to become a part of him, shape his flesh.

Part of him, like the cottage. Only it wasn't his anymore. He was suddenly aware, after all the hurrying and adventuring and fighting and worrying, how very still the world seemed to be.

He'd gone away, and so had the place he'd loved. It wasn't the same, though he wasn't really sure why. It had changed, or stood still while he'd changed, and he didn't fit anymore. It didn't want him. Tristan beat his fist against a log, and squeezed his eyelids tight together, but not before tears streaked his face.

The kindling went back on the woodpile. He touched the lion-dog's head just once, very softly, and then he locked the door again. For the last time.

Elisena was standing in the orchard, waiting. She touched a branch, and one white blossom balanced at its tip. Sunlight broke through the clouds to limn it.

Tristan stood in front of her, looking down at his travel-stained boots and his much mended breeches. There were tiny yellow flowers springing up in the grass between his feet as he watched, and a butterfly lit on his toe. Its wings were salmon and green.

He touched her face, lingeringly, fingered one of the shimmering crystals beside her cheek.

"All right. I'm not sure you know what you're asking. I've never been much good at anything in my whole life. You've seen how I am with cities and strategies, with magics. I think you're making an awful mistake. But I'll try."

At least, he thought, the business of Nímir is finished. I can be lighter of that worry. The prophecies had fulfilled themselves, and all was well, would be well, forever. Blais' quest was done. Achieved at last.

The butterfly had brought others of his kind, joined by one gray and white canary with wings of gold. A halo of bobbing wings formed about their two heads.

"I pledge you my life, Allaire of the Nine Rings—plus one."

"And I pledge you mine, Tristan of Calandra."

*And they lived happily ever after?*

Tristan was sure he heard it, but Thomas was just then engrossed in washing his paws, and unavailable for further comment.

# Fontana Paperbacks: Fiction

Fontana is a leading paperback publisher of both non-fiction, popular and academic, and fiction. Below are some recent fiction titles.

- [ ] THE ROSE STONE  Teresa Crane  £2.95
- [ ] THE DANCING MEN  Duncan Kyle  £2.50
- [ ] AN EXCESS OF LOVE  Cathy Cash Spellman  £3.50
- [ ] THE ANVIL CHORUS  Shane Stevens  £2.95
- [ ] A SONG TWICE OVER  Brenda Jagger  £3.50
- [ ] SHELL GAME  Douglas Terman  £2.95
- [ ] FAMILY TRUTHS  Syrell Leahy  £2.95
- [ ] ROUGH JUSTICE  Jerry Oster  £2.50
- [ ] ANOTHER DOOR OPENS  Lee Mackenzie  £2.25
- [ ] THE MONEY STONES  Ian St James  £2.95
- [ ] THE BAD AND THE BEAUTIFUL  Vera Cowie  £2.95
- [ ] RAMAGE'S CHALLENGE  Dudley Pope  £2.95
- [ ] THE ROAD TO UNDERFALL  Mike Jefferies  £2.95

You can buy Fontana paperbacks at your local bookshop or newsagent. Or you can order them from Fontana Paperbacks, Cash Sales Department, Box 29, Douglas, Isle of Man. Please send a cheque, postal or money order (not currency) worth the purchase price plus 22p per book for postage (maximum postage required is £3.00 for orders within the UK).

NAME (Block letters) _____

ADDRESS _____

_____

_____

While every effort is made to keep prices low, it is sometimes necessary to increase them at short notice. Fontana Paperbacks reserve the right to show new retail prices on covers which may differ from those previously advertised in the text or elsewhere.